A MOTHER'S HEART

BOOK YOUR PLACE ON OUR WEBSITE AND MAKE THE READING CONNECTION!

We've created a customized website just for our very special readers, where you can get the inside scoop on everything that's going on with Zebra, Pinnacle and Kensington books.

When you come online, you'll have the exciting opportunity to:

- View covers of upcoming books
- Read sample chapters
- Learn about our future publishing schedule (listed by publication month *and author*)
- Find out when your favorite authors will be visiting a city near you
- Search for and order backlist books from our online catalog
- Check out author bios and background information
- Send e-mail to your favorite authors
- Meet the Kensington staff online
- Join us in weekly chats with authors, readers and other guests
- Get writing guidelines
- AND MUCH MORE!

**Visit our website at
http://www.zebrabooks.com**

A MOTHER'S HEART

Veronica Ashley
Elizabeth Graham
Martha Hix

Zebra Books
Kensington Publishing Corp.

http://www.zebrabooks.com

ZEBRA BOOKS are published by

Kensington Publishing Corp.
850 Third Avenue
New York, NY 10022

Copyright © 1998 by Kensington Publishing Corp.

"Cassandra's Quest" © 1998 by Veronica Chapa
"Best Laid Plans" © 1998 by Elizabeth Graham
"His Mother's Gauntlet" © 1998 by Martha Hix

All rights reserved. No part of this book may be reproduced
in any form or by any means without the prior written consent
of the Publisher, excepting brief quotes used in reviews.

If you purchased this book without a cover you should be aware
that this book is stolen property. It was reported as "unsold
and destroyed" to the Publisher and neither the Author nor the
Publisher has received any payment for this "stripped book."

Zebra and the Z logo Reg. U.S. Pat. & TM Off.

First Printing: May, 1998
10 9 8 7 6 5 4 3 2 1

Printed in the United States of America

Contents

Cassandra's Quest

Veronica Ashley

Chapter One

Lady Olympia Phaedra Heraclius was dreaming about the sea when the singing started. The gentle rise and fall of the nuns' chanting barely touched the surface of her dream: she was five again, standing beside her father, watching sailing vessels on a calm turquoise sea. Her father was leaning over a marble balcony, pointing out the ships, guessing where they were from. His deep voice carried above the crash and slide of the waves and made her feel important and safe. In her dream, the warmth of the sun and the bracing, fresh scent of the water filled her with happiness. She saw herself smiling, then parting her lips to taste the air. The wind teased her, blowing golden strands of her hair into her mouth; with a touch she pulled them free.

Such peace. Calm. Simplicity. Lady Olympia sighed. Satisfied with her journey back in time, she smiled and let the singing lead her, like a friend's hand, out of her dream.

"Ave . . ."

Lady Olympia opened her eyes. There was serenity in

her gaze. A gaunt, regal woman in the brown robes of a nun, motionless, hands folded in her lap, she sat in her chair and looked quietly around her. Her profile gave the impression of great nobility, her chin slightly raised as if in expectation of giving a command or receiving a compliment. Her skin was as fine as parchment and pale, but the lines around her eyes and mouth were few and delicate, as if etched by butterfly wings. Her hair, a lusterless wheat color streaked with gray, was softly gathered in a braid that crowned her head. In her amber-colored eyes the life force that was slowly draining out of her body was still strong, and anyone who looked at her directly would never have thought that she was ill.

The garden of the Convent of the Holy Cross was Lady Olympia's sanctuary. It was lush and green with spring. Enclosed by stone walls tall as the gates of Heaven, the garden was a marvel to behold with its myrtle and Judas trees, flowers swelling with buds, and hedges of yew. It was a miracle, since the land surrounding the convent was rocky and inhospitable to all living things. Legend had it that the tears shed by the convent's founder, a mystic and hermit, and a sliver of the true cross had created a spring of fresh water. The water nourished the land; there was enough to sustain fruit orchards, an olive grove, and a vegetable garden, all of which lay on the other side of a wall, through a locked door. The sacred water made it a sanctuary for the sick who prayed for a miracle to make them well.

Each morning, Lady Olympia's daughter and one of the novices carried her here, to her chair, so she could pray in the life-sustaining sunshine. She had been praying for two years. Lately, her prayers had been opening doors to dreams and memories.

Perhaps it is time, she thought to herself. *Time to prepare*

*myself and Cassandra. To set her on her way. The Lord himself
knows she can't stay here much longer without causing a rebellion.*

The nuns of the Holy Cross had taken vows of chastity,
obedience, and humility. They were taught to speak rarely
and work hard to avoid idleness. Cassandra worked hard
and had embraced the vow of chastity. She had even been
willing to cut her long, silvery-gold hair, but the rest were
thorny issues. At eighteen years of age, she was a woman
with a mind of her own, and she rarely hesitated to let the
world know it. She could not mind her tongue, nor stem
the tide of reason when her obedience was put to the test.
Cassandra's restlessness tried the patience of the Abbess
and distracted the novices. Cassandra was a problem.

A laugh barely made itself felt in Lady Olympia's throat.
Her mouth softened. Although she was staring at the fountain in the middle of the garden, she was picturing her
daughter in her brown robes, climbing trees. Cassandra
liked to sit in the boughs and gaze out over the walls at
the orchards and the fields and into the horizon.

Lady Olympia turned her head as she heard steps coming across the stone floor of the colonnade. It was Cassandra, walking fiercely, kicking her coarse brown robes out
with every step. Lady Olympia turned calmly back to the
fountain. *Does she know of my plan?* she wondered. *I've told
no one save the Abbess, who would never reveal my . . . Could it
be? Has Cassandra seen into the future? Has she used her powers?
Here? She and I know how it upsets my sister, the Abbess.*

The singing stopped. Lady Olympia heard the crunching
of small stones as Cassandra stepped onto the garden path.
The coarse brush of her daughter's robes scared the birds
perched on the fountain's rim, beaks ready to dip into the
water. They darted, scattering into the air, chirping wildly.

"Mother?"

In an instant, her daughter was standing before her.
Lady Olympia looked up, shading her eyes from the sun.

The light illuminated her daughter's gold hair like a halo. But it was not a saint's mooning gaze that met hers. There was concern in her daughter's amber eyes; her mouth held a question, and Lady Olympia read it easily. *What have you been up to?*

"And why are you not at Mass?" Lady Olympia stalled. Squinting into the sun was going to give her a headache. She closed her eyes and waited.

"I wanted to be with you. Shall I move your chair beneath the tree? Or—" Lady Olympia felt her daughter move slightly to the left. The strong light disappeared, blocked by Cassandra's body.

Lady Olympia lowered her hand and opened her eyes. Cassandra had tied her long, heavy hair back with a piece of hemp. There was a streak of dirt on her cheek that told her that Cassandra had been helping Sister Mary in her herbarium. And there was a peach blush to her skin, which was usually so pale it seemed lit by the moon. The serious look in her eyes made her look older than eighteen.

Lady Olympia cleared her throat. "Sister Agnes requested that, as long as we are here, we follow the schedule of the nuns. That includes attending Terce."

"You know I do. Usually. But we must speak."

Lady Olympia noted that her daughter, arms held across her chest, had slipped her hands into the sleeves of her nun's robe. Cassandra may not be zealous about following the nuns' routine, but she is beginning to adopt a few of their mannerisms, thought Lady Olympia.

"You're going to send me away."

Lady Olympia arched her brow at her daughter's directness, but secretly she admired Cassandra for it.

"Yes."

Cassandra scrunched up her mouth, looked away, then back. "It's not right."

Lady Olympia watched as her golden-haired daughter

straightened like a soldier. It seemed as if a mantle of iron had just fallen onto Cassandra's shoulders. There was a warrior air to her bearing, and the sight made Lady Olympia think of the Amazons. She knew without asking who her daughter wanted to fight. It was God.

Cassandra saw the glint of understanding in her mother's eyes and in the softening lines around her mouth. But it did not brush aside the anger Cassandra felt tightening her limbs, spurring her heart to beat faster. She whirled around, away from the love she could feel sweeping toward her, and, raising her face to the sky, secretly called to God to show himself so she could fight him, wage war on him, for allowing her mother to become sick.

Cassandra took a deep breath and tried to relax her shoulders, but the weight of her questions was too much. She rubbed the back of her neck and looked sideways at her mother.

The last two years had passed like sand beneath their feet. The sacred waters had not helped her mother; she was just as ill as the day they arrived. Although now her mother seemed more at peace with the sickness. A truce of some kind had been made, and her mother bore the bloody coughing fits, aching muscles, and headaches with calm resolve. But Cassandra would have throttled God and his archangels if given the chance.

The patter of footsteps streaming across stone and the swishing of robes lured Cassandra's attention. She watched the nuns, in two brown files, walk past the open arches of the covered walkway. Only one novice, her head covered by a short, white kerchief, slid a glance toward the garden.

At the end of the procession, walking side by side, whispering, were the Abbess and Sister Mary, the herbalist. Like a doe sensing an intruder in the forest, the Abbess stopped and looked out at the garden. She met Cassandra's gaze. Turning away, the Abbess said something to the nun which sped her on her way, then continued into the garden.

The efficient snap of her robes ceased when the Abbess stopped before mother and daughter. She was uncommonly tall, older than Lady Olympia, with a dry agelessness like stone. Her pale, even features were tense with dedication.

The beauty that had faded from her face was in the Abbess's voice. "How are you feeling this morning?" she inquired, her voice rich as honey.

Cassandra's mother waved her hand in the air. The gesture was noble, queenly; Cassandra could almost see the heavy jewels she remembered from her childhood, flashing from her mother's fingers.

"I'm thankful God has permitted me to greet yet another beautiful day."

The Abbess's face softened. "I, too, give him thanks." She paused, then whispered, "Sister."

The Abbess's intelligent, amber eyes held the amber gaze turned up to her. They both smiled. To Cassandra, watching quietly, time seemed to rush backward. The austere Abbess and the beautiful noblewoman were gone for a moment: Cassandra saw two ten-year-olds, sisters, sharing a secret.

Cassandra knew she and her mother had been fortunate to gain admittance into the convent. Pilgrims were welcomed, but family members—that was a different story. The walls were built to guard the nuns from the lust of men and from the world, including families, which could only remind the nuns of that other world. The convent gates had swung open with the Bishop of Constantinople's blessing. It hadn't hurt matters that her mother had made a gift to the plump, squinty-eyed bishop, of a gold reliquary, filled with coins that had been in her family since the dawn of the Church.

"I'm glad you've joined us. I was just about to tell Cassandra about my plan," said Lady Olympia, causing her daughter to arch her brow. "And I might as well tell you, too."

"It's very simple, really." Lady Olympia turned her beautiful gaze upon her daughter. "I need you to find something for me."

Lady Olympia looked expectantly from Cassandra to the Abbess and back again. She wet her lips before continuing. "It's a swan, rich with gold and enamel work, no larger than my palm," she said, holding her hand out gracefully, palm up. "It's one of the last treasures in my family. It was a gift from the Empress Theodora."

The Abbess snorted at the mention of the lascivious empress. Lady Olympia narrowed her gaze at her sister, then continued, looking up at Cassandra.

"I'd like to see it one last time."

"Mother!" Cassandra winced, jerking her head back. "Why must you say things like that?"

"I'm not afraid of dying," she soothed, but it sounded a little too rehearsed to Cassandra. "I've made my peace with God." *What I am afraid of is what will happen to you if you remain much longer. This convent cannot contain you.*

"Peace?" Cassandra cried. "You must fight. Fight this thing that sickens you! Fight God!"

The Abbess sucked in her breath at her niece's blasphemy. But Cassandra could feel something like a wild beast stirring inside her and her boldness grew. She felt her color rising. "When did God ever hear your prayers? When?"

The Abbess crossed herself and mumbled, "Ave Maria gracia plena dominus . . ." Lady Olympia cast a wary glance at her sister.

"When Father gambled most of your fortune away? When he used to come home sick and drunk, stinking of other women? When he drank himself to death? I want to know. When has God—"

Her mother cut her off. "Enough, Cassandra." Her voice was low and even, and would be obeyed.

The Abbess's praying came to an abrupt halt. Her eyes narrowed on Cassandra, who began pacing in an effort to stem the flow of her anger. She balled her hands into fists. She was a girl of average height but her energy made her a towering force.

"God answered my prayers when you were born," said her mother. It became so still, it was as if the water in the fountain, the garden, and all the creatures in it paused to listen. Cassandra stopped, but would not face them.

"He listens. When you talk to him, you must be willing to listen with all your heart."

Cassandra looked over her shoulder, saw the tears glistening in her mother's eyes, and fell to her knees before her.

"Please don't leave me."

Alone in the world, Lady Olympia read in Cassandra's eyes. She gathered her daughter in her arms and, bending, pressed a kiss on the top of her head. The unspoken words were like a wound, and her daughter had used her anger to protect it. Her mother meant to kiss the hurt, smooth the salve into the wound that went clear to her daughter's soul.

"But you'll never be alone," her mother said as Cassandra lifted her head. Lady Olympia brushed a wayward curl off her daughter's face, caught a tear, and smoothed it away.

At that moment, at the touch of her mother's hand, Cassandra felt as if a great light had blazed into being, illuminating the dark place in her mind, creating warmth where there had been cold emptiness. Cassandra knew that her mother's touch would be something she would remember forever. And because of the memory, and others like it, she would indeed never be alone.

Cassandra sat back on her heels with a sigh and placed her hands over her mother's.

"What else do I need to know about the swan?"

Lady Olympia straightened in her chair and turned her hands over to hold her daughter.

"When I was a child, I heard the swan possessed a secret . . . the secret of immortal beauty."

"An old wives' tale," muttered the Abbess.

At her sister's comment, Lady Olympia narrowed her eyes and pursed her lips. She cleared her throat, then proceeded.

"Inside the treasure lies a special compartment that holds the secret." Lady Olympia saw her daughter's eyes light up with curiosity. "You must find the swan lest such magic is discovered and misused."

"Hmph." The Abbess looked up and away as Cassandra and her mother both turned to follow the sound. When they were sure another doubting murmur was not forthcoming, mother and daughter turned to each other once again.

Leaning forward in her chair, Lady Olympia whispered, "Use your power of sight to find it."

Cassandra felt the Abbess's disapproval like a chill in the air.

"Such pagan ways you speak of, sister," the Abbess muttered under her breath. Lady Olympia pursed her lips again. Her eyes flashed Cassandra a warning to ignore the Abbess.

It was a sin to believe that anyone other than God the Father and the Son could divine the future. But in times past, before the coming of the Savior, there were men and women who had the gift and were praised for it. Cassandra had been named after a woman from Trojan times who had the ability to see into the future. And like her namesake and many of her female ancestors, Cassandra could read the future in a pool of water.

Cassandra thought of the sacred bowl of hammered bronze hidden away in her mother's room. The Abbess had taken the bowl away from Cassandra when she discovered the novices had been asking her to foretell their futures. She had never complied, but she was still guilty, if not of an actual act, then of a power that was dark, dangerous, pagan.

"I will return the sacred vessel to you tonight," said Lady Olympia.

"But—" The Abbess, eyes flashing between mother and daughter, puffed up like a thundercloud.

"And as long as you remain in the convent, you will use it only for this purpose," said Lady Olympia, arching her brows.

Cassandra nodded. She noticed the Abbess relax. All the anger that had made her puffy appeared to seep into the ground.

But Cassandra didn't need the sacred vessel to know that the swan had probably been pawned by her father to pay his gambling debts. It had been five years since her father's death.

"The swan could be anywhere in the Empire," Cassandra said, thinking out loud. "It could have been traded to the barbaric lands of the north!" She paused. A smile tugged at the corners of her mouth and spread slowly. "An adventure."

Cassandra's interest in her mother's request intensified at the thought of leaving the walls of the convent far, far, *far* behind. Imagine: running through open fields; walking into a sunset; racing the wind on an Arabian stallion; gazing upon the limitless blue of the sea and breathing its mussel-like smell. Walls would now be behind her. Never again would they keep her in, keep life out.

"There is one more thing," said her mother. She bit her lower lip. She wanted the hopeful look on her daughter's face to last forever, but instinctively, Lady Olympia knew that what she was about to say might dash it to bits.

"I've hired a bodyguard for your protection," she said, watching Cassandra's smile fade, "in the city, and throughout this quest." It was just as she feared; the light in her daughter's eyes vanished.

By the saints! Another wall, Cassandra thought to herself. Another protecting, shielding, limiting wall. And the name of this wall is . . .

"I'm not a child. Why do I need a bodyguard?" she scoffed, the fire back in her eyes.

"The ways of the world are—"

"—Dangerous, dark, evil," finished the Abbess.

"My beautiful, proud, strong daughter, you cannot go about this alone. You must be protected."

"I'll learn to fight and use a sword. How hard can that be?"

"Cassandra!"

"I'll use my power of sight to keep me from harm's way." No response from her mother except a heaven-sent gaze. Desperate, she tried again.

"I'll wear these robes!" she exclaimed, gripping the coarse fabric between her hands, liking the idea as she said it. "No one would dare harm a nun."

Her mother shook her head and defended her reasoning, but Cassandra would have none of it. She closed her mind, and her mother's words moved through her, words about how the man had been highly recommended by the Strategus of the Imperial Army, and how he had escorted the Empress herself on a pilgrimage to the Holy Lands, and how noble of spirit he was. They meant nothing to her. A wall was a wall.

By the evening meal, a low, whispery, velvety murmur had woven through the convent. Cassandra was being sent out into the world on a dangerous quest. And she was going to be protected by a bodyguard—a man. At the long trestle table, over their simple meal of bread and a soup of early spring vegetables and lamb, the novices could barely sit still. As one of the nuns read aloud from the Book of Psalms, the four novices, sitting at the far end, fidgeted, elbowed one another, and sent silent messages with their eyes. Sipping her soup, Cassandra caught the questioning look cast by Eudocia, sitting across the table. Pink-cheeked, with cheerful blue eyes, Eudocia glanced down the table of nuns and, feeling safe, looked back at Cassandra and mouthed the words, *Is it true? You're leaving?*

Cassandra nodded as she bit into a crust of bread.

"When?"

Cassandra shrugged.

"You're going back to Constantinople?" Eudocia's eyes widened with disbelief or fear, Cassandra couldn't tell which.

"Yes." A nun nailed her with a squinty look; Cassandra was not as good at this game as the others.

Cassandra froze and gazed piously at her food. She looked up tentatively. They were all staring: the three novices sitting across from her and the one on her left. Their fresh-scrubbed faces were bright with expectation and excitement. Sitting stiff and straight enough to balance apples on their heads, they all, as if of one mind, leaned closer. Eudocia asked the question that was firing color in their cheeks.

"You're to have a male protector?"

Cassandra narrowed her gaze. What was this fuss about a protector? A man? She knew Eudocia came from a prominent family with many brothers, uncles and male servants. And the others . . . it wasn't as if they'd never seen a man before. Of course she hadn't seen a man, save the priest who came to say the Mass and hear confessions, for close to two years. But the novices, who had been here longer than she, had not seen one in years. A man was something foreign, exotic.

A man was just another wall, mused Cassandra, nodding, "Yes. A protector."

But as they filed out of the refectory, Eudocia caught up to her.

"Do you think your protector will be as great as the Leopard?"

"Who?"

"Why, 'tis said the Leopard is the most accomplished of men. Legend has it he is a beast."

"A beast of a man," came the high-pitched whisper behind Cassandra, causing her to turn. It was Catherine— Cat, as she was called by the novices. Her eyes were like deep green pools.

Cat continued, reaching out to touch Cassandra's robe. "He is a beast known for his ability to stalk and *hunt*," she said, drawn to the word, relishing it on her tongue, "the empire's enemies."

"That is the kind of protector I would want," squeaked a voice.

Cassandra turned to the front and looked down on Thea, who was only eight. The little novice had been dumped at the convent by her widower father when she was six.

"Maybe you will be lucky," Thea continued. "Or, if the guard your mother has chosen is not suitable, you can hire the Leopard."

"How do you know of such a man?" Cassandra finally asked. For a convent, the place was a treasury of information about, of all things, bodyguards!

Eudocia lowered her eyes demurely and giggled behind her hand, as did the other novices. "We just . . . know. We may be cut off from the world, but the Convent of the Holy Cross isn't the end of it."

That night, moonlight streamed through the window in Cassandra's sleeping cell and pooled across the floor-boards. A votive candle cast a soft nimbus of gold beside her bed. The scent of rosemary and lavender cut through the damp, moldy smell of the stone walls.

The window was no larger than Cassandra's head. Its shutters had been bolted shut when she had first walked up to it two years ago. It was always open now, sometimes even in the winter. At night, when she was unable to sleep, she would lean against the wall next to her window and run her hand around the opening as if she were blind and studying the face of a friend.

Her back to the familiar stone wall, Cassandra turned her hands this way and that in the moonlight. She could feel the diamond-bright light washing over her. She could feel the cool of it. A wind brought the sound of new leaves dancing in the breeze and the earthy smell of growing things. She breathed in deeply and thought about summer: what bliss to smell the peaches and apricots from the orchard. And in the fall—the apples and pears. Figs and dates were her favorite foods, but neither was allowed inside the convent because the priest said they invited lascivious thoughts. But now that she was returning to Constantinople, she could have all the figs and dates she wanted!

But as with all good things, this one had an unpleasant side. The bodyguard. Cassandra groaned, already sensing the struggle that would undoubtedly ensue once he started curtailing her freedom. And there was the matter of her stubbornness, which was legendary; at least that is what the Abbess, with her martyred glances, seemed to think. Cassandra doubted a man was capable of the same *how you make me suffer!* type of a look. A man was capable of making you feel much worse. Cassandra was sure of it. Especially the bodyguard her mother had hired. She could feel it in her bones.

Perhaps . . . perhaps I could use my gift to see him, she thought to herself. The water will tell me something about the man. The water will tell me what I need to know.

She had discovered her gift when she was twelve. Her mother had not been surprised; many of the women in her family had been similarly blessed. Because it seemed such a natural part of her being, Cassandra had never been frightened of her power.

Only she wished she didn't have to use it for such a ridiculous purpose. Cassandra yanked the leather string holding her hair off her face and swore. "Christe!" She scrunched her nose and knitted her brows as she crossed the room. But before she reached under her bed for the package wrapped in silk, she paused and took a deep breath. She tried to clear her mind of dark thoughts. When she felt she could give the sacred vessel the reverence it was due, she picked it up. Carefully, she unwrapped the bowl, poured water from the little carafe she kept next to the candle, and set the bronze vessel in the middle of the pool of moonlight. She knelt before it.

The bowl looked old as Troy. It was beaten, worn, and dented. It glowed in the light and drew her close. Cassandra breathed in and out deeply, her gaze focused on the sacred vessel, her hands turned palms up, ready to receive the power.

Surrender and claim the strength that is yours. The voice in her mind was like an old friend. Cassandra relaxed and opened her mind to the visions, dreams that would come and be caught and gathered by the sacred vessel.

Leaning forward, Cassandra stared into the water. A breeze rippled the surface, breaking her reflection. Her surroundings blurred . . .

Through the ripples, a room appeared. Cassandra saw that it was a tent, a pavilion, hung with crimson draperies, illuminated by bronze lanterns and candles on ornate stands that glowed like gold. There were carpets on the floor, a leopard skin. And there was someone in the tent. A man. Black hair. His back was facing her. She could tell he was a soldier from his sword, sheathed at his side, his metal . . .

The water settled. Cassandra could see that the man was hunched over a little as if he was holding something close to him. No. He was holding someone, a woman, judging by the hair, which was long and silvery blonde . . .

Cassandra's eyes widened in recognition. It was she! And the man was . . . kissing her!

She felt the heat rising inside her and, magically, the feeling transformed her and she was there, in the tent, and the man was holding her in his arms.

She felt the fire of his lips on hers, his breath. He was whispering her name against her mouth. His hands were in her hair, drawing her closer, toward his heat. She could feel the urgent press of his body through her gown.

She heard her breath coming hard. And the heat. Like little explosions of fire. The animal fierceness of this stranger's passions unlocked something inside her. She felt it, a thing so liquid and hot she couldn't describe it. She moaned and the sound moved the water, breaking the image and the sensation of arms around her, a body pressing to become one with hers.

With a gasp, Cassandra sat back on her heels. *Christe! Is that my bodyguard?*

Her heart was thundering beneath her breast. She pushed her hair behind her ears and noticed her hands were shaking. *Control yourself. It meant nothing,* she said to herself. She gripped her hands together in her lap. *Nothing. He is not the one. It's a mistake.*

She swallowed and looked at the water. The vision had to be wrong. She dared not believe otherwise.

Chapter Two

The convent's chapel became quiet and still as the last nun departed, her robes swishing across the faience floor, leaving Cassandra and her mother to their prayers. It was just after Lauds on the morning Cassandra was to begin her journey back to the world, to the city of Constantinople, *Sodom and Gomorrah all in one* according to the Abbess. Two weeks had passed since Cassandra's mother had informed her daughter of the journey. There had been no more visions, because Cassandra had not turned to the sacred vessel for guidance. Somewhere in her mind, safely locked away, were the images of her in the arms of a man— her bodyguard. She refused to believe that the images had any prophetic value.

The rose light of the sun was pouring in through the windows. Only moments ago, the music of chanting voices had soared toward the dome of the chapel, filling the space with a calm certainty. So soothing was the sound, Cassandra had felt she was being held by caring arms. Now the quiet made her uneasy. She swore she could hear the dust motes dancing in the bright light, hear her heart beating with anticipation.

She could not keep still any longer. Pulling back the edge of her veil, she glanced sideways at her mother, who was kneeling beside her and moving her lips in silent prayer. Her amber eyes held the noble profile for a moment before rising to the murals above her mother's head. Her gaze swept the scenes that showed the life of Christ from the point of view of the Virgin. Her gaze lingered on the Annunciation and the Angel Gabriel before rising further, to the great golden dome and the mosaic of Christ Pantokrator holding the book of Gospels. He seemed so far away, whereas Mary, in her blue robes, with her large, beseeching eyes, appeared within reach.

Something about those eyes, Cassandra thought to herself. Feeling something inside her open, she bowed her head, closed her eyes, and started to pray.

"Hail Mary, full of grace, bless and keep my mother safe in this sacred place. Give me the strength to leave her so that I might fulfill her wish. And if it is not too much to ask, guide me in my search. I am not afraid of the world beyond these holy doors, but I fear that my temper and impatience might lead me into situations that are best to be avoided. The gift of prophecy helps me to see, but not all things. Only you and Christ, Our Lord, have the power to know all. With all my soul I believe that, with your divine help, I will return with the swan and my mother will live to share her wisdom with me again. All honor and glory are yours, most blessed Mother. Hear my prayers," she whispered, believing her words, squeezing her hands together.

During Lauds, Lady Olympia had sensed her daughter's impatience, but it was not enough to lure her from praying. She meant to lay a protective path of prayers that would carry Cassandra forward into the world, and nothing was going to keep her from her mission, even her fidgeting daughter. When Lady Olympia felt Cassandra lower her head and heard the soft whispering, she smiled. It was a change so slight, it suggested peace and serenity instead of pleasure. It was a mother's smile, a smile echoed in the mosaic of the Virgin and Child.

But Lady Olympia wasn't smiling when it came time to say good-bye to her daughter. The Abbess, standing just outside the convent's gatehouse and to the side of mother and daughter, caught the frantic, fearful look in Lady Olympia's eyes as she watched the chairbearers approach the convent, winding up the hill of yellow rocks and stones. Cassandra was unnaturally still and quiet, the sight of the caravan that would bear her away holding her like the dance of a snake. Suddenly, the girl looked at her mother. The Abbess saw the hope in Cassandra's wide gaze, a look that waited for the turn of a mother's head and a wordless message that would end this waiting, a look that meant, *I've changed my mind. Let's go back inside.*

With no walls to stop the wind, great gusting blasts of spring air made their robes flap, their veils flutter like the wings of restless birds. But no one moved.

Finally, Lady Olympia turned to her daughter. Sighing, she shook her head and reached out to touch the edge of Cassandra's veil. The Abbess had objected strongly to Cassandra's request to leave the convent dressed as a nun. It had taken the will of a bull to break through the Abbess's wall of *No!s.* But Cassandra's stubbornness eventually won out: she convinced her mother and the Abbess that it was God's will. She wasn't committing a grievous sin, she was doing it for her own safety. Who would harm a nun? She promised to put the robes and veil aside once she reached Constantinople. But until then, she was a nun from the Convent of the Holy Cross.

"You will remember to give Anne the key?" said Lady

Olympia, referring to Cassandra's nursemaid, who would be meeting her, along with two servants, at the abandoned villa. Lady Olympia had sent word of Cassandra's arrival weeks ago. The key, hanging from a belt around Cassandra's waist, would open a steel box of jewels that was hidden beneath the floor in the triclinium, the dining room.

"I will."

"And you will not do anything that will upset her?" Lady Olympia's face was a study in seriousness, but her eyes twinkled with memories of her daughter hiding garden snakes and other green, slimy creatures from the garden in her nursemaid's bed.

"I . . ." she began and met her mother's imploring gaze, "will try, but you know it takes very little to set her off, clutching her breast, claiming I've given her another attack."

"She's your nursemaid, Cassandra. Family. She deserves your respect. I will not remind you of it again."

"I know my duty."

"I know you do." Lady Olympia closed the space between her and her daughter and laid her hand against Cassandra's face. "May God be with you, my brave, beautiful, all-too-willful girl."

Cassandra knelt before her mother to receive her blessing. Lady Olympia made the sign of the cross, then bent forward to kiss the top of her daughter's head. She helped Cassandra to rise. They stood looking at one another until the noise and heavy breathing of the tired chairbearers and the escort reached the convent's gatehouse. Lady Olympia drew her daughter into her arms and rocked her as if she were still her baby. With a sigh, Lady Olympia released her daughter. After one last kiss, Cassandra ran to pick up a small box, her sole possession, and, robes crackling in the wind, approached the chair that would carry her to the city.

The Abbess noted the paleness of Lady Olympia's skin and frowned. Hesitantly, she said, "Are you sure you must go through with this?"

Lady Olympia shook her head to imply *no*. She watched her daughter glance back, wave, then climb into the chair. "When is a mother ever sure when it comes to the raising of a daughter? How can a mother know?" She paused and turned to the Abbess. "But I know one thing," she said, arching her brows. "I cannot bear to have her watch me grow weaker and weaker."

Lady Olympia turned her focus back to the chair. As she watched the escort draw the curtains and give the signal to leave, she continued, as if speaking to herself. "She must use her strength, not for me, but for the path which lies ahead. Cassandra will find the swan. She will come back." Her throat filled, painfully tight. "And I . . ."

". . . Will welcome her back with open arms," finished the Abbess. *"Dieu le veut.* God wills it," she said. But behind her pious declaration was something else, and it made Lady Olympia slide a quick glance at her sister. She knew all too well that the Abbess was glad to see her daughter leave.

In silence, hands tucked in the sleeves of their habits, Lady Olympia and the Abbess watched as the chairbearers lifted Cassandra's chair on the supporting poles and began their descent down the hill and to the road to Constantinople.

After one last look at her mother, Cassandra settled back into the depths of the chair. She wrinkled her nose. The cushions smelled musty. She parted the curtains to let in the sweet air. She fidgeted and fussed with her robes. Finally, spotting the reliquary, she scooped it up and set it on her lap. It was made of chased silver and, according to the merchant, it had once held the veil of St. Agnes. Of course, she'd never believed the merchant, but it was good for holding things. Carefully, as the box was old, she removed the cover. Inside were papers of parchment with the recipes for fragrances and creams. She moved these to the side to look at her mother's emerald ring, recalling her mother's startling advice.

"Sell the ring first. It's no more than a bauble. But the recipes . . . they are your inheritance from the women of my family. They are priceless. If you must sell one, use *Moonlight in the Garden*. Take it to a shop on the Mese called . . ."

The memory was abruptly cut off by a chairbearer who stumbled, sending Cassandra tottering over onto her side. In a heartbeat, the other bearers righted the chair. There was a heated exchange of words then, as if they'd suddenly remembered that they were carrying a nun—dead silence.

The chair swayed and bounced along without any further mishap, reaching the City gate by late afternoon. At the gate, the chief of the bearers spoke to the gatekeepers, and passed along a piece of money. The land wall that protected Constantinople was made of the same dark yellow stone as the Convent of the Holy Cross. But unlike the convent, it rose twenty feet high to a top surface as broad and smooth as a road. It was said that the Virgin Mary guarded the walls. Many soldiers had seen the Virgin when she came to warn them about a surprise attack by the Arabs. It had been a miracle, and it had happened a long time ago. Cassandra knew the story but, peering out between the curtains as they entered the city and craning her neck to see the top of the wall, she could not help thinking that she might be exchanging one enclosed world for another.

* * *

Alone in the courtyard of her family's villa, Cassandra turned, her eyes sweeping over the cracks in the stone pavement, the terra cotta pots crowned with dead herbs, the trees and shrubs overgrown into spindly shapes like monsters from a child's nightmare. It looked like the perfect place for an old family ghost to take up residence.

The chairbearers must have thought so, too, because as soon as Cassandra stepped out of the litter.

Cassandra sighed as she walked toward the stone fountain. She couldn't fault the men for running away. The place looked as if someone had cast a dark spell over it.

She looked into the fountain and wrinkled her nose at the smell and the sight of slimy green water. This had been one of her favorite spots to sit and play when she was a child. Her father had made her a fleet of sailing ships, and she had commanded the fountain's waters as if they were the seas to new worlds. Lured by the memory, she moved to dip her finger in, but at the last moment, stopped. She brushed her hands against her robes, as if to clean off the dank and haunted gloom of the place.

Mother! Cassandra's throat filled with tears at the ruin that surrounded her. Why was she going through this alone? She wished her mother was with her. She wished her father was still alive. She wished . . . she wished . . .

"Get a hold of yourself, Cassandra," she said softly to herself. "There's work to be done. Mother is counting on you." Cassandra knew she would never be able to banish the darkness from her past. All she could do was keep moving forward. So with steely resolve, she lifted her chin and turned to face the iron gates. They were still open, gaping wide. She crossed the courtyard. Using all her strength, she pushed the rusted, heavy metal of one side closed, then the other. She tried to be careful and not let

the two ends bang together; how her father hated that
sound! But at the last moment, the gates seemed to lurch
out of her hands, almost catching her thumbs, and closed
with a resounding screech and thud.

The villa's hollow emptiness echoed Cassandra's mood.
What little courage she had summoned in the courtyard
drained out of her the moment she saw the garden in the
atrium. She slumped against a marble column and shook
her head in disbelief over the weeds and thorns and ugly
curling masses of things just beginning to turn green with
spring. All her mother's work—destroyed. All the flowers
her mother had coaxed into blooms—gone. Cassandra
listened and looked for the birds that used to live in the
tree branches. There was only the heavy silence of dead
things.

Anger welled up inside her like a red-hot fist. How dare
this happen to her home! No longer shocked by the
destruction, she kicked the leaves and debris that dared
to hide the cream marble floors. Her arms lashed out at
the cobwebs that filmed the walls and frescoes. She grumbled at the birds that had built a nest on the gold wall
sconce in the hall. She screamed at the mice in the empty,
shallow reflecting pool. When she yanked the protective
coverings off the cedar chairs and divans, she sent clouds
of dust billowing in the air. At the cedar doors to the
triclinium, she paused briefly, then pushed the doors open.
The shrouded divans set up around the table looked like
ghosts. But it was the fresco of the nine Muses with Apollo
that commanded her attention. Noticing that the painting
was unharmed, her narrowed, glittering eyes softened. Cassandra smiled at the scene that greeted her, and for the
first time, she was glad to be home.

Hours later, to the golden light of beeswax candles she
had found in her mother's study and stuck into the cande-

labrum, Cassandra sat eating in the dining room, staring at the fresco. The nuns had packed her a simple meal of cheese, bread, and olives. She was still wearing her brown robes and veil, but she was sitting most un-nunlike, with her feet tucked up under her, on one of the divans. She had swept the floors as best she could and wiped away the cobwebs. She could hear the family of mice scurrying about in the hall, but she didn't care. She smiled as she popped a green olive into her mouth.

The flickering candlelight made the saffron-colored dining room walls shimmer like gold. The images of the nine Muses looked like they were dancing. Cassandra took account of all the goddesses that graced the room. The Muses were dressed in sheer, flowing white gowns. No doubt their state of dress was responsible for the gleam in Apollo's eyes as he hid behind a tree, watching. All of the goddesses were well shaped and had long, flowing hair and beautiful eyes. Of all of the art—the paintings and mosaics that had once graced the house—the fresco had been her father's favorite piece. There was not much left in the form of decoration, as everything had been sold to pay off her father's debts, including the enameled swan her mother wanted her to find. But the fresco was the heart of the villa.

Tired, happy, and sad all at once, Cassandra stretched and yawned. "Tomorrow I'll work on the garden," she said aloud to the nine goddesses. Curling up on the divan, her nun's robes blanketing her, she closed her eyes. With the Muses looking on, Cassandra slept.

"Haghia Sophia! Who's this? A thief? There's a thief in the house!"

The screeching woke Cassandra, then she felt the slap of a cloth in her face. "What—" She put her hand out to protect herself from another blow, but it came anyway. "Stop!" She struggled up onto her side and watched her nursemaid about to deliver another blow.

"Anne! It's me. Stop."

Anne's arm froze in mid-swing. The woman's eyes widened, taking account of the nun's habit and veil. "A nun! I've been hitting a nun! Haghia Sophia! I'm damned, damned. I'm—"

"You're not damned. It's me, Cassandra."

Cassandra sat up and swung her legs over the side of the divan.

"What? Mistress Cassandra? You're a nun?"

"Well . . . in a way."

Anne's head pulled back and she backed up like a confused pigeon.

"It's a long story," Cassandra said. She stretched and yawned, all the while keeping her eyes on her nursemaid, waiting for Anne to clutch her breast and feign an attack of the heart.

Anne glanced at what remained of Cassandra's dinner on the table. "Your dear mother's letter said you would be here." The nursemaid peered at Cassandra as if in doubt of her identity. Her forehead and the area around her mouth wrinkled in concentration. "But she made no mention of a nun."

"I'll explain everything later."

Anne sighed as if she were the greatest martyr on earth. "Where have I heard that before?" As if the matter was closed, Anne began to clear off the table. Cassandra reached out to help.

"I promise," Cassandra whispered, placing her hand over Anne's.

"Oh, mistress!" the nursemaid cried out, flinging herself into Cassandra's arms. "I've missed you so. And your mother?" Anne pulled away just enough to look up into

Cassandra's face. "Has the blessed water helped? How does she fare?"

Cassandra felt her nurse's soft arms and frail bones through the old woman's tunic and dalmatica. Anne's hair was completely grey and rolled into a braid that crowned her head. Her eyes, still youthful and alive, were ice-blue.

"My mother grows weaker every day," Cassandra admitted, releasing the woman. "Although she would have me believe that she is feeling stronger. You know how she is," she said, looking over her shoulder as she bent to clear off the bread and remaining olives. But when she saw the older woman's eyes film with tears, Cassandra looked away. She turned back to her task, saying, "Now she's sent me on a quest. To find a swan of enamel with mechanical, flapping wings."

"I remember it," said Anne, wiping her eyes, nodding her head. "I think your father, God rest his soul, sold—"

"Yes," Cassandra finished for her. "I know. It could be anywhere in the Empire. But I'll find it."

She turned again, her hands full, and breathed deeply. "I'm glad you're here."

"Well, of course I'm here!" Anne puffed up her chest. The sadness vanished from her wrinkled face as duty propelled her to take the food from her mistress and carry it away. "Good thing, too! A young girl like you, alone here! Humph! I can't imagine what might have happened had I not arrived when I did," she said, more to herself than to Cassandra as she walked out of the room, still talking. "Even with the bodyguard coming. No telling when he might arrive. Like most men, he probably won't be here until he's good and ready."

The bodyguard. Cassandra moaned.

Anne appeared suddenly in the dining room doorway. "Are you ill?" she asked, concern knotting her forehead.

Cassandra smiled weakly and shook her head.

"I wouldn't be surprised. Olives, you know," Anne said matter-of-factly, walking away.

Nervously, Cassandra started to push her hair behind her ears, then stopped as she remembered, and felt, that she was still wearing the veil. She tugged it off and slumped back onto the divan.

The image on the water. Remember?

Something was released in Cassandra's mind. The memory of a vision—a man holding her and kissing her—filled her head and swept through her body like a wave of heat.

"The bodyguard?" she muttered to herself. She frowned. "Impossible."

The villa came to life. Cassandra and Anne, joined by two of the servingwomen who had served the Heraclius family for many years, cleaned the villa until the floors gleamed and the walls shimmered with the colors of the harvest and the sea. The smell of camphor lingered on the second floor; Cassandra remembered her mother using it to disinfect the bedding every spring and fall. Lavender, mixed with herbs crushed between Anne's hands, scented the first floor. The smell of bread baking seemed to put everything right; Cassandra could almost hear the villa omit a contented sigh of pleasure.

With the chores in Anne and the servingwomen's capable hands, Cassandra turned her attention to her sleeping chamber. The white marble floor, veined with pink tendrils of color, gleamed. Cream-colored linen covered a cedar bed piled high with white and gold silk pillows. She looked at it wistfully. She couldn't wait to sleep in her own bed. Then she surveyed the pile of silk and woolen tunics and dalmaticas spread out on the floor in a circle around her.

"Now if only I could find something to wear," Cassandra muttered. She frowned and held up another tunic. The shoulders! The length! It looked as if it had been made for a little girl!

"Too small," she sighed, dropping the garment onto a pile. She sat back on her heels and crossed her arms. What was she going to do? She'd promised the Abbess and her mother that she would put aside her nun's robes. She couldn't possibly continue to wear them. That would be a sacrilege. Or some kind of sin: probably the kind that would mean a very long stay in purgatory, she mused. She pushed her hair behind her ears, then tapped her fingertips together. "Think, Cassandra, think."

Mother's clothes!

With the idea to search her mother's wardrobe, she rose to her feet.

"Mistress? Cassandra?" the whispery voice from the doorway made her pause. She looked and saw one of the servingwomen nervously twisting her tunic. "Mistress? You have a visitor."

A visitor? But who knew . . . ? There was something about the woman's eyes; they had that startled, powerless look.

"Anne says he was sent by your mother, the Lady Olympia."

The bodyguard.

"Christe!" she swore under her breath. She growled low in her throat, then stopped abruptly, catching the servingwoman's eyes on her. Cassandra smiled ruefully. "Tell Anne I'll be right there."

She grabbed a tunic from the mass of silk at her feet. A mirror of bronze caught her scowl as she held the garment to her and smoothed its folds. Impossible, she thought. It would barely cover her knees!

She paced back and forth. There was no time to look in her mother's room for something suitable. She would have to . . . she would have to . . .

Cassandra froze. She walked to the mirror as if her life

depended on it and studied her reflection. Her face, clenched and tight with seriousness, began to relax as her mind explored the possibility of a disguise. She grinned mischievously and, without another thought, picked up her nun's veil, secured it, and dashed out of the room.

Chapter Three

Nicephorus Acominatus, tall and dignified, paced the hall like a caged animal. The heavy scrape of his boots on the marble floor, the metallic bite of his silver body armor, and his sword, tucked in its leather scabbard and banging against his leg with each step, made it sound as if an army had descended. His blue cloak swirled dramatically around him each time he turned. His obvious irritation made Anne's skin prickle. She stood watch, eyes on the black-haired soldier, guarding her domain proudly. But every now and then, she sneaked a hopeful glance at the stairs.

Nicephorus gripped the pommel of his sword. He moved his right shoulder, as if to work the stiffness out, or to shrug off the old woman's stare. Weren't they expecting him? he asked himself. Why was he kept waiting? Who was he waiting for? This was no way to treat the next Strategus of the Imperial Army.

He puffed up his chest, rolling the thought in his mind: Strategus, General. He deserved it. In another year he would be leading the Imperial Cavalry. He was sure of it. He just needed time for his arm to heal.

He sneered, baring his teeth at the thought of his wound. He felt the old woman take a step back, and derived a bit of pleasure from her discomfort. It was nothing compared to the humiliation he felt for being ordered, by his commanding officer, to accept this post as a *bodyguard*. He narrowed his eyes contemptuously at the description. He'd had no choice but to accept the position. It was either this or a dull stay at his officer's villa in the country. "Give your arm time to heal, Nicephorus. I can't afford to lose you. But if you stay on active duty, you'll do more damage, and the Turks will be singing with joy when they learn that you're a threat to them no more."

Nicephorus crossed his arms over his chest. A hot, lancing pain shot up his arm to his shoulder. He ignored it, using the pain to fuel his impatience. He couldn't wait to meet the imbecile who was keeping him waiting. By all accounts, judging from the location of the villa and the decoration, the person had money. Probably some wretched old goat who had made a pack of enemies from his crooked business deals. "Well, I just might double my price," Nicephorus thought, his upper lip curling in a sneer.

Lost in his thoughts, Nicephorus didn't hear the soft footsteps on the stairs. He didn't see the exchange of glances that passed between the nursemaid and Cassandra: the amazed look of wonder on the older woman's face at Cassandra's daring; and the pleading amber eyes that beseeched Anne to go along with whatever was about to unfold.

As he was turning, he caught the old woman's gaze and followed it. He froze: there, poised on the steps in brown robes and veil, her eyes downcast, was a nun. He heard himself gasp. Christe! He'd be guarding a nun? Why, in

God's name? All the surprise attacks he'd dealt with throughout his career had never prepared him for this!

His shock calmed Cassandra. Her heart had started beating with alarm the moment she saw him: black hair, tall, powerful. Was the prophecy coming true? Was this the man who had been revealed by the sacred waters? It wasn't possible. She could feel the color draining from her face. She reached out to hold the wall as she took another step down.

Nicephorus opened his mouth to greet her, but nothing came out. He swallowed. She was so pale! Her eyelids, nose, and mouth so delicately carved . . . like a statue of marble, he thought.

He could picture her standing in a niche in the Haghia Sophia, with candles lit around her feet. He could see people praying to her, asking for forgiveness and help. He could hear the soft, velvety whisper of their prayers.

Nicephorus watched her continue her descent, all the while keeping her eyes downcast as if she were afraid of being turned into a pillar of salt if she looked at him. He slid a glance at the old woman—she was frowning at the nun. That's strange, he thought to himself. The woman's eyes were like little dagger points.

The nun stopped in front of him. The top of her head came barely to his chin. He looked down at the veiled head bowed before him. He felt the color rising in his cheeks, he felt like a beast, unworthy of standing before the bride of Christ.

The nun cleared her throat and slid a glance at the old woman, which prompted Anne to speak.

"Welcome . . ." the old woman ventured, ". . . Captain?" she asked hesitantly.

"Captain Nicephorus Acominatus, at your service."

Anne held out her arm. "This is . . . Sister . . . Cassandra."

"Welcome, Captain."

The words were so hushed, Nicephorus had to bend over to hear. Perhaps she's never spoken to a man before, he thought. Some of these nuns spent their whole lives in the company of women.

"I apologize for keeping you waiting. I wasn't expecting you this early."

Her words were like velvet. He fought the urge to move closer, so drawn was he by the deep voice. Such a contrast to her humble and meek manner, he thought, narrowing his eyes on the bowed head before him.

The icon of meekness anxiously gripped her hands together in a tight ball beneath her sleeves.

Silence locked the nun and the captain together. A disturbing thought continued to ring through Cassandra's mind: was this the man from her dreams? She could not risk the chance that he was the man the waters had revealed. She had to make him leave!

"I trust you will find protecting me quite dull. It was the wish of my . . . superiors that I have a guard while I am in the city. If, for any reason, you believe that this position is not suitable for one of your standing, please, Captain, feel free to tell me." She paused and raised her face to look at him. "And I shall release you of this charge."

"Release you," he echoed to himself. Never, came the vow automatically in Nicephorus's mind as he stared into the amber eyes. The naked meeting of their eyes gave him a thrill like no meeting of naked skin ever had. Her eyes were the color of honey. He saw innocence in their depth . . . and more. There was a spark that seemed to challenge him again.

The man's frank, open look made Cassandra feel shy. She bent her head before him. She felt him shifting his weight, heard the soft jingling of his mail, the creak of his leather belt. She could not help herself—she looked up at him again.

Cassandra felt a change in Nicephorus, a softening and yielding in his body and gray-blue eyes that enticed her to look closely at him. She noted the broad planes of his face, his strong mouth. His voice, when she'd first heard it, had reminded her of early morning summer rains and polished bronze. The black-haired beast she had caught pacing back and forth in her hall was gone. She tilted her head, lost in her musings. *This is a different animal,* she thought to herself.

She was perfectly still, and yet she felt herself being drawn toward him. She wanted to place her finger on the scar on his chin. She wanted him to speak to her—no, whisper, again.

Like a lily opening its face to the warmth of the sun, Cassandra felt something inside her turn and grow. Looking at him, standing so close, made her feel warm and quiet. She was glad to be wearing the nun's robes, for there was a part of her that wanted to hide. She shoved her hands further up her sleeves and dropped her gaze to the floor.

She cleared her throat of the feelings that had become lodged there. "Please, you mustn't feel any obligation to stay. I am quite capable of caring for myself. I can write to my superiors tonight and tell them of the change."

"Nay . . . Sister. I am yours, er, your servant. I am duty-bound to remain at my post."

Cassandra's grimace was hidden by the folds of her veil. "Then perhaps—tomorrow, if you wish—you can return. I will reveal my plan then."

"But I have orders, as your protector, never to let you out of my sight," he answered gently.

"Never?" Cassandra replied, a sarcastic lilt to her voice. She looked up at him, her eyes sparkling mischievously.

"There are some things, Captain, that, I'm afraid, you will not be permitted to . . . view."

The captain's mouth curved in a smile and it made her weak in the knees.

She steadied herself. "I'm sure that my Lord, my God, is pleased that you take your orders so seriously, Captain," she answered, lowering her eyes once again.

At the mention of the Lord's name, Nicephorus swallowed uncomfortably and shifted his weight from side to side. He glanced sideways and steeled himself against the stare of the old woman, which was so intense, he was sure she'd been reading his thoughts.

"Now you've done it! He's making a place for himself in your garden," complained Anne through her teeth as she stood in the dining chamber's doorway, spying on the man.

Cassandra winced at the news and dropped onto a divan in the dining chamber. The captain had left the villa, only to return a few hours later with enough equipment to stage a siege. His horse was in the stable. His bedroll was plumped up against one of the columns in the atrium. Christe! It was happening too fast.

"And now he thinks you're a nun. *Sister* Cassandra. I've never heard of a Saint named Cassandra, so I know it can't be true." Anne was tapping her hand over her breast, so Cassandra knew the woman was preparing herself for one of her attacks.

What was she going to do? How could her mother do this to her? She didn't need anyone to take care of her. She was perfectly capable of looking after herself. But no. Her mother had to secure a captain, this man, to look after her. Handsome though he was, she didn't want him here. He was in her way. He was just another wall!

And now she was caught in a web. *Sister Cassandra*. She gritted her teeth and shook her fists. *I can't do this.*

You must, she answered herself. She breathed deeply in an effort to calm herself, but the image that had been revealed to her by the water kept surfacing. *But what if it's not he?* she thought. She'd only seen him from behind. There had to be scores of tall, black-haired men in the city.

But wait . . . the man hadn't been kissing *Sister Cassandra!* Her mind reached out and grasped the simple detail. Her eyes narrowed in concentration. Was that it? Could she have the power to alter the course of events? Maybe the prophecy couldn't come true . . . for Sister Cassandra.

She jumped to her feet. "Then the way out is to keep my identity as a nun," she said to herself. "Hide in these nun's robes and hope the man will get bored or tired. Why would he possibly wish to keep company with Sister Cassandra? Devout, meek, obedient Sister Cassandra?" She smiled to herself.

A little detail reared its head. Cassandra sighed deeply at the prospect of behaving like a nun from the Convent of the Holy Cross. But in the next breath, she vowed it would be a performance that would make the Abbess proud.

Cassandra saw a lot of the villa's floor in the days that followed. A study in meekness and humility, she walked about in her nun's habit, her eyes perpetually cast toward the ground in front of her. But most of the time, she simply stayed away from her bodyguard. Anne helped, telling him, when he asked for Sister Cassandra, that she was in meditation or prayer. It was all Anne needed to say, and he would back away. But Cassandra still felt as if she'd grown a shadow, a protective presence, but not like an angel's.

It was more like an animal's, a beast protecting what belonged to him.

At night, whenever her mind turned to thoughts of the captain, she'd scold herself. "You're no wiser than the novices back at the convent," she'd complain aloud, at night, in her room.

She felt invisible in her nun's habit. And she liked it. But when she ran into him, their hands and bodies would graze, sending shocks of heat through her, reminding her that she was very real. As was he. She knew he felt it, too, by the way he held himself, close to her, breathless. But he was always the one who turned away first, as if he didn't want to look too long at her, and be reminded of her vows.

She fought the memory of her vision—his touch, his lips on hers, his mouth whispering his desire. A pagan prophecy. She knew that the robes and veil would be enough to shield her. They had to be enough. As real as it had felt, she had no choice but to believe that she was safe as long as she remained Sister Cassandra.

"You should let her look at your arm."

Nicephorus looked up at Anne, but continued rubbing his arm and rolling his shoulder to stretch it, for he was afraid the wound, although it was healing, would leave his fighting arm stiff. He was standing by the courtyard's fountain, his booted foot on the rim. His hair was wet where he'd splashed himself to cool off. He'd just finished brushing down his horse and cleaning out the stall. Anne had been helping Cassandra plant herbs in the terra cotta pots that lined the brick walkway.

Nicephorus turned his gaze to the far side of the courtyard where Sister Cassandra was adding fresh earth to an urn. He returned his attention to the old woman.

Anne tugged at the kerchief tied around her head and

said, "She has a gift for ministering to wounds and such. Knows which herbs and creams can aid in the cure."

"Does she?" They'd spent the last two days staying out of each other's way. He felt she'd been going to great lengths to avoid him, for they were never in the same place at the same time. She'd already told him about her quest to find a treasure, an enameled swan. He thought it an odd thing for a nun to do, but kept his opinions private. He reminded himself that he was being paid to protect her, not to give his opinions.

"I imagine the convent is a good place to learn tasks of that nature."

"Mmmmm. Taught by her mother, as well. Fine lady. The most gracious woman in all the Empire." Anne sat back on her heels and let her gaze wander to Cassandra. Squinting, she cupped her hand over her eyes to shield them from the sun. "Had high hopes for her. Prayed that she'd marry well, an educated nobleman with Roman blood. Have a brood of children . . ."

"One might say she *has* married well," he pointed out. He watched Cassandra tugging on her robes as she rose to her feet.

"Humph," Anne snorted.

Startled, Nicephorus looked at the nurse and was reminded of the anger in the old woman's eyes the day he met his charge.

As though Cassandra had sensed the meaning of their conversation, she suddenly turned. Like any ordinary, shy, young girl, she blushed.

Nicephorus felt like touching her. Shocked by his own crudeness, he blinked and snapped to attention as if he'd been issued an order.

"How's your arm, Captain?" Cassandra cried out, moving toward him, her robes rippling gracefully. "Has it been troubling you?"

"It's fine."

"Tush. He was just moving it about as if it was ailing him," corrected Anne. Moaning, her hand on the small of her back, she rose to her feet in a hunched position. Slowly, she straightened and walked out of the sun.

"Indeed?" Cassandra stopped directly in front of him and, as if her habit was just an ordinary gown and she just an ordinary woman, she looked him in the eyes.

"I can look at it, if you like," she offered.

Afraid? he read in her eyes. Or, at least he thought he saw the faint glimmer of a challenge.

"We won't be damned if I just have a look," she cajoled. "Sit," she ordered.

After a moment, Nicephorus obeyed, sitting on the rim of the fountain, hoping he would not regret it.

Cassandra craved opportunities to test her knowledge, so with singular purpose, without noting the muscular strength of his arms and back, she poked and prodded, innocently touching him through his tunic. She pulled the neck of his tunic aside, as far as she could without tearing it, to check the wound. The cut ran from the front of his shoulder to the middle of his upper back. A sword, no doubt, she thought to herself. The look of the wound told her that the assailant had probably intended to cut off the captain's entire arm. He'd nearly succeeded.

She marveled at the stitches. They were the work of an artist, precise and even. There would be a scar, but it would not disfigure him or leave a ghostly ripple of white, shiny flesh. She touched it, pressing the flesh around the wound, too. It was healing nicely.

Nicephorus drew in a deep breath as a sharp wave of desire crashed through him. Bigod! How could she assume that he'd just sit here and endure her touch as if it were the most natural thing? But then, it did feel natural. And right. He squeezed his hands into fists and gulped as her fingers moved with feathery lightness to the middle of his back. It took all his power not to pull her down into his lap. As she pressed and studied and whispered, he knew not what, under her breath, he became afraid. He was not fearful of going to Hell for obliging her; he was afraid she would stop. And that she would look at him without a glimmer of feeling, as a surgeon would regard a patient.

Cassandra noticed his chest rising and falling with quick breaths. The innocence of her actions became filled with a meaning she did not quite understand, but she felt enough to be ashamed. With a start, she backed away from him.

"Forgive me," she whispered.

At her apology, Nicephorus looked up and met her gaze and became lost in the amber beauty of her eyes. His stare deepened. She blushed.

For a moment, it was all different: Nicephorus felt their roles falling away. He felt stripped of his role as soldier and protector. He was just a man. And she—a woman.

By the third day, she'd had enough of her captivity, for she had no doubt she was being held captive in her own home. The day was cloudy, damp and close with the smell of a storm in the air. She was pacing the floor in her room, her brow furrowed in thought. She pulled her veil off and tossed it onto the bed.

When she'd left the convent, she thought she'd be free and could come and go as she pleased. But the captain had made certain that his charge would not be leaving the villa. Ever. All the shopping was being done by Anne and the servingwomen. She didn't have to do anything . . . except avoid Nicephorus.

And begin her task of finding the swan. She walked across the room to a wooden chest with wrought iron filigrees, on an iron stand. She dropped to her knees and smoothed her palms across the top. Safely tucked inside was the bronze bowl. Tonight, she knew there would be a full moon. The sacred bowl would help her see the swan. She hoped to use what little moonlight the storm would permit to guide her visions.

But first she had to find some way to get the captain out of her villa. Get him far, far away from her. With a great sigh, she sat back on her heels. She was following the grain of the wood with her finger when an idea came to her. As if God had advised her, she rose to her feet, grabbed her veil, and went to look for her bodyguard.

She found the captain clearing the atrium's garden of fallen boughs and dead branches. Sweat stained the back and front of his sleeveless tunic, which was cinched by a wide leather belt. He had rolled and tied a piece of cloth around his forehead. He reminded her of the gladiators she had seen in the murals that decorated the Hippo-drome.

She could smell the earth, the scent of storm on the breeze, the clean maleness of his sweat.

"Uh-hmm," she said, clearing her throat to get his atten-tion. When he turned to see who it was, she permitted herself to look at him.

The man was looking at her with his gray-blue, far-seeing eyes, which made her turn her face away a little. The speech she'd prepared vanished.

Nicephorus turned away briefly, and tossed the dead branch into the pile with the others. He winced slightly at the pain in his shoulder, then returned his attention to the nun. He thought her beautiful and found her shyness attractive. But there was something about her he did not understand. He felt it whenever they were standing

together, like this, or when they'd run into each other,
their bodies colliding. He was not a clumsy man, but being
under the same roof with the nun seemed to befuddle his
center of balance and sense of direction. There was a
strong womanly presence about her, a sense of femaleness
that he thought unusual for a nun. And there was the
scent of flowers about her. Musky and sweet. The smell
made him wonder what it would feel like to be held in
her arms.

"I was wondering if I might have a word with you?" she
asked in her soft, rather breathless voice, looking unconsciously into his eyes again.

The captain, sensing her discomfort, took command of
the situation. "Of course," he answered.

"You're so . . . kind to take an interest in the garden,"
she said, looking about her, noticing the strides he had
made in clearing the dead branches, ridding it of the
gloom that had settled in. Even the birds, she noticed,
were returning.

"It's been a long time since someone looked after it,"
he said, following her gaze.

"Two years," she said under her breath, forgetting that
she had not told him anything yet about the villa, her
family, her quest.

"What's that?"

She decided to tell him a little. "This is my family's
home. My father died five years ago. My mother is . . . ill.
She is at the Convent of the Holy Cross."

"I'm sorry. It is good, I suppose, that you can now call
the Church your family, and that you are not completely
alone." There was a wistfulness to his tone that gave her
the impression that he had no living relatives, or even
friends. She looked at him closely. To see him, standing
so self-assured, tall, and powerful, even without his sword,
she would have thought he didn't need anyone.

"Our Lord God takes care of all those who turn to him."
She truly meant it. It didn't matter to her that she was not
a nun. She still had the right to think it.

She continued. "What I came here to say is that you've
been so patient, giving yourself tasks here, that I was wondering if you'd like the evening to pursue . . . whatever
relaxing pleasures men in the city pursue." Christe! How
could her tongue get so tied up?

He looked taken aback by her proposition, his brow
furrowing with little lines, for what did a nun know about
pleasurable, manly pursuits? Then a devilish gleam came
into his eyes. "What pleasures do you advise me to
pursue?"

"Oh," she said and waved her right hand, feeling as if
he were backing her into a corner. "You know of what I
speak, Captain." She could feel herself blushing, and hated
it. The man was daring her to continue!

A spark ignited inside her. She squared her shoulders
and lifted her chin. The Abbess would be displeased, but
she could not ignore a challenge. "You know . . . gambling,
drinking . . ."

"Yes?" he encouraged. Cassandra could read the expression in his eyes; he couldn't believe he was discussing such
matters with a nun. It drove her on.

"And women." She paused. "My father was such a
man."

His eyes met hers and held them for an instant before
turning away guiltily. Beneath the nun's robe was a woman
who'd lived as an ordinary child.

He took a step to resume his task.

"Here," she said, stopping him. He watched her remove
a leather pouch from the belt around her waist. She
stepped forward, moving gracefully, as if she was at the
Imperial Court. She reached and took his hand.

It was as if a flame had leapt between them. She knew

he felt something, too, by the way he looked at their hands, then at her face. Her heart stopped beating as she watched the side of his mouth begin to curl into a smile.

Nicephorus had a mind to pull her into his arms. Shy and bold all at once. What kind of creature was she? A woman, indeed, despite her vows and her robes.

She pressed the pouch into his open hand. He felt the coins. She was paying him to go, to "pursue whatever relaxing pleasures men in the city pursue." Without a word, she turned and left him standing in her garden, his hand heavy with coins.

He stared after her, then at his hand. He flexed his arm, his sore arm, and squeezed the life out of the pouch. The pain in his shoulder nearly made him cry out. Rage swept through him in waves. He didn't want her money. Why did she think she had to buy him off to have a few hours to herself? What kind of man did she think he was? Or, did she take him for a beast—a gambling, drinking, whoring beast?

He growled under his breath and flung the bag of money aside, giving no attention to the soft thud as it landed in the overgrown tangle of weeds near the brick wall that separated the villa from another garden. Reminding himself that she was Christ's bride did nothing to curb his rage. The voice of reason, whispering in his ear, only heightened his fury and fanned the flames of his anger into a dangerous force.

Chapter Four

Wispy veils of clouds streamed across the evening sky borne by a wind that held the promise of rain. The sun had set in a blaze, painting the heavens in broad brushstrokes of pink and orange and red, with careful touches of purple. The rioting colors had quieted for the evening and slid from the heavens like silk, leaving a blue as pure and deep as the Virgin Mary's mantle in the mosaic that decorated the convent's nave.

There were diamonds in the sky. And a white moon ringed in a softer shade, like a saint's halo. The moonlight was soft and became softer still when the clouds moved past, veiling it. But it was enough to guide Cassandra.

She felt light and free in the white linen tunic that served as her sleeping gown. It was the only garment from all her tunics and dalmaticas she thought worth saving; however, its length and tightness across the bodice made it appropriate only for bed.

Her hair, newly washed, hung loose and long in undulating waves of silver. With the sacred bowl in her hands, she walked from the house, out into the garden, and stood in a pool of moonlight.

She knelt on the white marble walk and set the bronze bowl in front of her. At her side, laurel leaves burned on a copper plate, sending a plume of smoke into the air. She was unafraid of the sacred ritual she was about to perform, and yet she felt tense and cold. She knew that the money had angered Nicephorus. She had found the pouch in the weeds when she was preparing herself for the ritual. She had seen him leave the villa and walk to the stables like a thundercloud. She winced and wished she could do it over again; she knew she would approach the matter differently.

She tried to push the incident aside. She knew that the laurel would help ease her tension and free her mind.

Sitting back on her heels, she closed her eyes and exhaled a breath slowly. She took another breath, then released it. Then another. She repeated the breathing sequence over and over until she felt completely at peace and entwined with the moment. She opened her eyes and leaned forward, staring at the water and at her reflection. Calm. The water. Her breaths. Her surroundings blurred . . .

She closed her eyes and felt her pulse drumming in her temples; a strange lightness flew up her spine, making her face warm. She opened her eyes.

She saw the swan—it was white enamel with wings and bill edged in gold and two blue sapphires for eyes. Someone was holding it, then using the little gold key to adjust a special mechanism that gave the swan a unique quality. Cassandra smiled, remembering the first time she had seen the little swan flap its wings. As the watery image began its magical performance, she heard the sound of clapping and the high pitch of a woman's laugh.

Cassandra leaned closer, and as her hair spilled forward, she pushed it back, behind her ears.

Where was the swan? "Show me," she said, narrowing her eyes on the water, willing it to tell her.

The swan rippled away, and she began to see the image of a ship rising from the water; its white sails were puffed with wind, and it rose and fell on white-capped waves.

She closed her eyes in concentration. The swan was on a ship. But where was it going? She squeezed her hands together in anticipation, then looked.

But the ship had disappeared, and the image on the water was that of a man's face—Nicephorus.

She fell forward, losing her balance, then righted herself. In the time it took her to catch her breath, the image did not change: she saw the captain astride his horse, holding something in front of him. She knew it was he; his face, his eyes, were clear. But what was he holding? Something, someone, in brown with a . . . It was she! And there was a mob of people swarming around them, shouting and screaming, waving sticks, their faces inflamed with rage.

The captain's horse snorted and wheeled around. It reared onto its hind legs and pawed the air before stamping the earth and flying into a gallop, out of the hell of the mob.

Cassandra watched herself and Nicephorus flee through the narrow stone streets of the city. He controlled the beast as if it were a part of his body, urging it through the tightest spaces, around the sharpest corners. She could hear the sharp bites of the steel-shod hooves against the cobblestones, hear the captain breathing heavily behind her, feel the horse beneath her and the jarring bounce that rattled her bones, and feel the arm that held her so tightly she could barely breathe.

Then it was over. The captain reined the horse to a trot. She watched, spellbound, as Nicephorus gentled it with soft words of praise, then reined it still. She watched him take great gulps of air. Then the captain looked down at her. Gently, he lifted her chin up, to look at him. She could feel his breathing, still coming fast, as were her own breaths. She could hear the blood pounding in her ears. Slowly, he leaned down. A quiet signal passed between them. As she watched, Cassandra could feel the moment when they both moved without moving toward the promise of a kiss. Now. She watched as he spread his fingers against her cheek. Holding her possessively and still, he brought his mouth down on hers.

Cassandra took a sharp breath. She felt the savage, hungry press of the captain's lips. Time and place blurred; she was in his arms, living the prophecy. Now. Now. His lips were hard. The flame of his tongue was branding her. She felt herself returning the fire, and a luxurious heat filled her mouth and swept through her body.

"Nicephorus," she moaned against his lips.

With the word, the sensation of being in another place vanished. But not the vision. Heart hammering, senses made senseless, she watched as she put her arms around him to draw him closer. She saw herself lost in the heat of the captain's kisses and knew that his passions were branding her, and that she would never be the same.

After one cup of wine, one roll of the die, Nicephorus had had enough. He rode through the sleeping city, visions of himself waking the nun and lecturing her about her stubborn ways filling his mind. But as he drew close to the villa, he dismounted and walked his horse to the stable. Quietly, he saw to the horse's needs, then walked to the back of the villa where he'd discovered a gate in the garden wall. Its forbidding size mocked him; the thickness of the metal made him groan.

The gate was heavy. He pushed with his good shoulder, but it didn't move. He pushed again. It screeched. He stopped. Listened. Then carefully pushed again. He opened it only far enough to squeeze through, and when he was in the garden, he crouched down. He'd noticed a flickering light through the leaves. Staying low, he moved forward, taking care not to break or snap the branches in his way. It was easy, like a game.

Peering between the branches, he saw where the light was coming from—there was a small fire, smoke. And then he saw her: a pale nymph with silver-blond hair, pacing the garden. She was moving away from him, so he couldn't see her face. She was holding her arms close to her, as if she were cold. The moonlight lit her tunic and revealed the perfection of her body. She could have been standing there naked, so enchanting was the sight that held his gaze. The slope of her back, her hips and legs, every graceful curve was revealed by the light.

She turned.

"What the devil!" he swore under his breath, his eyes fixed on the face of the nymph. *Sister Cassandra?*

He lurched back, losing his balance, but reached out for a branch to steady himself. Cassandra looked, her body jerking with awareness, and Nicephorus ducked down behind a shrub and hoped it was full enough to conceal him. Sensing she had turned away, he lifted his head and peered through the leaves.

Is that what nuns wear to bed? And what a strange ritual. Did her order practice rituals from a more pagan time?

Nicephorus studied her, trying to see and memorize everything—the way he'd had to, because he'd learned a long time ago that it was crucial to his survival. He saw the long, heavy waves of her hair shining in the moonlight, the slimness of her calves, the gold bracelet around one ankle. He saw a bronze bowl at her feet. He noted the pale, beautiful face of the nun he'd vowed to protect and saw her moving her lips as if she were talking to herself. He noticed the ease with which she stood there, in her diaphanous shift, like some pagan temptress from another time, and it confused him.

Cassandra shivered. She could still see the image of herself in Nicephorus's arms, kissing him. She could still feel it happening, his arms tightening around her, the crush of his mouth on hers. She could smell their heat. The feeling in the center of her being—was it longing? She wanted the kiss to continue. She wanted more.

Pagan. Pagan Little Prophetess. It was the Abbess's voice invading Cassandra's thoughts.

What if the Abbess was right? Cassandra asked herself. *What if my power of sight, these feelings I have, damn me to hell for all eternity?*

She hugged her arms to her chest. Unaware that she was being watched, she stood quietly in her garden and fought the feelings, the voices, tugging at her. At some point in the future, Nicephorus would save her. He would kiss her. He would . . .

She felt the first drops of rain on her skin and looked up. She listened to the soft pattering sound on the leaves as it anointed her face. She looked ahead, into the garden, the garden Nicephorus had been tending, and swept her gaze over the dark shapes and shadows of trees and bushes. As if the sky had suddenly been torn apart, the rain fell, hard, fast, drenching her skin, pressing her shift against her limbs. She loved the feel of the rain, the freedom of standing in it and letting it have its way with her.

For a moment, Cassandra forgot the images revealed on the water. She twirled in the rain. She danced, sweeping her arms in graceful arcs, bending at the waist like a lily in the wind. Innocent of the eyes that followed her, she pulled her shift over her head and cast it aside.

Pagan, said the voice in her head.

Then so be it, she answered.

The rain drenched Nicephorus, who stood tense with shock at the sight of the dancing girl.

Chapter Five

Cassandra spent the next morning in her mother's study, copying the recipe for her mother's fragrant cream, *Moonlight in the Garden*. Her quill scratched across the parchment she'd found, along with quills and ink, on the shelves which lined the back wall. The shelves climbed to the ceiling and were filmed with dust and crowded with the objects of her mother's pastime. There were dried herbs and flowers, a mortar and pestle, delicate glass bottles for perfumes, and row upon row of alabaster jars, some filled with oils, others empty. A small bronze brazier stood in the corner. The desk was cedar with carved legs that ended in lion's feet. Silk rugs in all the colors of the sea, sun, and sky covered the floor.

Biting her lower lip, she worked quickly. Her vision had revealed that the swan was most definitely not in the city, but on a ship, bound for . . . she knew not where. She was confident that another vision would tell her, but, in the meantime, she knew she had to prepare for a voyage. Whether the swan was being taken across the sea to Egypt, to Venice, or out through the Straits of Gibraltar, she knew she would need money. To start, she had her mother's emerald ring and this recipe. She must go to the market, to the shop her mother spoke of. She would have to tell the captain.

Or, she could go alone.

Nonplussed by the direction her thoughts had taken, she finished her task and, only when she was satisfied with her script, laid her quill aside and sat back in the chair. She crossed her arms in front of her. She hadn't seen the captain since he'd stalked out of the villa the evening before. She didn't count the visions. She shivered, remembering, and pulled her robes close and shifted in the safety they provided. If he was still angry, then she'd have to talk to him and smooth things over. She didn't want to. She wanted as little to do with him as possible, until she knew what course to take to prohibit the prophecy from happening. Of this she was certain: she had awakened with the cold resolve to do everything in her power to keep *that* prophecy from coming true. She didn't know if she had the power to alter the future, but she had to try.

Nicephorus caught Cassandra just as she was about to leave the villa. Anne had seen to all the preparations, procuring a chair and bearers to take Cassandra to the marketplace. She was bending down to climb in, sighing with relief that her ploy had worked, when he stopped her. Since he was fully dressed in his armor, his sword strapped to his side and ready to skewer giants and villains, his horse saddled and tugging at the reins, she knew that somehow he'd guessed her intentions.

She stood outside the chair, nervously fingering the worn fringe that decorated the curtains, as the chairbearers sighed with impatience.

"You've been very busy this morning, Sister," he smiled.

She detected a little barb in his tone. *He's still angry at me*, she thought to herself.

"I have business to attend to in the marketplace," she said, keeping her eyes downcast.

"Surely your servants can see to the provisions and the purchase of any items that you might need. Won't a *nun,*" he said and paused sharply, "alone," he added and paused again, "raise suspicions?"

Hearing the point, as sharp as a dagger, at the end of the word *nun,* she looked at him. His gray-blue eyes were stormy, but she ignored them. At first. She studied him further. He was looking at her rather oddly, she thought, raking her with his eyes as if she was a courtesan standing outside the entrance to the baths. She felt the color rising in her cheeks. She stuffed her hands into the sleeves of her robe and looked away, steeling herself with the knowledge that she had a voyage to prepare for.

She turned back to the chair. "I must go."

She heard his approach. "Then, as your guard, I must escort you," he announced. She saw his hand reach out and pull back on the curtain in a gesture more brutal than it was gallant.

He bowed formally and held his other arm out to assist her.

Cassandra brushed past it, wincing at the contact, and climbed in without his help.

Cassandra peeked out between the fringed curtains; the sunlight was almost blinding after the dark, cool confines of the litter. She looked up at the white walls of the homes that lined the street. She'd never ventured alone to the marketplace before. Her mother had been very strict and had never allowed her out of the house without a chaperone. She smiled to herself. Ahh, freedom, she mused.

She leaned out a little more, to get a better look. Nicephorus, riding ahead of her, chose that moment to turn around. He caught her in his gaze and, as if he had thrown a net around her, she froze.

Can't wait to meet your lover, he thought to himself. The twisted thoughts and visions that had visited his sleep after witnessing the little nun's performance in the courtyard were still with him. But the vision that held him in the strongest vise featured Cassandra as the lover of a very prominent nobleman, hence her disguise. And now she was hurrying off to meet him. It made him mad with a feeling that he could not define or dispel. He just wanted to growl and swipe the air with his sword.

"Impatient, Sister?"

"Of course not," she answered demurely. Without paying him further attention, she retreated back into the litter and pulled the curtains closed.

His face dark as a thundercloud, a distrustful look in his eyes, he turned back to the road and urged his horse to quicken its step.

All the riches of the world flooded through the Mese, the great Middle Street of Constantinople. Cassandra wanted to shout her happiness over the sight that lay before her, but she didn't, knowing full well that nuns didn't shout. She contented herself with a smile that, unbeknownst to her, made the people around her think she was lost in a vision of the divine.

She couldn't hear the water splashing in the fountain in the middle of the square because of the steady stream of people on foot and on horseback. It was a colorful crowd: bearded monks, mercenary soldiers towering above groveling beggars, patricians in their white and purple robes, noblewomen in their gilded chairs. She could see the colonnades of white marble, the string of silver, perfume, and jewelry shops, like pearls, that opened onto the Mese. A gold statue of the Emperor Constantine on a column of porphyry gazed down upon the marble colonnades, on the sirens and hippogriffs of bronze, and the statues of emperors and empresses that decorated the porticoes. In the distance a church of rose marble, the Sancta Sophia, rose like a hill. The sun reflected off the gilded dome and made it shine with an intensity that seemed to sanctify the air.

She only had to walk a small distance before finding the shop, Pandora's Box. But before she stepped inside, she turned to tell the captain, who had been following her like a brooding black cloud, not to wait. Words of dismissal poised on her lips, she turned. But he was gone. She looked about; there was no sign of him or his horse. She shrugged and turned her attention to the shop. Here she would sell the recipe *Moonlight in the Garden.* And after pawning the emerald, she would have enough money for her journey.

In her nun's habit Cassandra had thought herself to be invisible. In her mind, the coarse brown robes and white veil shrouded her in a magic so powerful that no one could see her or guess her real identity. It was a belief as fragile as glass. Pandora's Box was about to open her eyes to the truth.

Members of the Church were bad for business; they reminded the common man and woman that catering to the pleasures of the flesh and beauty was a superficial pursuit, a game played in cooperation with the devil.

The silence that greeted the nun was crushing. Attention flew from the items for sale—the perfumes and creams in their decorative glass vials, alabaster and terra cotta jars—to the nun. She was, for all practical purposes, pinned against the shop's wall, a brown butterfly with the life pressed out of her.

The cold silence that greeted Cassandra made the hairs rise on the back of her neck. The weight of her veil and robes increased tenfold. She could not move.

"I imagine they don't receive very many nuns," she murmured softly to herself. She tried to keep her eyes on the ground, but it was hard. She glanced sideways to the right and left; the shop was full. All eyes were on her.

"Christe! You'd think the Virgin Mary had just walked in," she said under her breath in an attempt to lighten her spirits.

When the shopkeeper, a balding little man with bushy brows and busy eyes, dressed in blue silk that announced his success, jumped away from a patron to assist Cassandra, he didn't mean to lavish her with special attention, but to see to her needs and get her out of his shop.

But what a beautiful, white-as-the-finest-silk complexion, the shopkeeper thought to himself, marveling at the nun's skin. That luminous glow must come from all that praying and fasting, he thought. Then he had an idea: he would invent a new item for his shop, and call it something like Saint Agnes' Holy Face Cream.

With a genuine smile on his face, for it wasn't often that inspiration came to him so quickly, he approached the nun and gestured with his arm for her to follow him.

Cassandra found her feet and followed him to a little back room. It smelled of sandalwood and spikenard and was lit by a single lantern that hung from a beam running across the ceiling. Shelves stocked with urns and jars surrounded her on all sides. Feeling at home, she sighed with relief.

When she first showed him the parchment, the shopkeeper stared wide-eyed at it, as if she had decorated the recipe with a picture of a satyr embracing a nun. Knowing that there was nothing unholy about the paper, Cassandra didn't follow his gaze. Impatiently, she tapped her foot and waited for his response.

"Where did you get this?" he said in an accusatory tone. His eyes softened a little, and he cleared his throat. "Sister." He looked straight at her.

"It's my mother's recipe. I'm to sell it . . . to raise money for our convent."

"Ahhh. The convent," he echoed, nodding with a satisfied smile. All the dark, stressful feelings fled the room. "And your mother? She is . . . ?"

"Lady Olympia Phaedra Heraclius."

"Well, why didn't you say so?" The light seemed to shine a little brighter, friendlier. "I've heard of her. Who has not? It's a wonderful blend," he said, tapping the parchment, "this mix of oil of Damascus roses, sandalwood, and a hint of musk and vanilla. Brilliant!" He looked at Cassandra and began tapping his fingertips together. "Have you any more?"

"More?"

"I'm willing to make a sizable donation to your convent. If there's more."

She shook her head. "No. Just this," she said and caught the droop of his shoulders, adding, "for now."

He brightened. "Yes. Maybe you'll come back?"

She glanced over her shoulder toward the interior of the shop. It was still too, too quiet.

The shopkeeper noted the direction of her gaze. His eyebrows twitched. "You must admit, Sister, Pandora's Box is an odd place for a nun to show up. Now I have a very nice incense that would fill your chapel with the holiest of fragrances. Perhaps you can convince . . ."

Cassandra let the shopkeeper continue to talk; her mind

was on other matters. Lifting her eyes to heaven, she wondered where she could pawn her mother's emerald ring.

Her purse heavy with gold solidi, Cassandra nearly danced out of the shop. Tugging her veil around her face to hide her smile, she began to cross the market to the jewelers' shops. She was halfway to the Gilded Peacock when she felt a hand on her elbow, steering her gently around, back in the direction she had just come from.

"What the devil—"

"And a pleasant 'God Bless You,' too, Sister. Tsk. Such devout talk for a nun!"

She'd know that voice anywhere. Nicephorus!

Glaring at the captain, she demanded, "Where are you taking me?"

"Home," came the curt reply.

"But I'm not ready," she argued, yanking her arm away to be free of his touch.

But her actions only made him tighten his grip. "Yes, you are. It may already be too late."

"Too late?"

She felt him draw nearer to whisper in her ear. "A mob's been gathering near the Taurus Market since we arrived. It seems the increase in the price of bread has our citizens in a foul mood. I'm afraid there might be a riot."

She stopped and pulled her arm free of his possessive hold. He noticed the color in her cheeks and thought it quite charming, until he reminded himself that she had deceived him into believing that she was a nun.

"You must permit me to make—"

But he wasn't listening. Or noticing the strange looks being directed their way. He didn't care. Whoever she was, her safety came first. Eventually he would discover the truth. But for now . . .

He took her by the arm again. He loosened his hold slightly when she shrieked. "Unless you can work miracles, I suggest that we leave, Sister. Now."

But even a miracle would not have stopped the mob from charging through the streets. There was menace in people's eyes. Their faces glowed and sweated with the heat of their conviction: the Emperor intended to starve the citizens of the most illustrious city in the world! He and his henchmen were evil and deserved to be destroyed.

Strangers, allies now against a common evil, joined hands and shared weapons, from clubs to daggers, even tools used in the kitchen. Young and old, men and women, took to the streets, turned their anger loose, and destroyed everything in their path.

Nicephorus felt the sea of anger and discontent before he saw it. Even though he had chosen a seldom-traveled street that ran parallel to the route he was sure the mob would take, he could feel them. The mob was moving toward him. He damned himself for not being more forceful with his charge; he should have picked up the little nun and thrown her across his horse the moment he heard about the riot. Now he and Cassandra and her chairbearers were caught.

After a crooked bend in the street, Nicephorus found himself facing the mob. He reined his horse still and held up his right arm, signaling the chairbearers following him to stop, which they did, abruptly, sending Cassandra falling forward inside the curtained chair. The mob, a stream of anger, lurched to a halt, but it could not be stilled; it bubbled and boiled with raised lances, clubs, and flaming torches. Clear voices filled with venom filtered through hushed murmurings. All it took was one cry.

"It's the rich that's done this! Driven the prices up to

fill their coffers with gold and starve us poor folk. Death to the rich with their fancy chairs and escorts. They're murdering our children!''

As if an invisible hand had come up behind the mob and shoved, the stream lurched forward, quickened its step, started running.

"Damn!" Nicephorus wheeled his horse around and spurred it into a leap that closed the distance between itself and the chair. The chairbearers, eyes wide with terror, trembling at the sight of the mob, turned this way and that, looking for a way out of danger. Spun by the slaves, the curtained chair rocked and dipped and was near to capsizing when Nicephorus reached in, grabbed Cassandra, and lifted her onto his lap. Without hesitating, ignoring her shrieks, he spurred his horse again and they flew, retreating down the street, away from the mob.

She didn't even have time to grab hold. She heard the yowls, the angry yells, but when she turned around to see, Nicephorus pulled her up against his chest and wouldn't let her move. They veered down one street after another, as if the stream was just behind them, threatening to drown them. The horse's hooves hit the cobblestones and the sound echoed through the empty street.

When Nicephorus was finally certain they were out of danger, he let go of his fierce hold on her. He pulled back on the reins, slowing the horse to a trot, then a walk. He caught his breath and felt the anger inside him battering against his chest. The great Captain Nicephorus Acominatus, baited by a stubborn woman, pursued by a mob! What madness had possessed him to agree to protect her in the first place?

But the feel of her against his chest shattered his wall of anger. There was silence between them—not a wall of quiet, but something soft, touchable. He heard her breaths, which had been short and fast, easing into a gentler rhythm. The smell of her. He leaned in closer, reining the horse still.

Cassandra held her breath; she knew what was going to happen. The prophecy! It was coming true. Here. Now.

No! she cried to herself. She struggled to be free of her guard, but Nicephorus, mistaking her agitation for fear, whispered in her ear, "We're safe, you have nothing to fear." Then he began stroking her head to calm her.

At his touch, at the care that enveloped her, something opened inside her and she relaxed against his chest. The memory of the vision released itself throughout her body. She closed her eyes. She could feel it happening, his arms tightening around her, the crush of his mouth on hers, and the velvet fire of his tongue tasting her. She could smell their heat. The flame at the center of her being licked her and made her sigh.

She felt so small and vulnerable against him. This delicate nun, flesh and blood woman. Whoever she was, she was his now. Nicephorus gently nudged her face up, to look at him. He meant to tell her that they were out of danger, but he forgot his intention the second her gaze met his. She parted her lips, as if to say something, but no word marred the perfection of her mouth, held soft, open. He rubbed his thumb across her lower lip. He felt her tremble and read the frantic look in her eyes. He felt both powerless and powerful. He had to taste her, possess her mouth and know the feel of her. Slowly, he leaned down, giving her time to move away, but she didn't move. I'll kiss her lightly, chastely, he thought as he brushed his lips against hers.

So sweet. A moment so simple and pure. That it could be everlasting was never his intent. Because at the first feel of her parted, defenseless lips, he knew he wanted more. And the wanting and yearning that had plagued him rose with a growl. He clasped her jaw. A virginal gasp brushed his face, and he ignored it.

His mouth worked slowly, as if time moved like honey. She was trembling, but she wasn't fighting him or begging him to stop. Her mouth opened, beckoning, and he wondered if she knew what effect that little gesture would have on him before he took the opportunity offered and swept this tongue inside to mate with hers.

At the hot flame of his tongue, she tried to pull away from him, though only for heartbeats. He was kissing her so slowly, so thoroughly, she was sure he intended to eat her from the inside out. So this was what kept the older novices, the ones who had sampled the world of men, awake late at night. She sighed and pressed herself against him. The butterflies in her stomach had long since departed, replaced by a heat that moved through her in silky waves. She had never known such pleasure, but she knew instinctively that this was more than a physical response. She felt safe and open and beautiful, all at once. She was reborn.

She felt the horse shift and stamp beneath her, felt her bodyguard's body tighten in the saddle. She wrapped her arms around his hips and clung to him. Her tongue moved with his, and she quickly learned that he liked the teasing, darting movements of her tongue best of all from the growls that surfaced. She wanted to please him. She wanted to be able to do and say anything.

Unafraid, she met him kiss for kiss and prayed it would never end.

Passion raged between them as they tightened their hold and deepened their kissing. His mouth took her mouth again and again, slanting over hers with a fierce possessiveness that made him wish they were in his bed. It was then, with the realization of how much he desired her and would not be content until he was making love to her, that he forced himself to stop.

He pulled away, stunned that he had gone so far, here, in the street, where anyone could have seen them, a nun and a captain of the imperial army. He could tell by the look on her face that she was confused. Or was it shame that darted in her eyes, making the amber brilliance die suddenly. Her lips were swollen. He moved to touch her, but caught himself. He felt her stiffen and pull away. *No, no,* he said to himself as he gentled her back close to him. He hoped she could trust him enough to reveal her true identity. Especially now. *Who is this nun, this creature who performed sacred rituals in the moonlight and rain, this woman who kisses not just for the pleasure of it, but because of something deeper?* He knew the difference. This was a woman he would never be able to let go.

Who are you? he asked himself, looking down at the veiled crown of her head. *I know you do not belong to God.*

And with the name of his old rival on his lips, he jerked the reins of his mount and sent them moving toward the villa.

Chapter Six

The smell of a storm was in the air as Nicephorus and Cassandra rode home in silence. Thunder grumbled in the distance. A sultry wind played with the edge of Cassandra's veil. She paid no mind to anything save those disquieting minutes of passion.

She closed her eyes so that she might see better and focus on what she had just done. She relived those minutes in his arms. The taste of him, like something ripe, waiting to be eaten. His strong, flexing strength. His hand under her jaw, holding her steady. The smell of his skin. She saw it all and told herself that neither Nicephorus's action nor her yielding had any meaning. It was folly. A young girl's silly game. *The act of the devil,* said the Abbess's voice in her head. That was all.

But her blood thrummed through her body at a new pitch. She felt like a just-plucked peach, all wet and warm, bitten, her juices flowing. The feel of him behind her made her want to lean into him. She wanted to rub her scent into his. She could deny all she wanted. But she felt everything.

And so she decided to tell Nicephorus that she could not permit him to guard her any longer. It was over. The quest to find the swan was still the most important thing to her, and she would not have anything or anyone stand in her way. The fact that the prophecy had come true was a warning to beware of Nicephorus's powerful force. She was sure that if their lives became entwined, she would never find the swan. She would write her mother and explain how wrong it had all turned out.

By the time they were home, her mind was made up. As Nicephorus helped her off his mount, he caught the cold, passionless look in her eyes, the pinched mouth. He held her too long, forcing Cassandra to break away. But Nicephorus had other intentions. Even though he felt that the passionate woman had vanished and the nun had returned, he heard the thunder rumble over his shoulder and held on to her, half-turning her in his arms.

The feel of his imprisoning hands prompted her to speak.

"I want to thank you," she said. "You saved my life." She looked up at him, then down at his hands, which felt like manacles around her arms. "You can let me go now."

"When I'm ready," he whispered.

She felt the smile in his voice moving through her like a flame. His bravado and confidence needled her. How dare he play games with her.

With the taste of him still on her lips, she said, "I will be forever grateful to you for your quick actions this day. But as of now, I relieve you of your duties. You are free to . . . go."

"Go?"

The look he gave her seemed to pierce her and bite her backbone. She hesitated only a moment. "Yes. I need someone who . . ." she paused thinking, *someone who will not kiss me.* "It's for the best."

He raised an eyebrow over the forced, confident tone of her voice. "Is it, Sister Cassandra?" *And just who was this someone?* he thought to himself as he let her go and stepped back.

He brushed his hand through his hair and looked away. He swore to himself. *Nicephorus, you fool, you scared her. You never should have kissed her. She's too young. Too young to know anything. And stubborn, inexperienced . . .*

He turned his gaze back to the nun before him and glared at her. His thoughts were as rational and straightforward as if he were planning his strategy to ambush the enemy. *How inexperienced could she be if she thought of disguising herself as a nun? The pagan wench from the night before did not look inexperienced to me,* he thought, recalling her undressing and dancing naked in the rain. *How dare she play me for a fool.*

His face had taken on a hardness that made Cassandra flinch. She decided she had been too abrupt. She should have taken her time, told him over dinner.

"I realize I probably sound ungrateful for everything you've done, for rescuing me, for—" She stopped trying when he shook his head at her.

"Perhaps now you'll tell me who you really are."

"What?" Cassandra swallowed. She felt the hairs stand up on the back of her neck.

He read fear in her eyes, but it did not stop him. "Who are you? You're not a nun, unless your religious order allows you to wear your hair long, perform mysterious rituals by moonlight, and dance naked in the rain. In what convent are such things permitted and taught?" He paused before he attacked. "You are an impostor, Sister Cassandra. Now that we are to part company, surely you can tell me the truth."

Christe! The man had spied on her! Pulling her robes

around her, she glared back at him and met his challenge. "You had no right—"

Nicephorus grunted and crossed his arms over his chest. "It was quite a performance." He read the vulnerability in her face, saw how she fought to master her feelings. He should have stopped and let things be, but he could not. "There was a sense of innocence that I found especially refreshing. Who was it you were practicing for? Trust me, you do not need to practice. And if I were you, I would replace the door to the garden, or your midnight dances might start drawing a crowd."

That he had seen her perform the ritual . . . He might as well have stripped her of all her robes, for she felt completely naked and exposed.

What did it matter now? She tore the veil from her head, releasing her hair, which tumbled over her shoulders and down her back, and with it the scent of lavender and musk. Suddenly, she felt free and bold, as if she had just unlocked iron chains. She lifted her chin and told him the truth.

"You're right. I'm not Sister Cassandra. I'm Cassandra Heraclius, and I've spent the last two years in the Convent of the Holy Cross tending to my mother. She's dying— *ill,*" she corrected herself. "But with God's grace she will recover."

But her gift of the truth did not have the effect she expected. Nicephorus narrowed his eyes in doubt and flexed his arms as if he wanted to reach out and shake the truth out of her. His disbelief, mixed with anger, flared and came at her like a wave of heat. Why didn't he believe her? she wondered.

Then she recalled the second part of his accusations, something about practicing her dance *for someone.* Did he actually think she was a harlot practicing for her lover? Christe! That was it! The man believed she had a lover!

She laughed. She had never even been kissed by a man until today.

She coughed to disguise the laughter, but she couldn't help herself. His glare was meant to silence her, but she could not remain silent.

"I have no lover, Captain," she admitted innocently. "Why, until today, I'd never been ki—" She caught herself at the brink of foolishness. Cassandra felt her cheeks redden. She looked away and nervously pushed her hair behind her ears. Innocent though she was in the ways of the world, she knew instinctively that a noblewoman never admitted to a man that his was the first kiss.

The thunder grumbled, the green sky darkened with ink-black clouds, but the sun shone in the villa's courtyard in Nicephorus's smile. It was a smile Cassandra did not trust. She backed away from him, and turned to enter the villa. But Nicephorus had other plans. Before she knew it, she was in his arms.

"Captain!"

He pinned her against him and buried his free hand in her hair. It felt like silk and shone like starlight. He imagined it fanned across his bed, or falling like a curtain around him as they made love.

"Let me go, please."

Her request went unanswered, but to quiet her resisting body, he began massaging the back of her neck, behind her ear. He heard her sigh and leaned down and kissed her. Just a gentle brush of his lips against hers. He pulled away to look into her eyes, and the amber gaze that met his, so full of hope, life, and passion, made him tremble. "Cassandra," he whispered, burying his face in her scented hair.

She collapsed against him at the desire held within the sound of her name. To think that a word could sound so intimate and have the power of touch . . . Aroused, she put her hands around his neck and drew him down to her. She moved to kiss him, held back at the last moment, then answered his whisper without making a sound.

Hers was the gentlest of kisses, like a veil of silk, gently falling across his lips. But he caught it and turned it deep, hard, and hot. The hungry press of his lips branded her with a fiery jolt that diffused into warm, pulsing waves. With an innocence that shook him, she teased his tongue with hers. She responded aggressively to his low growl of satisfaction, moving deeper, breathing her desire into his mouth. Harder, said her mouth. More. More.

No part of her was sacred. She felt his hands slip between her nun's robes and her linen tunic and move down her back, boldly caressing her, cupping and shaping her sensitive flesh. She moaned, enslaved by his hands, which were molding her against the length of his body, igniting a need to fill an aching emptiness building deep inside her. She loved the hard press of his body, the strength of his arms around her, the taste of him. She wanted to lose herself inside his kiss.

Suddenly, the image of the jeweled swan rose behind her mind's eye. She jolted, breaking the spell that had claimed them both.

In the second she stopped, Cassandra had time to focus on what was happening. She broke loose from his embrace and turned away.

"This is wrong!" The words came unbidden as her senses continued to crave his masterful touch. She pushed her hair from her face. She swallowed, aware that he was staring at her back, aware that her beating heart sounded louder to her than the howling wind. What had she done? She could not steady herself. The sooner she found someone to help her in her quest, and left Constantinople, the better. Some beast of a man who would do his job—no more, no less.

"Cassandra?"

She shuddered; his voice had the power to move her as much as his touch. She dared not turn around for fear of showing how deeply and completely he had affected her. Forcing herself to take deeper breaths, she turned her head to the side, but would not look at him.

"You must go," she said. "I have work. I must find the swan. I've, I've told you everything." She finally looked at him.

Nicephorus's dark eyebrows knotted in thought. "Yes. Your quest," he answered, his voice clipped and gruff.

Was he hurt? Cassandra wondered. Surely she didn't mean anything to him. He probably had a lover, she thought to herself. What would he want with someone like her, a girl who'd spent the last few years in a convent. Was it possible that he felt something for her? It couldn't be, she argued.

The storm seemed to close in around them; the black clouds were so low now that it seemed all she had to do was reach up to grab a fistful of the angry air. The wind howled and ripped her robes open.

"Who will you contact? To help you. At least allow me—"

She lifted her hand to stop him from continuing, and Nicephorus cursed the dismissive gesture under his breath. They were back to their little game.

"You've done more than enough already, Captain. I don't know who . . . I need someone like . . . the Leopard." The name had fallen from her lips, but now that it was out, she agreed. Yes, the Leopard.

Hearing her request, Nicephorus arched his brow. Calmly, he said, "The Leopard? I doubt the man has time for such . . . ." He didn't know what to call her quest. She was talking about a man who was used to hunting down assassins and the enemies of the empire. *Treasure hunt* sounded too frivolous. ". . . an enterprise." He watched her turn toward him. She pulled her robes close to keep them from snapping in the wind. Or to hide from him. Her hair whipped around her face.

"I can make it worth his while."

A smile played at the corner of his mouth. "Indeed? I know you have been selling your pretty fragrances and mean to pawn your jewelry to finance your quest. How will you pay for—"

"I will find a way," she said, cutting him off. "Will you take me to him?"

Nicephorus grinned, startling Cassandra, for she felt her request was probably asking too much of him.

"It's said he likes a pretty face, comely figure." His eyes dared her to follow his thoughts. The memory of a vision flashed in her mind; she saw herself lying naked on a leopard skin.

She looked away, burned by the spark of desire in his eyes, a flare of heat that suggested that he had seen the image, too. She bit her lip, sneaked a glance, and damned herself for looking. He was grinning at her! He did not look at all like a man who had just been pushed aside. *Does he think he has some kind of power over me now?* she asked herself. *It was just a kiss, nothing more. Once I meet the Leopard I'll be off in search of the swan and he'll know it meant nothing to me, nothing.*

The thunder rumbled at the edge of her thoughts, and before she had a chance to look, or think of what to do next, the sky ruptured with rain.

Cassandra had not foreseen putting aside her nun's robes so soon after Nicephorus's arrival. With all her powers, she had not been able to see the inevitable, as if the part of her that dreamed and saw the visions had believed with an unshakable authority that she was truly a nun. The brown robes had disguised herself from her self. The shield of coarse fabric had worked so well, that when she went to her room to remove the robes, she felt naked to her soul. She didn't know herself anymore. Who was she, if she was not a nun from the Convent of the Holy Cross. Who was she? Daughter? Woman? Prophetess?

While rose-fingered dawn was painting the sky, Cassandra sat on the edge of her bed, nervously rubbing the hem of her nun's robes between her fingers. She did not want to let them go. The quest that stretched before her did not frighten her. Nor did meeting the Leopard. It was something else, a trembling that could have been from the feel of a cold breeze over her naked skin, or the touch of her bodyguard's lips on hers. Who was she? she asked herself.

Finally, with a look in her eyes that defied her paralysis, she let the robe slip between her fingers and rose to her feet. Bravely, she stepped over the pool of fabric, the shell of who she was, and moved toward the bronze mirror. She pulled her shift over her head and looked at herself, touched her cheek, smoothed her fingers across her lips, her neck and shoulders. She beheld the reflection of her breasts and the sweep and curve of her waist and hips. She had never looked at herself before. It was an awakening. The image in her head had been that of a scrawny little girl who had escorted her mother to the convent. But the image in the mirror was that of a woman.

"So this is Cassandra," she murmured, looking. This is who Nicephorus saw that night in the garden.

The realization did not shame her into covering herself. Her body, so long concealed by the dark, mournful robes, and as if by a thousand invisible veils as well, bid her to see the woman she had become. She touched her breasts and felt their fullness and weight in her hands. She fanned her fingers across her belly and vowed to anoint her skin with perfumed creams. She would create a new fragrance for herself, a scent that captured this creature staring back at her—this woman.

"Perhaps after I've found the swan," she mused, "I'll ask Mother to teach me the skill of scent-making." She paused in her thoughts. "But first, my venture with the Leopard," she said to herself, wrinkling her nose disagreeably as if she could already sense his beastly nature.

Bathed, smelling of lavender, her hair a silver cloud down her back, Cassandra set herself to work to complete her transformation. With her mother's wardrobe at her fingertips, she dressed herself in a cerulean blue silk *tunica talaris,* or undergown. Over this drifted a layer of deep blue, shorter in sleeve and hem length than the tunic, decorated with bands of pearls. So long accustomed to her nun's robes, she was amazed at how light the clothes felt and the freedom of movement that they offered. Cassandra slipped on a pair of blue silk slippers embroidered with tiny silver beads. She adorned herself with her mother's emerald ring and gold enamelled earrings decorated with delicate strands of tiny seed pearls which hung nearly to her shoulders. On her head she placed a circlet of silver decorated with more pearls and an attached white silk veil. After adjusting the headdress in the middle of her brow, she left her room—and the convent girl—behind.

Chapter Seven

Nicephorus regarded the transformed creature before him with quiet respect. She had found him deep in the garden, attempting to fix the lock on the garden gate. He was on his knees, his focus on a small mechanism that activated the hinge, when she appeared. He had not heard her coming from behind. The silk gown made a whispery, silvery sound against the glossy leaves; it was a different, softer music than that made by the coarse brown robes. She appeared all in blue, like some foam-borne creature of the sea. The sunlight played among the leaves and in her hair, which was loose and long. Her body, freed from the nun's robes, moved differently and reminded him of the woman he had seen dancing in the garden.

He knew why she had sought him out. The night before, he had promised to send a messenger to the Leopard and ask for an audience with the great warrior. They had been dining on lamb kebobs, a salad of cresses, and saffron rice when she made the request. He had barely been able to swallow a succulent morsel of lamb, which had suddenly become dry and hard and too large for his throat. Nicephorus had known what the answer would be; nevertheless, he had followed through with his promise. Today she was expecting an answer.

He rose to his feet, forcing Cassandra to step back as his presence seemed to consume all the available space between them. He leaned toward her, silent with his yearning to take her into his arms. Days had passed since their first meeting when her pale, beautiful face and amber eyes had vanquished his heart. Now a woman stood before him, a stunning creature made beautiful not so much by her silk gown, but by the sense of pride and power that enrobed her like her scent. Here was the precious swan she was seeking, he thought suddenly to himself. Was this the real reason behind the quest? Were there actually two swans Cassandra's mother wanted her daughter to find?

The thought stopped him for a moment, the idea of sending a daughter out into the world on a quest to find herself was remarkable to him. What kind of mother would see to such a thing? What an amazing woman, he thought. He tried to imagine what Cassandra's mother was like. Perhaps Lady Olympia had the same deep amber eyes and challenging glance as her daughter. He hoped some day to meet the mother who could claim such a fiery, stubborn, tempestuous creature as her own.

Nicephorus felt Cassandra challenging him with her newly discovered identity. *Say something,* her aura seemed to say. *I know you notice me.* It appeared to have happened overnight, this change from girl to woman, but he sensed that she had been struggling for some time. She had not struggled overmuch with his kisses, he remembered. But the smile that quickened, quaked at the sudden realization that Cassandra had transformed herself for another man— the Leopard. He frowned and crossed his arms across his chest.

But his eyes gave him away. He could not mask his longing to reach out for her. Cassandra read the desire and turned away too quickly, sidestepping a tree trunk and pulling at her clothes as if they were coarse and brown.

Captain Nicephorus Acominatus escorted his charge for the last time to the camp of the Leopard. Everyone knew that the Leopard and his special force of warriors preferred living in tents outside the City walls. They would not be caged. Nicephorus laughed to himself, thinking Cassandra was not so different from that band of men. She had been vehemently opposed to riding like a caged bird in a curtained chair, and had put up a fuss in the courtyard that most likely rocked the gates of Heaven. Nicephorus had argued that the Leopard was expecting a noblewoman. What would the warrior think if he saw her approaching his camp on a horse?

"He'll think I have a mind of my own when it comes to such things," she had replied. She had dared him with her furious eyes to force her into the litter, but he'd merely brushed aside the white veil that the wind blew across her mouth.

Watching her now, out of the corner of his eye, he could tell that she had been taught to ride by someone who had known what he was doing. Her balance, confidence, and command of the reins and her mount made him smile. She did not deserve to be caged, he mused. If it were up to him, he would see to it that she rode whenever, however, she liked, and was allowed to sleep and dance under the moon whenever she wished. For the first time in his life, Nicephorus felt he had learned something about women, this woman. He liked knowing. He wished to know more. There was still a chance, at the Leopard's camp, he told himself.

He sat straighter at the prospect, narrowed his eyes, and surveyed the road with a predatory air.

As dusk fell, Cassandra and her escort reached the camp. It was spread out over the low crown of a hillock north of the City walls. A ring of bonfires lit up the border of the camp and were manned by armed guards, who saluted the riding party as if they had been expecting them. Three large silk tents, two white and one black, stood on the flat ground, and many smaller shelters filled up the sloping spaces.

As she walked through the city of cloth, following Nicephorus, a noise caught Cassandra's attention. She looked up to see a black banner with the symbol of a leopard flapping in the air above her head. She gulped the knot of anticipation—of course it was anticipation, not fear, she reasoned—that was stuck in her throat. He was a fierce warrior, but there was nothing to be frightened of, she told herself. She recalled the novices at the convent telling tales of his exploits, how he had beheaded a giant with just one sword blow, assassinated a barbarian from the North with a bow and arrow, duped a witch trained in the art of poisons into poisoning herself, and destroyed creatures sent by the devil, like three-headed hydras and such. Not one story, that she could remember, mentioned the Leopard harming good, decent citizens. She wiped her palms on her tunica. Now she would see for herself.

Nicephorus stopped before the black tent, and turned to Cassandra.

"You can wait for him here," he said, lifting the silk to the side and making an entrance for her.

Her eyes widened with concern as he gestured toward the dark of the tent. "But I thought you would—"

"—Wait with you?" He chuckled. "You made your desires clear, lady. You prefer to seek the help of the Leopard. So our journey ends here." He could not help himself;

with his free hand he smoothed her cheek and jaw. "Farewell, Sister Cassandra," he whispered.

She could not find her way through the thoughts and emotions that suddenly held her in their massive grip. *Farewell*. Was that it? After all they'd been through? And then in the next moment she chastised herself for even considering the thought that she deserved more than a cool farewell. After all, she had dismissed him. What did she expect?

With a tremulous smile, she moved past him and entered the cool darkness beyond his outstretched arm. She turned to tell him something, but he was gone, the black silk falling, shutting her out, leaving her to contemplate her impending meeting with the beast, alone.

Chapter Eight

It wasn't entirely dark. Brass lanterns and beeswax candles in ornate stands burned in the far corners and on a leather trunk worked with bronze, with a massive lock that shone like a burnished sun. They illuminated a simple chair of metal, backless with a white fabric seat, standing beside the trunk; a screen of intricate latticework; and a bed.

Cassandra's eyes widened at the crimson silk hangings that surrounded the bed, which was covered in red as well. It was elevated on a dais. Pillows fanned the sides nearest the tent walls. It was a setting of opulence and comfort, which surprised her, considering the Leopard was a beast known for his prowess with sword and dagger, his ability to sniff out enemies of the empire.

Unconsciously, she moved toward the bed. The softness of the tent's floor lured her attention. She gasped, seeing the leopard skin and knowing its importance, all at once. She had seen it in a dream, seen herself lying naked upon it. She stood rooted to an Oriental carpet, afraid to move.

A sound, like a deeply drawn breath, raised the hairs on the back of her neck. She whirled on her feet and looked about her. Someone was watching her. She could feel a presence, a presence like an animal's, ready to pounce.

Light and shadow rippled behind the carved screen.

"Who's there?" she demanded through her veil at the shadow behind the screen. "Show yourself. I'll not be fright—"

"My apologies. I did not mean to frighten you, Cassandra," said the deep, gentle voice.

Cassandra tilted her head toward the voice. When it touched her name, she felt touched by a hand as well. A gentle hand. Strong. Caressing. Familiar.

Cassandra narrowed her eyes. *It can't be.*

The shadow paced back and forth behind the screen.

"Who are you?"

The shadow quickly answered, "The one you seek."

"The Leopard."

"Yes."

"Why do you hide from me?"

"Have you not heard the stories? I am a beast."

Unconsciously, Cassandra twisted a bit of silk between her fingers, all the while forming in her mind the picture of the beast that would not show itself to her. What if what the novices had said was true? That he was scarred and marked beyond human recognition. That he had black hawk eyes that could turn you to ice with their deep, tormented stare. That his dark hair and beard were matted with the blood of his enemies. Christe! What had she done?

"You've come for my help," he said gruffly, as if she were all of a sudden a torment to him.

She answered with a defiant, "Yes," sweeping the frightful images aside.

"And what will you give me in return?"

"Money," she answered him as if it were manna from Heaven.

"Humph," he snorted. "That chest is already full of gold. I don't require any more. What else do you have?"

As her hands rose to remove her earrings, the voice answered, "No. No jewels."

She sensed him licking his lips, and she remembered what Nicephorus had said about liking a "comely figure."

Delicately, to show him she was not afraid, she removed the veil that concealed her mouth.

"Aahhhh," he sighed appreciatively. "A kiss, then? A good enough start, I think."

Cassandra watched the shadow step from behind the screen into a deep pool of darkness. With another step, she screamed and backed away. "No!"

Nicephorus Acominatus bowed to Cassandra. "It will be my honor to help you in your quest."

The Leopard was Nicephorus? There was no question. Here he was. The man begotten from Hell and her bodyguard were one and the same.

Cassandra threw a murderous look at the tall figure dressed entirely in black. Before she realized what she was doing, she was moving toward him, ready to strike, and lashing out through gritted teeth, "How dare you play me for a fool!"

But as his animal instincts were finely honed, he immediately grabbed her hands by the wrists and held her steady. This fanned her fury all the more and she moved to kick him, but he dodged her too well to give her satisfaction.

"May I remind you of your own little ruse, *Sister* Cassandra? It appears that both of us are masters of this game."

She stilled slightly under his control.

"That's better," he said, feeling her anger wane. He released her, but, when he sensed her intention to back away, he reached out and gripped her upper arms.

"Why?" she said, refusing to meet his gaze. "Why did you do this?"

"Would you have believed me? That I was the Leopard? You wanted nothing to do with me, Nicephorus, remember?"

At first, Cassandra could not bring herself to look at him—this man, who had agreed to help her in her quest once, and who had now agreed to it again. But she felt his eyes, eyes with the power to touch like hands, and they lured her attention away. Held by his blue-grey gaze more tightly than any muscular arm or chain, she felt the pull between them like a strong undertow. This was what she wanted to fight. This *thing* between them that made her words catch in her throat, her heart pound like waves crashing against rocks, her bones turn to water.

"You cannot stop me from finding the swan," she whispered.

He went very still. His eyes locked with hers. "But I believe you have already found it."

Her look turned deep and questioning. "What do you mean? I've found nothing."

He shook his head. "If only you could see what I see."

For a moment her thoughts flashed to the image of herself in the mirror. Cassandra recalled what she'd seen— a woman, not a girl from the convent. Not someone who cared to hide any longer in the robes of a novice.

She lowered her head and stared at the Leopard's leather vest, thinking how the sacred waters had always revealed the little jeweled swan, and then herself, one after the other. Two swans? Had her mother intended this to happen all along? It would be just like her mother to say one thing and mean another thing entirely, she thought, frowning. Nothing was as it seemed, she thought. And the ultimate proof was the man now standing before her.

When she looked up at him again, Nicephorus thought

he would drown in the depths of her amber gaze. Had she finally accepted him? he wondered. Elation crashed through him.

"I don't understand anything anymore," she confessed, touching his arm.

Her innocence opened him to her vulnerability, and to his own. His need to make love to her was so keen, he felt a tear rise and shimmer. It was more than an animal's need to mate. It was a human desire to mate with all that was pure and good in the world.

He didn't want words to mar the depth of the emotion between them, but he felt the need to reassure her that yes, she did understand. She understood in her heart what had happened to her and what was happening now.

He reached out and cupped her chin in his hand. "You understand, Cassandra. You see and understand."

His lips were closer than a whisper. She understood that he could claim her mouth for the pleasure of it if he so desired. She saw something flicker in his eyes and, at the same time, felt his hands move up her arms, tighten and pull her closer to him. She didn't fight him, didn't try to pull away. She remained still, feeling his heat engulf her, his fingers fan apart on her arms to touch more of her. In a flaming instant she saw them on the leopard skin. She shuddered, realizing how very much she wanted it to happen.

Nicephorus felt her unspoken desire enveloping him like a scent, and swooped down and captured the lips raised innocently to him. His mouth was teasingly gentle at first, his lips barely tasting her. But as she began to respond, his mouth became hard and demanding.

Cassandra gave herself over to his kiss. The touch of his tongue, flicking over her lips, encouraging him to allow him entrance to the velvety domain beyond, set fire to all her questions and confusion. She parted her lips and his tongue drove deep, exploring and caressing. The depth of his kiss pulled her out of herself and into a moment of heat and desire.

She felt him trembling with passion. His response stirred her all the more and she moaned against his lips. She felt his hands slip down her arms to grasp her waist. He stroked her through her tunic, then with the desperation of a man who has long dreamed of this moment, he grabbed her firmly and pulled her hard against him. His mouth grew hungrier still, increasing the sensations sweeping through her. A soft, frustrated cry slipped from her parted lips when his lips moved on to the sensitive hollow beneath her earlobe. His mouth sucked her gently here, tasting the scent of her, then slipped down her neck, leaving a trail of fiery kisses in his wake.

Her tunic stopped him. He pulled himself slightly away to look at her.

"What do you see, Cassandra?"

His voice caressed her with the same wild urgency as his mouth had and she gulped down a shallow breath. She read in his eyes the restlessness within his body, felt the pounding of his heart against her breast. Shaking with thirst for the continued press of his mouth on hers, she lifted her hand and with her finger slowly traced his lower lip, still wet from their kissing.

"I see you. I see this," she said, raising her face to him, kissing him lightly, like a dream.

But this wasn't a dream. Her bold action took Nicephorus by surprise. But he was quick to make up for lost time. His hand moved to cradle her head as his mouth possessed hers with bruising ferocity. Deep within her, in that part of her as yet untouched by a man, she felt something melt and turn and pull and yield. She shuddered, and the mouth on hers softened.

She lost herself to the exquisitely wanton kiss that kept

building, pressure on pressure, heat on heat. More and more reckless. More and more shameless. Building it together. It was an intimacy that made her ache for more. Breathless, she tore her mouth away. Could he feel it? Could he see?

She did not have to speak her desire. Nicephorus read the piercing look she gave him, read the meaning in the way she bit her wet, swollen lower lip, and the unguarded manner in which she held her body, tilted forward, as if she wanted him to lift her and carry her away.

He moved to stand behind her. His fingers touched her neck, just the tips first, sending currents up her arms, down her back, making it hard for her to breathe. He began to rub her neck. She felt the rhythm of his fingers loosening her muscles, separating the strands of her hair, rubbing himself into her.

She sighed and moaned. She moved under his hands, lifting her arms, removing the silver circlet and the veil. He turned her around by the shoulders to face him. He helped her lift her tunica over her head, then her under-gown, until she stood naked and beautiful. A woman.

Chapter Nine

They reached for each other at the same moment. Nicephorus lifted her into his arms and put her in the center of the bed. The candles illuminated his movements as he unbuckled his sword belt and removed his black tunic. He was wryly chagrined to see that his hands were trembling. He turned to the side and took a deep, steadying breath before continuing to undress. When he turned to face her on his bed, he could almost feel the hot blush that spread across her cheeks. He feasted on her beauty—her face framed by magnificent, wild hair, her lush body that no words would justly praise or rightly honor. But in his own time, with his lips, his body, he would find a way.

Cassandra took in the tousled black hair, wide shoulders, and magnificently formed arms and chest. Having left the convent girl far behind, her look was bold. Still, she shied from looking any further than his hips, which were slim and sleek. She caught his gaze as he approached her. She lifted her arms to him and, when he took her hands, she drew him down. Impatient to touch him, she met him halfway; she buried her face in the soft hair of his chest and breathed a trail of feathery kisses across his skin. His eyes slitted with passion as he watched her. He plunged his hands into her hair and pulled her head back to cease her teasing.

This beautiful woman had sought the Leopard and had found him. He would help her find the jeweled swan. But now, he would honor the gift of this woman God had placed in his path. Nothing stood in his way. Nothing else mattered.

He cradled her head between his hands and claimed her mouth with his. Nicephorus groaned as he felt her hands tentatively rest on his hips, his legs, then boldly move up his thighs. All semblance of control gave way to his animal instincts. He felt the heat and the power of his need to take her and mate with her. She was in the Leopard's den now. She was his.

He came down on top of her, claiming her body, and separated her thighs with one of his own. Bracing his weight on his elbows, he covered her body completely with his and moved, ever so slightly, as if to rub his scent into her. Desiring to know her essence, he shifted his weight so that he might touch and look at her.

He placed his finger on her brow and began a slow descent down her aquiline nose, over her lips, her chin and neck. While touching her, he held her gaze, watching how her eyes closed slightly in pleasure as his finger smoothed the hollow in her neck and circled her breasts. Each new place that he touched, he did it slowly, his touch and his eyes asking her permission. She gave it to him, her breasts, her arms, the slope of her belly and hips. She sighed and breathed his name.

He prepared her carefully. All that he had learned at

the hands of other women was lavished on Cassandra. His fingertips glided leisurely down to the soft insides of her thighs, making her writhe and tremble beneath his hands. Softer than a breath, his fingers fanned across the pale gold hair that guarded the treasure just beyond his reach. She bucked and went to cover herself with her hands, but he shushed her with his voice, his hands. Watching her, his own desires flamed with impatience: touching her was no longer enough.

He felt his control slipping away. Hungry for her, to know her essence, he leaned down and kissed each virgin thigh and breathed in her scent. With the heat of her urging him on, he covered her with his mouth and tasted her. He paused. He waited for her to refuse him, to make those inhibiting sounds or protests that would force him to stop. But to his pleasure, she parted her thighs. He moved to lie between her legs and take her at his leisure.

Trembling with raw pleasure, she clawed the pillows above her head. She could not help moving beneath his tongue. It felt like fire and waves all at once. Trusting him, she opened herself to him, lifting her hips, giving him her body, her soul. She looked down at him and nearly came undone; he looked like a beast sprawled between her legs.

Then she was spiraling down into herself. And the heat between her legs rooted her to his mouth, his bed. The pleasure came with a crash that set her free into the sky, and she cried out with the power and the joy that made her tremble and cry and want to laugh and to be held and never let go of again. This was a magic she had never foreseen. She, Cassandra, with her bronze bowl and all the powers of the women in her family in her blood, had known nothing. The veil that had shielded herself from her self had been torn away. And she knew the freedom that came from making love and how it set you free to kiss the sky.

Nicephorus held Cassandra's shaking body in his arms, smoothed her hair, and kissed her. Before she could stop him, he moved on top of her. He was careful when he lifted her hips and brought her to him, rocked back on his heels and held her against him, rocking, rocking, patiently moving inside her. He wanted to give her enough time to adjust to him.

"Cassandra, Cassandra," he breathed her name as he lowered his body over hers.

Christe! He was going to tear her in two! She breathed deeply, trying to relax and make the pain go away. She held his face between her hands and met his gaze. He stilled his body; she knew what he was thinking. She moved her hands to his lower back and pressed down to reassure him that this was what she wanted. But he would not move.

"I had heard you were a beast in all things," she teased.

He narrowed his eyes at her, then nuzzled her neck. "Where did you hear such a lie?"

"In the convent, of course."

He laughed and kissed her neck before raising his face to look at her again. "Remind me to pay a visit to your convent. Those little novices need to get their facts straight."

She arched beneath him as the discomfort began to give way to another sensation entirely. "No doubt you will inspire even more stories, and perhaps earn a few followers for your army as well."

He smiled and marveled at the fact that, until a few days ago, she was a nun from that same convent. Now, here she was, in his bed, mating with him. He kissed her nose and captured her mouth in a long, deep kiss. He was a beast, he thought to himself. And the beast would not rest until ecstasy consumed her.

With steely control, he moved inside her, rekindling her desire. They didn't look away or close their eyes. They moved together, primitive sensations driving them on, until the pleasure moved in watery waves. It clenched them one moment, released them the next, until their passions peaked and they came with wild cries and became one source of heat.

Chapter Ten

Golden halos of candlelight softened the darkness inside the tent. Cassandra opened her eyes and felt Nicephorus cupped around her body. On her side, wrapped in the captain's arms, she listened to his breathing, felt the soft air behind her ear, against her neck. He sighed and nuzzled her. He moved slightly, stretching his leg over her and pinning her to the bed. The appreciative sound of his sigh moved through her like a ripple of water.

She waited until his breathing evened out, then gently turned to face him. In the shadows of the dark, his face looked so peaceful, she could not believe he was the same man who had been ordered to be her bodyguard. And now he was also the Leopard. Cassandra could not tie the beast to the real man. She shivered, thinking of the ways he had possessed her body. Maybe he was a beast, but a different kind than the stories and tales had reported.

And now the beast was her lover. She watched his chest sinking and rising. There was a trail of a scar that ran from the middle of his chest to his lower rib. She wanted to touch it, follow it, kiss whatever hurt might still be there. She wanted him to wake up and touch her again.

She glanced up at his face and found him watching her with an open, admiring gaze. Joy fluttered through her body. She tried to think of something to say.

She cleared her throat. "I'd like to start off on the journey as soon as possible."

His hearty laugh caught her off guard; she didn't think her request was particularly amusing.

"Ahhh, so it's back to business, is it?"

"Well . . . It's just that I thought . . ."

He wanted her to know how he felt. How he'd loved her from the first day he saw her on the steps, in her nun's robes. He loved her, and he wanted her to know. But perhaps she could already see that she was loved?

He grabbed her and pulled her up on top of him. She tried to move, but his hands were quicker, sweeping over her buttocks, caressing her into stillness.

"I want you to look into my eyes and tell me what you see," he said.

His apparent ease and comfort at having her spread across his body prodded a spirited lack of self-consciousness. Resting her elbow on his chest, she propped her chin into the cup of her hand. And she did as he'd asked—looked into his eyes.

"What does the future hold for us, Cassandra?"

She was ready to tell him that she couldn't divine the future without the bronze bowl, but something kept the thought from continuing, something soft and accepting in his eyes. There was something that he wanted her to see. But could she?

She lowered her bent arm and her gaze narrowed in seriousness. She could feel his heart beating. His gray-blue eyes reminded her of the sea, as did the rise and fall of his chest. In the quiet intimacy of the moment she felt borne away, and in that instant, she experienced a vision that was more heartfelt than anything she had seen before: she saw them together, but it wasn't the togetherness of friends, or lovers, but—

She blinked and pulled herself away, rolling off him, off the bed, and rising to her feet in graceless movements as if she were propelled by fear.

Startled, Nicephorus sat up and asked, "What is it?"

She paced like a tiger.

"Cassandra! What?"

"I can't marry you."

As if he'd seen her vision, too, he answered, "Why not?" The edge of cold steel was in his tone.

"I will not live behind more walls!" She saw it all, walls like the convent's, only higher. And a bodyguard, who was also now her husband, for every hour of the day. No. She was free and she would stay free.

He moved in front of her and blocked her way. "Walls? This is not about walls. I love you. I wish to marry you. Where do you see walls?"

"Eventually, you will close me in," she accused, looking up at him. "That's how people live, husband and wife. Don't think that I don't know."

"Cassandra," he whispered, gently holding her by the arms. She felt so cold. He looked at her and swallowed, for he knew she was partly right. Women could not move about as they pleased, not wives, or daughters, or nuns. They were protected by men, by walls, by laws. And, Christe! he would protect her forever.

He searched his mind for an answer that would still the little beast she had become. "I promise you only my heart. No walls," he added with a whispered gentleness, shaking his head. "Besides, I can't imagine a fortress strong enough to contain you. You would think nothing of disguising yourself as a—a man! to escape." He paused to gauge her assessment of his feelings. He'd meant every word, and he knew, through experience, that she wouldn't hesitate to devise another identity to secure her freedom.

Cassandra's resolve wavered in the face of his promise. She looked up at him, hoping he would never forget this moment, his words, his pledge. She placed her palms on his chest, stepped closer, and kissed the scar on his chest. Could she trust him? There was only one way to find out.

"Cassandra, Cassandra," he whispered as she weaved a trail of kisses.

He pulled her down with him to the leopard skin rug. And she let his voice take her in its persuasive arms.

The sun was over Lady Olympia's shoulder as she sat on the fountain's stone ledge, reading Cassandra's letter. Birdsong spiralled from the branches of the trees that sheltered the convent garden. The fountain was playing its soothing dream song, and the wind was carrying the sweet, plush scent of ripening fruit from the orchards beyond the walls. Lady Olympia's mouth moved with the words of her daughter. Her amber eyes shone with the light from her soul. She followed the last lines with her finger, looked up from the letter, and smiled.

Tipping her head back, she closed her eyes and gave a great sigh . . . of relief. *My deed is done,* she said to herself. *Cassandra has seen herself for the woman she is. And she has a partner, a mate, who, I think, will never let her forget it.*

She sighed again, so deeply that anyone entering the garden at that moment would have thought Lady Olympia was experiencing a moment of blessed ecstasy.

In the next breath, she sat up straight and crossed herself. Still smiling, she re-read the passage about Cassandra and Nicephorus's journey to Venice, where her daughter had seen the jeweled swan in a dream.

She's discovered the important swan, Lady Olympia mused to herself. *She's discovered love. And more.*

Lady Olympia recalled Cassandra's animal fury and refusal to leave the convent to go on the quest. She remembered that, on the morning Cassandra left, her daughter had been wearing the robes and veil of a nun. She had used the garments as a disguise, but Lady Olympia had known that Cassandra was hiding from no one but herself. As if her daughter were standing before her now, Lady Olympia could see Cassandra's wide, round eyes, eyes that had been filled with such longing that she had nearly changed her mind. And now . . . her brave, beautiful girl had cast her robes aside and had emerged to be the woman she was meant to be.

A twinkle in her eyes, Lady Olympia folded the letter and was slipping it into the pocket of her robe when the Abbess, with a keen, sharp look about her as if she'd been hunting something or someone, appeared and strode across the garden path.

The Abbess stopped in front of her sister and opened her mouth to say something, but stopped as the face lifted to hers, so pale and delicate, was transformed by a smile. Suddenly, it was her little sister, Olympia Phaedra, who was sitting before her. The Abbess felt her heart lurch and the tears rise.

And then her little sister was gone. But the smile remained.

"They're going to have a baby," Lady Olympia announced. "A girl." She removed the letter from her pocket and handed it to the Abbess.

The Abbess's eyes never left Lady Olympia's face as she unfolded the letter. The older nun's attention darted from her sister's smile to the letter and back and forth, again and again. A question deepened the creases of her wrinkled brow as she held the letter up in her hand and shook her head. "Where does it say that? There's nothing here that says Cassandra and this captain are expecting a child. I see no—"

"Don't you see?" Lady Olympia said excitedly.

The Abbess quickly scanned the letter again. "No," she answered, confusion in her eyes.

Lady Olympia rose to her feet slowly and touched her sister's arm. "I can see it, Mary," she whispered, saying her sister's name out loud with the hopes that the older woman would, for a moment, be her sister and not the Abbess.

Lady Olympia turned to face the water and, placing her hand on her heart, said, "I see it here. And in my soul."

Looking at the fountain, seeing in the sacred spray of water Nicephorus and Cassandra, holding a baby in her arms, she said to herself, "A mother always knows."

For a few moments, Mary watched her sister. There was love in the Abbess's eyes. And years of unsaid words trembled in her throat. She forced a dry swallow as she took quiet note of Olympia Phaedra's noble profile, the finely etched lines radiating from around her sister's eyes, and her chin, so perfect it looked carved from alabaster.

Following her sister's gaze, Mary looked at the fountain and whispered, "Then perhaps they will name the child Phaedra, after her beautiful, wise grandmother."

"Perhaps." An all-knowing smile lit the noble face of Lady Olympia Phaedra Heraclius. She could see the wondrous path that lay before her daughter. And she rejoiced.

Best Laid Plans

Elizabeth Graham

Chapter One

The best laid schemes o' mice an' men gang
aft a-gley

> —Robert Burns
> "To a Mouse"

Crane Island, Virginia—1876

"I now pronounce you man and wife."

Plying her paper fan and sighing happily, Phoebe Crane glanced at her daughter sitting beside her on a pew in the small, old church. It was crowded with a large percentage of the island population. And filled with August heat and humidity.

"Isn't Margaret the loveliest bride ever wed on Crane Island?" Phoebe whispered behind her fan.

"I'd say that's going a trifle too far, Mama," Serena whispered back from behind her own fan.

The radiant couple began walking down the aisle, the

bride tossing flowers from her bouquet toward the guests in the pews.

Phoebe sighed again, not so happily this time. She should have known how Serena would react. "I'm beginning to think the only weddings I'll ever attend are friends' and acquaintances'."

"We've had this argument a hundred times before and you know how I feel. Besides, this is hardly the time or place."

"What better time or place to remind you of the happiness you're missing out on?" Phoebe persisted. "You're twenty-four. Peter's been gone two years. He'd want you to have a happy life."

"My life is just fine. I need a husband no more than you do—and you insist you don't pine for another one."

"I've already lived my life. You haven't."

A pink rose landed in Serena's gray sateen-clad lap.

"There! That's a sign if ever I saw one." Phoebe realized she was pushing too hard, but couldn't seem to stop.

Serena didn't reply. A few minutes later the two of them picked up their long, full skirts and joined the stream of people leaving the church. Phoebe was surprised to see that her daughter carried the rose instead of leaving it on the pew as she'd expected. Was it possible the beautiful wedding they'd just witnessed had made Serena finally take her mother's words to heart? Give the idea of marriage some thought?

Jonas and Gavin Mead fell in behind. Phoebe gave them both a warm smile. "Lovely wedding," she offered.

"Guess so," Jonas said, a little brusquely.

Jonas's bark was worse than his bite, she knew, after sharing many a dinner sitting across from him at her dining room table. He was one of the kindest, most decent men she'd ever met and he looked uncommonly well today. His gray hair was newly-trimmed into distinguished-looking sideburns, and his gray-blue eyes gave her a keen glance. And seemed to linger a moment.

Amazed, Phoebe felt her cheeks pinken.

"Yes, it was," Gavin answered, returning her smile. He gazed at the back of Serena's blond head.

Phoebe hurriedly brought her attention back to Gavin. My goodness! He looked as if he wanted to grab Serena and give her a kiss like the one Hank had just given Margaret.

She knew, of course, that Gavin had an eye for Serena, but she'd never realized that he felt this deeply.

His black hair was slicked back and his dark eyes still held that intent look, which somehow made him appear more handsome than usual. He was a fine young man, even if he and his adopted father weren't native Islanders. They'd made a lot of improvements to the old general store in the year since they'd bought it and moved here.

Phoebe had decided he'd make an ideal mate for Serena almost as soon as she laid eyes on him. New blood was certainly needed here. Serena had shown no interest in any of the Island's eligible young men since her fiancé's death, although several had tried to court her.

Unfortunately, she'd also shown no interest in Gavin.

"Are you two coming along to the boarding house for the reception?" Phoebe asked, hoping they were. It certainly couldn't hurt for Gavin and Serena to share this atmosphere of wedded bliss for a while longer.

"Sure am. Wouldn't miss a chance to sample some of your cooking."

Jonas's grin made a funny little flutter go through Phoebe. She'd never met another man quite like him. He could go from almost gruffness to that warm grin in a matter of seconds.

She collected herself. Never mind Jonas. She wanted to keep Serena and Gavin together a while longer.

Not that Serena seemed even to have heard any of this.

She just walked with the crowd to the door, her head still straight forward.

Phoebe moved a little closer and poked her discreetly in the side. Serena jumped and gave her mother a dazed look. "You're being rude," Phoebe whispered.

Serena seemed to come back from a long distance. At last her blue eyes cleared and she turned to give Jonas and Gavin one of her sweetly distant smiles.

"I'm sorry, Jonas . . . Gavin. I . . . guess I was woolgathering."

Again, Gavin gave Serena an intent look. But this time he looked at her face, Phoebe happily observed, his glance moving up to her daughter's eyes and lingering.

Just like Jonas's had . . .

Phoebe quickly turned this thought off. What on earth was wrong with her today? The wedding atmosphere must be rubbing off on her, too.

They'd finally reached the door, and a welcome breeze swept over them. After they'd all congratulated the newly-married couple, Phoebe said, "We'd better go on ahead and get everything ready." She glanced at the two men.

As she'd hoped, Jonas and Gavin fell in behind them.

"Margaret couldn't have had a better day for her wedding," Phoebe said, turning to include the men. "You know that old saying, 'Happy is the bride the sun shines on'." She gave them a wide smile, then turned back to Serena. Her daughter's face still had that bemused expression. "But of course, since it's August, it's not surprising the weather is sunny."

Phoebe realized she was prattling, but couldn't seem to stop during the remainder of the short walk along Crane Island's main road, only a lane, really, to the old Crane house. Gulls called overhead, and a fresh sea breeze cooled the sun's rays. The oyster shells covering the lane crunched beneath their steps.

Oh, this little island in the Chesapeake Bay was a wonderful place to live!

Yes, but . . . there's something missing, a voice in her mind said. She swallowed, unsettled. Of course there was.

Her daughter needed a husband.

They stopped in front of the big, white-painted frame house, with its wraparound front porch. Even after six years, the neatly lettered sign on its post gave Phoebe a deep sense of satisfaction.

"Room and Board," the sign announced, and underneath that, "Dinner Served Monday Through Saturday." Yes, they'd come a long way since those fear-filled days right after Arthur's death when she hadn't known which way to turn.

"Jonas, you and Gavin might as well stay out here and enjoy the breeze," Phoebe announced when they'd climbed the porch steps. "I'll go get everything on the table."

She paused, then glanced at her daughter. "You may as well stay out here, too, Serena. It won't take both of us." She gave Serena a guileless smile. "I'll let you clean up afterwards."

Serena smiled back, but her blue eyes glinted. *I know what you're up to,* that glance said. "I'll do that gladly, Mama—but I'll help you now, too."

To Phoebe's chagrin, Serena swept inside, leaving her mother to follow. In the kitchen, Serena got her apron off its hook, tied it around the waist of her second-best dress, then turned to her mother.

"That was a good try, Mama, but when are you going to give up on me? How many times do I have to tell you I don't intend to marry?"

"I can't give up," Phoebe replied. "I want you to be happy."

"If it takes marriage to make a woman happy, then why don't *you* marry again?"

Trying to make her voice firm, Phoebe said, as she had at the wedding, "I've already lived my life."

Serena gave her mother a slow glance, making Phoebe conscious of her gray-streaked blond hair, her still-trim figure.

"No, you haven't. You look years younger than your age, and you're plenty vigorous, too. You've got lots of life left. *You* need to share it with a nice man. Like Jonas."

Something in Phoebe's chest jumped at her daughter's last words. She frowned, unable to think of the words to refute Serena. She *was* hale and healthy. God willing, she very well should have years more left to live.

She cleared her throat. "Let's not discuss this any more. We have work to do."

"That's fine with me." Serena pumped water into the pail on the washstand and checked on the tubs of ice cream in the corner, kept frozen with salt and ice and covered with burlap sacks. She turned to the table where the pretty little cakes she'd baked earlier were now cool and ready to be decorated with frosting.

Phoebe wasn't able to resist one last try. "Oh, Serena, you'd make some man such a wonderful wife."

Serena glanced up at her mother. "So would you, Mama. So would you."

Going to the big old cookstove to get the rolls ready for reheating, Phoebe firmed her mouth as she deftly performed her familiar tasks.

She didn't need to be yearning for what had once been and could be again. She'd had a happy marriage, but she didn't need another one.

But her daughter did. Serena just wasn't the spinster type. And if that look she'd caught in Gavin's eye after the wedding meant anything, Serena's life was about to be stirred up.

She brightened. Maybe her dreams of rocking grandchildren on the big front porch during her declining years would come true after all.

Jonas and Gavin sat next to each other in rocking chairs, watching the porch and living room fill up with wedding guests. Jonas felt sort of strange today. Kind of agitated. Well, no wonder. Weddings were for women, so they could puddle over with tears of joy, or something.

He should have figured out a way to get out of it. But since it was Sunday and the store was closed, he hadn't been able to come up with a good excuse. He never got sick, so that wouldn't have worked.

He gave his son a sideways glance. That look Gavin had given Serena in the church had startled Jonas. But the girl seemed completely oblivious.

Jonas blessed the day he'd taken in ten-year-old Gavin, who'd lost both parents from a fever. But he wanted grandsons before he died. Granddaughters, too. It was past time Gavin married and raised a family.

Time Serena did, too. He liked the girl. She was pretty and a hard worker. Sitting around the stove at the store with the fishermen last winter, he'd listened to the stories about how Phoebe and Serena had made the old Crane home into a boarding house when times were hard after Phoebe's husband died.

Phoebe was a damn fine woman. It was easy to see where Serena got her looks. Somehow, his mind lingered on that thought until he realized what he was doing.

"Wonder how long until we get to eat?" he asked Gavin. "Maybe we should just go on home."

Gavin gave a start as if his mind had been far away. He

turned to his father. "I don't think we can do that, Pop. Be kind of rude to leave now."

Jonas leaned a little closer. "You could go on inside," he said in low tones. "Serena might be in the dining room and you could offer to help her do something or other."

"Why? So she can give me that cool, friendly smile she gives everyone?"

"Would you rather she frowned at you?"

"Hell, no! I'd rather she saw me as a *man*, Pop."

"Then why don't you do something to make her?"

"What? Pick her up and carry her off somewhere like a caveman?"

Jonas grinned at the frustration in his son's voice. "You might try that. Could be it would work."

"I've about decided it's the only thing that will. How do you court a girl when she tells you she'll always be in mourning for her dead fiancé?"

Jonas raised his brows. "You never mentioned that before."

"Only happened a few days ago. I've waited a decent interval. Hell, we've lived here for over a year now! I caught up with her on the lane going down to the shore and asked her straight out if I could court her. She gave me this surprised look and said no—then told me why."

"So what did you do? Say 'sorry to bother you, ma'am,' and leave?"

"It stunned me so much I couldn't think of anything to say." He scowled. "But that wasn't the end of it. If Serena thinks it is, she's mistaken. I'll come up with something."

He paused and gave Jonas a long look.

A look that for some reason made Jonas feel uneasy.

Alice Hastings, the new schoolteacher, climbed the steps and took the rocker across from them, giving them a friendly greeting and smile.

Jonas and Gavin returned the greeting.

'Wasn't it a nice wedding?'' she asked.

''That it was, ma'am,'' Jonas said, noticing how her brownish hair gleamed in the light, how trim her slim figure looked in her light summer dress.

How her eyes lingered on Gavin.

He glanced at his son, who was giving the woman a very neutral smile.

You could do worse than this one, he told Gavin silently.

Tom Rawlins, the town carpenter, walked up the steps and sat down next to Alice, his adoring eyes fixed on her face.

So that was the way the wind blew, Jonas mused. No doubt Tom would have the woman wedded and bedded before Gavin ever got such an idea in his head.

No, Gavin *never* would get that idea in his head. He'd been a single-minded, stubborn little boy—and those traits hadn't left now that he was a man.

If anything, they were stronger. Once Gavin set his mind on something, he wouldn't give up until he had whatever it was. And now he wanted Serena Crane. Jonas felt Gavin was facing the hardest challenge of his life.

And this time he might not win.

Serena appeared in the doorway. ''Everything is ready!'' she announced. Her face was flushed; wisps of her blond hair were coming loose from her neat bun.

Gavin was looking at her as if he'd never seen a woman before. He rose with Jonas and the rest of the group on the porch and they went inside to the big, cool dining room.

The long mahogany table down the room's center had a white cloth spread over it and was laden with platters and dishes of food.

Wonderful smells drifted in from the kitchen. Phoebe entered with a napkin-covered basket of rolls, which she placed on the table. Like her daughter, she looked flushed from the kitchen heat, wisps of her own hair flying loose.

Fine woman, Phoebe, Jonas thought again. Odd she'd never remarried. Not too many to choose from on little Crane Island. But a few unmarried men of her age lived here.

Including himself.

Now where had *that* thought come from? He'd known from an early age he was a natural-born bachelor. And he was more set in his ways every day. He'd make no woman a fit husband.

It must be the wedding today. It seemed to have stirred everyone up, got them to thinking about courtship and marriage.

Tomorrow it would be all over and things would be back to normal.

Of course, not for Gavin. He wouldn't give up until he had won Serena. Or left the Island. That thought slid into Jonas's mind like a serpent and once there, wouldn't be dislodged.

When they'd left Baltimore behind and come here in search of a simpler life, neither he nor Gavin had missed the city or their life there. He didn't think Gavin missed it now.

But if Serena wasn't to be won, he knew Gavin wouldn't be able to stand living here seeing her every day for the rest of his life.

He saw Gavin giving Serena another of those looks that should have raised her temperature and got her to notice him. Just then she looked up. Her glance met Gavin's and held.

Her eyes widened and he could see her swallow. Jonas felt a small glow of hope come to life inside him.

He saw Phoebe had also caught the look passing between Gavin and Serena. A pleased smile curved her mouth. She must have felt Jonas's eyes on her, because she suddenly turned toward him.

"Help yourself, Jonas," Phoebe said. "There's plenty of food."

"Thanks, Phoebe." Her cheeks were rosier, too, he would swear. No doubt because she shared the same hopes he did that their children would find each other.

Yes, that had to be it, Jonas told himself as he picked up one of the light-as-air rolls.

Couldn't be anything else.

Chapter Two

Standing outside the wide front door of the general store, Serena smoothed the skirt of her brown cotton frock, tried to tidy her hair, then sighed at the futility of trying to tame her curls. And why did she care?

She'd known Gavin Mead for over a year and had never before cared about looking her best when she saw him.

Maybe it was because all this seemed so odd. Gavin finding her alone in the kitchen for a moment yesterday after the wedding and asking her if she'd come to the store tomorrow, then saying he wanted to talk to her about something personal.

She'd given him a startled look and he'd smiled wryly back and told her not to worry, that it didn't concern the two of them. She'd felt her face redden, embarrassed that he'd read her look so easily. She'd known he was referring to that day last week when he'd asked her if she'd let him court her, and she'd told him the same thing she'd told other would-be suitors these last two years. That she was still in mourning for her lost fiancé and probably always would be.

Recalling the incident, she shivered now as she had then. Gavin had given her a burningly intent look that seemed to last forever. Then he'd politely bade her good day, turned, and left. She'd stared after him, and an unexpected feeling of loss had welled up in her.

Gavin had given her another of those looks as they left the church after the wedding yesterday . . . and still another at the house later. That last one had done something to her insides that felt very strange . . .

Serena took a deep breath and opened the store's door. Gavin was alone, not even Jonas was in sight. She'd half-expected others to be in the store, since it was the only one on the Island. If so, she could have purchased the unneeded items she'd used as a pretext for coming here today, and hurried home without discussing whatever it was Gavin had in mind.

Pen in hand, Gavin glanced up from an open account book. He smiled when he saw her standing in the doorway. The smile lit up his face. Gavin was a handsome man. Why had she never noticed that before? *You have noticed it before,* her mind told her. *You noticed it yesterday after the wedding.*

"Good afternoon, Serena."

She returned his smile and greeting, then threaded her way down the center aisle past racks holding bags of flour, meal and animal feed, coils of rope, and implements. Overhead, swaying cedar-stave buckets hung from the ceiling.

Setting her basket on the scarred wooden counter, she forced herself to give Gavin a look she hoped showed only mild curiosity.

"You wanted to talk to me?" she asked, her voice brisk.

"Yes, I did," he answered, as briskly as she'd spoken. "I have an idea I'd like to discuss with you."

Serena knew she was staring because what he'd said was so unexpected. "An idea?" she echoed.

"Maybe I should say a proposed plan." He glanced at the closed door to the back, which contained storerooms and living quarters. "Pop should be gone for another few minutes."

Confusion mixed with her surprise. "Does it concern your father? Is that why you don't want him to hear what we say?"

Gavin gave her another smile, wry, this time. "Yes, it does." He paused for a moment, then went on, "Pop is a lonely man at heart, even if he doesn't show it."

Serena's surprise and confusion grew. Finally, she nodded. "You'd know better than anyone."

"Yes, I do. Your mother is a very nice woman—good looking, too. But I believe she's also lonely. I'd like us to try to get them together."

Serena gasped and moved back a step. *Was Gavin a mind reader? How had he known that she'd felt the same way ever since he and Jonas had moved here?*

Gavin frowned. "I'm sorry I sprang it on you like that, but I thought I'd better hurry up. Pop might come back in here."

Serena swallowed. He'd been blunt and honest. She would be, too. "I've had those same thoughts," she admitted.

His face cleared. "You have? Then you'll help me?"

Things were moving too fast. "I said I've had these thoughts," she protested. "I didn't say I planned to do anything about them."

"Why not? If we wait for them to do anything we'll be waiting forever. Pop's set in his ways. He thinks he's a born bachelor. That no woman could stand him. But he's mellow at the core."

Serena nodded. "Yes, I like Jonas. Mama does, too. But

she'd never admit she could feel any stronger about him or any man. She insists she's lived *her* life, but I—''

Appalled at what she'd almost said, Serena abruptly stopped. "What do you have in mind to get them together?" she finished instead.

Gavin's dark brown eyes lit up and he gave her a grin that did something funny to her stomach. "Then you'll help me?"

Serena worried her lower lip, then noticed Gavin's eyes were fixed on her mouth. She felt her face warming again. "I—I don't—" Listening to her faltering words, she made up her mind. "Yes, I'll help you."

"Good! I've been worried about this lately. Pop wouldn't know what to do with himself if I were to go back to Baltimore."

A strange, hollow feeling hit her stomach. "You're planning to leave the Island? But I thought . . . everyone thought you and Jonas were here to stay. That you'd take over the store one day."

Something flickered in the depths of Gavin's eyes. He shrugged. "I'm not sure. Pop wants and expects me to, but sometimes I get restless. There doesn't seem to be much to keep me here for the rest of my life."

His somehow disturbing gaze had settled on her face again, then it rose to her eyes and stayed, as if waiting for a reaction.

Was Gavin telling her this because she'd said no when he'd asked her if he could court her? Was this what that intent look had meant?

Could he be considering leaving because of her?

She pushed her errant thoughts away, trying to concentrate on Gavin's plan.

"Do you have any ideas about how to implement this?" she asked again.

"A few. If you could persuade your mother to take a

walk along the shore Sunday afternoon, I'd talk Pop into doing the same. We could all accidentally meet.''

Serena frowned. "A walk? Just a *walk?* But . . . Jonas and Mama have sat across the table from each other for dinner six times a week almost ever since you moved here.''

"This walk could lead to the next step. Do you have anything else in mind that would be better?''

Her frown deepened, then she shook her head. "No, I don't guess so,'' she admitted. "But what if it storms?''

Gavin gave her a blank look. "I don't know. I only got as far as the walk.''

The door from the back rooms opened and Jonas stood framed in the opening. "Gavin, where did you put the order I was making up for that drummer due here tomorrow? Afternoon, Serena. Didn't expect to see you here today.''

From his manner Serena felt sure he hadn't overheard. She kept her eyes away from Gavin and grabbed her basket, trying to remember why she was supposed to be here.

"Mama is running low on sugar and coffee,'' she said, fumbling in her basket and extending a glass jar.

"I'll get 'em for you in a jiffy.'' Jonas took the jar and turned to a shelf behind him, his back toward the room.

Silently, Gavin mouthed *Sunday, at three* at her.

She nodded and Gavin turned to his father. "I'll find the drummer's order and go ahead with the accounts if you're going to wait on Serena.''

The older man abruptly stopped measuring coffee beans into the jar. "Say, I just remembered something I have to do. You go ahead and help Serena.''

He hurriedly returned to the back, leaving Serena staring in surprise. Gavin put down his pen and got up to finish measuring out the coffee.

Serena gazed at his back. Gavin had very broad shoulders, she noticed, as if for the first time. He had a good, strong build. He was a fine figure of a man.

And what was that to her? She waited tensely while he measured out the sugar into a sack and placed both items in her basket.

"Will that be all?" he asked casually, but his eyes, his dark brows raised, gave her a different message. As if they shared a secret.

Which they did.

Serena managed a smile. "Yes, it will. Thank you." She pitched her voice so that if Jonas was close to the doorway, he'd hear her innocent words and not suspect anything.

She picked up her basket and left the store, wanting to break into a run, but forcing her steps to remain ladylike. Once on the porch, she allowed herself to hurry down the steps and the narrow lane bordered by enormous shade trees behind white-washed wooden fences.

She felt confused and unsettled, emotions not usual with her. Until the last few days. Until yesterday.

Everything seemed to be different since yesterday's wedding!

Did she have the right to try to change her mother's life so radically? Could she justify helping Gavin with his plan to try to match her mother and his father? Why not? Her mother had been trying to do that to her for the last two years, and besides, she truly believed her mother needed the companionship of another husband.

Needed love.

A shiver made its way down her spine . . .

Lulabell Higgens, the younger of the Higgens spinsters, coming toward Serena on the lane, stopped dead and gave her an astonished stare.

Serena realized she'd spoken her last thoughts aloud and felt her cheeks redden again, for the third time in a few minutes. The fourth time in two days. She'd blushed at the wedding yesterday, too.

She *never* blushed. What on earth was wrong with her?

"Good afternoon, Lulabell," Serena managed with a smile. "Isn't it a pleasant day?"

Lulabell recovered herself and smiled back a little uncertainly. "Yes, 'tis, S'rena. Though a trifle warm for my liking."

"It's August. We can expect more warm days before the summer's over."

"Suppose so," Lulabell agreed. "How's your mother?"

"She's fine. Stop in and have dinner with us some noon, why don't you?"

Lulabell looked alarmed. "Oh, I don't believe we could do that. Sister always wants to eat at her own table."

Serena knew that wasn't the true reason. Both sisters were extremely frugal. Serena understood their fear of becoming destitute. She and her mother had lived through many lean days after her father's death.

Serena said her goodbyes and kept on going toward the old Crane homestead.

She'd let Gavin talk her into a plan that might change her mother's life forever.

What about yourself? her inner whisper teased. *As your mother says, you're young. Most of your life is still before you.*

No! she denied. It wasn't. The best part of her life was buried with Peter. She'd love and mourn him forever . . .

Forever?

She shivered. Forever. How could she stand that?

Serena swallowed, resolutely turning her mind to her mother and Jonas. She straightened her shoulders and walked on.

Gavin's idea was a good one and she *was* doing the right thing to help him with it. And she'd keep her mind where it belonged, and not on any possible changes in her own life.

Oh? her mind asked, *and how will you do that when you're going to be with Gavin next Sunday? And many other times if this works?*

No, she wouldn't. There would only be a couple of outings with the four of them. After that, if things worked out as she and Gavin hoped, Jonas and her mother would want to be alone, not have their children tagging along.

How long do you think you can fool yourself into believing all this?

Forever! she shot back.

No, her mind answered. *I don't believe you can.*

Chapter Three

"Can't say as I've ever known Phoebe Crane to run out of anything before her regular order day."

Gavin, his pen idle in his hands, had been staring out the front door of the store. He laid the pen in the middle of the ledger and turned to his adoptive father.

"Neither can I." He paused, picked up the pen again, and rolled it over in his fingers.

He still felt surprised that Serena had agreed to his plan so easily. He'd had arguments lined up to convince her and none of them had been necessary. But that wasn't the only reason he'd set his plan in motion.

He tightened his jaw. God, what a little fool Serena was! How could she prefer spending her life mourning Peter when she could have a flesh-and-blood man who wanted her.

And who was going to have her.

He grinned wryly at his determined thoughts. Serena was stubborn, but so was he. Maybe she thought her refusal last week was the end of his courtship attempt. But she was wrong.

Did she realize his plan meant the four of them would be together at least several times? Had she thought of that when she agreed to help him? No, he decided. Or if she had, she'd dismissed it as of no importance.

His jaw clenched. Why couldn't he forget her? Settle for Alice, who'd made it clear more than once *she* wouldn't turn down any overtures.

Because he didn't intend to *settle* for anything less than the woman he loved. Either this all-out attempt would win Serena's heart or he'd leave here. He'd have to.

"Serena came to see me," he told his father.

Jonas's hazel eyes lit with interest. "Is that right? Think she's interested in courting after all? But can't come right out and say so yet?"

Gavin shrugged. This was going to be the hardest part. He was a straightforward man, and deviousness didn't come natural to him.

"Looks like it to me. She said she and Phoebe were going for a walk along the shore Sunday afternoon—about three. She seemed to be making a point of letting me know."

The interest in Jonas's eyes sharpened. "I b'lieve you're right! Are you going to happen along there?"

Gavin knew he had to handle this carefully. "It would look a bit too obvious if I did that—by myself, I mean. But if you were to come with me . . ."

Jonas's interested look changed to a frown. "You know I always take a nap on Sunday afternoons."

"Skipping one nap isn't going to kill you."

"All right, I'll do it—just this once, mind you. After this you'll have to make your own arrangements."

That's what you think, Gavin told him silently. Aloud, he said, "Thanks, you old codger. Getting out in the afternoon breeze will be good for you. Clear the cobwebs out of your brain."

"I know you're real worried about *me,*"Jonas shot back.

"Sure, I am. When Serena and I are married, you'll be all alone here."

Gavin thought he saw a momentary flicker in his father's eyes. Then Jonas snorted. "Pretty cocky, aren't you? You haven't gotten Serena to the altar yet. And there's no woman on this island I'd marry. Or even want to."

That might change, Gavin told his father silently, then felt a twinge of guilt. Had he any right to meddle in his father's life? Wasn't it Jonas's own affair if he wanted to stay a bachelor?

No, because as he'd told Serena, he knew Jonas was lonely at times—and the rest of what he'd told her was also true.

If his best efforts to win Serena for his wife failed, he *would* leave Crane Island. He couldn't live this close to Serena for the rest of his life and never have her. And if he left, Jonas would be devastated.

Unless he was cozily married to Phoebe.

So he was doing his father a favor, he told himself firmly. And himself as well.

"I don't feel like a walk today, dear. I have a bit of a headache. I think I'll lie down for a while."

Phoebe slid a sweet-smelling lavender sachet inside the snowy pillowcase on one of the un-let rooms' beds. They always kept any empty rooms ready for an unexpected overnight guest.

She smiled at her daughter. "But you go ahead and enjoy yourself. Maybe you'll meet some of the young people and have a better time without your old mother along."

Serena attended to the pillow on the opposite side of the bed, trying not to show her dismay.

"The fresh air will do you good," she said. "It's turned out to be a lovely day—not too hot and the breeze is still coming in."

She glanced up to see her mother staring at her. After a minute, Phoebe nodded. "Maybe you're right. That breeze was lovely coming home from church."

Serena smiled her relief. "Yes, and it will be even cooler now. Come on, this room is ready if anyone should need it."

Five minutes later, they headed down the lane leading to the shore, both still clad in their Sunday best. Phoebe wore dove-gray linen, with a wide-brimmed bonnet to keep the sun from her still-unlined face.

Serena's frock was a slightly lighter shade of gray, its plainness relieved by a lace collar and cuffs, and her own wide-brimmed bonnet.

She looked delectable, Gavin thought, his heart beating faster as he and his father neared the women.

In church he'd noticed that pale gray made Serena's hair even more golden, her eyes a deeper blue. He and Jonas had timed it just right.

This stretch of beach was wide—they could overtake the strolling women, then slow down and walk with them without it looking pre-arranged.

Grabbing his father's arm, he proceeded to do just that. "Good afternoon, ladies," Gavin said, drawing alongside Phoebe and doffing his hat. "Delightful afternoon for a walk."

Phoebe's expression was a mixture of surprise and something else—was it satisfaction?

"Why, good afternoon," she replied, including Jonas in her cordial nod and smile.

Jonas nodded affably. "Afternoon, Phoebe, Serena."

Serena gave them both one of her sweet, slightly distant smiles. But today it didn't seem quite so aloof. Maybe, Gavin thought, this wasn't going to be as hard as he'd imagined.

Or was that just wishful thinking? Jonas and Phoebe were no fools. Either of them might suspect their children were trying to rig something up.

The two men fell in step with the women.

"Pastor Erwin preached a good sermon today, I thought," Phoebe said in a moment.

Gavin's mind went blank. For the life of him, he couldn't remember the subject of their minister's weekly sermon.

"Sure did," Jonas said. "Need more like that one."

Thanks, Pop, Gavin told him silently. *That helped a whole lot to enlighten me.*

Serena gave him a smile with a touch of mischief in it that made his heart thump. God! He wished he could tell her right this minute what that smile did to him.

But he knew he couldn't.

They walked on, and their forced closeness made his shirt sleeve brush against the sleeve of Serena's dress. What would she do if he reached down and took her hand?

Jerk it away and this plan would be finished before it started. He had to take it easy, go slow, give her a chance to awaken to life and love again. The same things he'd been telling himself ever since they moved here a year ago and he saw her for the first time.

He hadn't looked at another woman on the Island since.

He heard Phoebe and Jonas talking away. Not that he was surprised by that. They'd always enjoyed talking to each other. Maybe a few of these outings would create more than talk between them.

He had to spark things up between himself and Serena, without letting her know that's what he was doing, but the silence stretched out.

"How are your plans for remodeling the store coming along?" Serena finally asked.

"Fine, fine," he answered, relieved she'd thought of something to talk about. "In addition to the new shelves, we've decided to put in a lunch counter."

She gave him a surprised glance.

He forced a grin. "We're not trying to take business away from you and Phoebe. It's just that a lot of people don't have time for more than cheese and crackers or a can of sardines when they come in to trade."

And they want to be able to cuss when they feel like it and spit out their tobacco juice, he added to himself. *Instead of sitting around a dinner table covered with a white cloth trying to make genteel conversation.*

Serena nodded thoughtfully. "Yes, I can see there's a need for that."

She glanced up at him again, her long blond lashes shading her eyes in an innocently seductive way that made his body tighten.

"But will that mean you'll have to keep the store open at noon—you and Jonas won't be eating with us anymore?"

He grinned. "We couldn't miss those meals—we'll take turns minding the store."

"Oh. Then that's all right." She smiled at him again.

His heart thumped, harder this time. She looked as if she really saw him, noted the color of his eyes, the way his face was arranged, for the first time.

It wasn't wishful thinking that made him detect the rosy flush that stained her cheeks for a few moments. Elation shot through him. This woman he loved was suddenly aware of him as a man.

The easy rise and fall of his father's and Phoebe's voices seemed to have ceased. Gavin glanced their way, surprised to see Phoebe's head close to Jonas's, and he heard the low murmur of their talk.

"Maybe this won't be as difficult as we thought," Serena whispered.

She was so close her breath tickled his ear. Gavin clenched his hands at his sides to keep himself from giving in to the urge to turn and put his arms around her.

Still not turning to face her, he answered, forcing a lightness into his voice he didn't feel. "You could be right."

"About what?" Phoebe suddenly asked, making him realize he hadn't lowered his own voice as Serena had.

"That we should have put in a lunch counter as soon as we bought the store," he said quickly, with an offhand grin.

Phoebe's blue eyes, so much like Serena's, widened. She turned to Jonas. "Why, Jonas, you never said anything to me about that!"

The older man shrugged. "That's all Gavin's idea," he said gruffly. "Don't know as we need it."

Phoebe laughed. "You're just like me, Jonas. Serena's always dreaming up newfangled things and I always think the old ways are best."

Jonas chuckled. "Lunch counters in stores aren't anything new, Phoebe, except on our little island."

Phoebe nodded thoughtfully. "I suspect you're right. We are behind the times here. But that's the way I like it!"

"Me, too," Jonas agreed. "Have to admit we're losing a lot of our young people, though. Crabbing and fishing don't suit everybody."

His father sounded as if he were one of the Island natives, Gavin thought. And didn't he feel the same way about this place?

"Oh, well. That's to be expected. Young people always think the grass is greener elsewhere. Many of them come back later."

"True enough. Guess I'll have to go along with Gavin or he might decide to try to find some greener grass, too."

Gavin gave his father a startled glance. He'd never said a word about leaving the Island—yet.

The older man's shrewd dark eyes gazed back at him and Gavin realized anew that his adopted father was as close to him as if they had been blood kin. He knew Gavin's thought processes as well as Gavin himself did.

They all reached the end of the wide shore and turned to retrace their steps.

"We've been talking about a little get-together at our house next Saturday evening," Phoebe said.

She gave Gavin a smile, then turned to smile at Jonas. "Of course, we want both of you to come."

Gavin blinked in surprise. He couldn't believe his plan was working so well—and so fast.

At least on Phoebe's part.

But not his father's, of course. Jonas wouldn't succumb that easily.

"Wouldn't miss it, Phoebe. I've heard a lot about those Saturday night get-togethers you used to have."

Gavin had to keep his head from snapping around. Jonas's rugged face held a bland expression. He certainly didn't look as if he felt railroaded into Phoebe's affair.

Gavin suddenly realized what that heads-close-together conversation between his father and Phoebe was about.

Instead of Phoebe developing an astonishingly quick interest in his father, as he and Serena had hoped, Serena's mother was doing some matchmaking of her own. As she'd done last Sunday after the wedding when she told Serena to stay out on the porch with them. And a few times before.

Why hadn't he realized this was happening?

Gavin couldn't keep his mouth from curving upward. It looked like he was going to get more help than he'd expected.

Serena hadn't said a word about the party. He gave her a quick glance.

Her eyes met his for an instant, and he saw they were wide with surprise and pleasure—and something else. An odd glint. She gave him an almost imperceptible nod. He grinned back, but felt an uneasy twinge.

Still, he couldn't wait for Saturday night.

Chapter Four

After Gavin and Jonas left them at the turn in the lane, Serena followed her mother into the house and closed the door behind her. A little more forcefully than necessary.

"Mama, I know what you're up to, and it won't work!"

Phoebe gave her daughter a blank, innocent look. Or at least she hoped it was blank and innocent. "Whatever are you talking about?"

"You know very well what I'm talking about. That sudden idea for a party next Saturday evening."

"It's not sudden," Phoebe protested. "I've been thinking about reviving them for quite a while. Now that the boarding house is on its feet, and we're making a decent living, we can take an evening off every now and then. Like we used to. No one should work all the time. It isn't healthy."

"Really? Then this wouldn't have anything to do with inviting Gavin?"

Oh, lord, she'd figured it out. Phoebe felt warmth coming into her face.

"Didn't you expect me to invite Gavin and Jonas? It would look odd if I overlooked them."

Serena's eyes shot blue sparks. "Stop twisting my words! You know what I mean. You're trying to match me up with Gavin. I thought we had this out the other day, and you promised . . ."

Serena's tirade came to an abrupt halt.

Phoebe stared in surprise. Her daughter's face, so full of indignation a moment ago, now had an entirely different expression. If she didn't know better, she'd swear it was a guilty look.

Phoebe collected herself. She'd been given a momentary advantage, she reminded herself, and she had to make the most of it, not waste time trying to figure out what was going on in Serena's head.

"I promised nothing," Phoebe said. "If you don't like Gavin there will be several other suitable young men there."

Serena's face looked as if she were fighting an inner battle. Finally, she took a deep breath and let it out.

"Of course I like Gavin—but only as a friend. And I've no intention of picking any young man to marry, suitable or not."

"So you're going to spend the rest of your life mourning Peter and wasting away . . ."

Phoebe paused dramatically, hand over her heart.

"You paint a vivid picture, Mama, but I don't think there's much danger of my wasting away. My appetite is as hearty as yours."

Stalemate.

"Be that as it may," Phoebe said, "I'm still going to have the party. And furthermore, I'm going to start having one every month. Just as we used to when your father was alive."

Phoebe realized she'd surprised herself. Where had that sudden decision come from?

For appearance's sake, Serena would have to attend. She couldn't spend the evenings in her room with a book as she so often did now that they'd gotten used to the boarding house routine and didn't have to work such long hours.

"You'd do well to get some nice cotton goods and make yourself a new frock for the party," Phoebe said. "Pink looks wonderful with your coloring."

Serena opened her mouth as if to argue, then closed it. "I will if *you* will," she challenged.

Phoebe started to protest, then stopped. If that was what it took to get her daughter in a pretty, young-looking gown again, then she'd do it.

"All right," she said agreeably.

Serena stared, surprised. "You will?"

"Of course I will. Now that I think about it, I could use a new frock, too. So, shall we go to the mercantile tomorrow?"

After a moment, Serena nodded. "Yes, let's do that."

"Good. If we get right on it, we can have them made up by Saturday night."

Phoebe gave her a pleased smile, feeling as if she'd come out the winner in this argument. "That's settled, then. Now, I'd better see to getting supper heated up. I believe that walk has worked up my appetite."

Serena returned her smile. "I'll help. I'm glad we don't have to cook Sunday evenings."

"So am I. Plenty of leftovers from dinner as always."

Phoebe left the sitting room and headed for the kitchen, Serena behind her.

"Oh, don't forget, our agreement included you choosing *pink* dress goods," Phoebe said over her shoulder.

She smiled again, mentally bracing herself for more arguing.

"I'll concede that point—if you'll agree to get *blue.*"

After a moment, Phoebe nodded. "All right. A blue dress would be a nice change."

It would, too. And would wonders never cease, Phoebe thought as she took her apron off its hook. In the space of a few minutes, she'd persuaded Serena not only to attend Saturday's party but also to make herself a dress in a color other than the grays and browns she always wore.

Something had happened to her daughter the last few days. She had been different.

You agreed to make a blue dress, her mind reminded her. *Something's happening to you, too.*

"Such a lovely party," Mavis Watkins simpered, taking the glass of fruit punch Serena offered. "We've all missed dear Phoebe's little get-togethers. Of course, in your reduced circumstances, everyone understood why she had to stop having them."

"We're doing fine and planning to have these once a month as we used to," Serena answered, ignoring the gossipy woman's coyly malicious tone. She felt odd in her new pink dress. Younger, somehow, and freer.

She wished Mavis would move on into the parlor, where most of the guests already were.

Gavin, his black hair tamed into submission, his Sunday suit fitting him well, showing off his good build, stood in the parlor doorway. He was talking to Alice Hastings, who sparkled in a green dress that set off her eyes.

If Alice's smiles were any indication, they seemed to be enjoying the conversation very much.

Not that she cared, of course, Serena assured herself. After all, people were supposed to be having a good time. That's what parties were for.

And she also didn't care how either Gavin or Alice looked. It was none of her business.

She wondered if Gavin had noticed her new dress.

"Since we saw so many lovely new furnishings at the Centennial, all this heavy, dark furniture looks so old-fashioned," Mavis continued, glancing toward the parlor. "We're going to redo our entire house in the French style."

Serena knew this was another not-so-subtle reminder that the Cranes, who'd originally settled this tiny island, had fallen on bad times. Remembering how hard she and her mother had worked since her father died, she'd suddenly had enough of this woman.

"I'm so pleased your husband's fishing business has improved that much," Serena answered sweetly. "We find our old furniture suits us just fine."

"Oh, well, of course it does," Mavis said. "I think I'll go talk to Miss Hastings. She's an excellent teacher. Timmy did so well last year, I want to thank her. My, don't she and Gavin make a handsome couple? Time that young man settled down."

Serena decided she'd stayed at the punch bowl long enough.

"Yes, and I'm going to see how everyone is doing. It's about time to get the charades going."

"Oh, of course, dear. My, it's been simply ages since I've played at charades. Such an old-fashioned game."

Serena escaped without answering, forcing a smile for the still-talking couple in the doorway as she passed them.

Phoebe and Jonas were seated on one of the settees in the parlor, also talking animatedly. Her mother was very attractive in her new blue gown. It made her look younger and her eyes seemed a deeper blue.

Jonas looked distinguished in his brown suit, his gray

head was tilted sideways, taking in every word Phoebe said, seemingly enjoying being the center of her attention.

Serena's spirits rose a little. Could it be that Gavin's plan was working after all?

Don't count on it, her mind told her. *You know your mother. They're probably discussing ways to get you and Gavin together.*

"Ha! Fat chance of that, with Alice throwing herself at him," she mumbled under her breath, then was appalled at herself. What was happening to her these last few days?

Briskly, she set about getting the charades organized. Earlier, she and Phoebe had strung a curtain between the parlor and dining room. Now, she drew it closed to form a stage of sorts.

She and Gavin were on the same team and despite Jonas's and Phoebe's protests, both of them ended up playing, too, on the opposite team.

Serena's team was up first. "Let's do 'wedding'," Lorna Meadows suggested brightly.

A lump settled in Serena's stomach at that choice. Ever since Margaret's wedding her safe, predictable world seemed to have gone askew.

Lorna turned to Alice. "You can be the bride, and," her gaze moved to Gavin, *"you* can be the groom."

The lump grew larger. "Oh, let's not do that," Serena said quickly. "It's too easy."

"We can make it harder," another girl put in. The other girls and women agreed.

The men groaned—all except Gavin, Serena noticed. Instead, he smiled at her, then at Alice. "All right, I'm willing to be the victim," he said.

"We won't use a veil," Lorna, who'd appointed herself unofficial organizer, said. "That will make it harder to guess."

Had Gavin's smile lingered a little on her before he turned to Alice? Serena wondered. She glanced at Alice, who certainly didn't seem unhappy to be cast in the bride role.

"That won't help much," Serena said. "No matter what you do, the other side will guess it instantly."

Lorna frowned. "Maybe you're right." Her face brightened. "I know—let's do 'baptism'. Since we don't have a baby, that won't be easy. We can still use Gavin and Alice."

Everyone except Serena enthusiastically agreed on the choice. She merely nodded and managed a smile.

What in the world is wrong with you? she chided herself. *This is just a game. You'd think you were jealous of them. You'd think you were attracted to Gavin yourself.*

At last their scene was arranged and the curtain opened to let the opposing team view it. Gavin and Alice stood close together, Gavin's arms curved to pantomime holding an infant, several others standing nearby. Tom Rowland, playing the minister, stood at the ready.

Tom didn't look any happier than she felt, Serena thought. He lifted his head and gave Alice an intense stare, then, his lips tightening, turned his glance away.

Serena suddenly understood. Tom was sweet on Alice! Why had she never noticed that before, when both of them boarded here?

Because you've been living in a fog for two years, her mind told her. *You haven't noticed much of anything. Especially anything to do with love or romance.*

When Gavin handed the imaginary baby to Alice, his motions were so careful, his smile at her so tender, Serena's breath caught in her throat.

How wonderful it would be to have someone look at you like that. Like Peter used to do.

And no one else had since.

How wonderful it would be to have Gavin look at you like that, her mind finished for her. Horrified at her wandering thoughts, she quickly pushed them back down deep inside.

The other side didn't guess until the minister began sprinkling the make-believe baptismal drops, then Phoebe yelled out, "Christening!"

"Exact word," Lorna called back.

"Baptism," Jonas said, smiling at Phoebe, who smiled back.

Serena tried to concentrate on that encouraging sign, and not on how glad she was this was over. It was time for her mother's side to perform.

Serena and her team members took seats in the parlor on the wooden chairs commandeered from the other rooms.

"Don't believe I'd ever make it as an actor."

She felt goose bumps rise on her arms at Gavin's unexpected voice. Turning to him with a forced smile, she was glad her sleeves came to her wrists so he couldn't see them.

"You did fine," she assured him.

He laughed, revealing a flash of teeth. "You're just being polite."

She'd never noticed how white Gavin's teeth were, what a nice smile he had . . .

She shook her head. "No. You were as good as anyone else."

He laughed again, and Serena hastily looked away. "I can always count on you not to flatter me, Serena. You're always down-to-earth."

Was that how he saw her? Somehow that description sounded so plain and dull. *And I don't feel down-to-earth,* she told him silently. *I feel very strange, not like myself at all.*

He leaned a little closer and the goose bumps came again. "How do you think our plan is working?" he asked in low tones.

She stared at him for a moment, too caught up in her physical reactions to take in what he was talking about.

"Phoebe and Pop," he said, still almost whispering, and this time she knew his smile lingered—his dark eyes, too.

"I—I'm not sure," she stammered. "They've been sitting together all evening."

"I noticed that, too. That seems like a good sign to me."

Serena nodded, not trusting herself to speak. He still sat too close for her to feel comfortable.

You don't need to feel comfortable, her mind told her. *You need to feel excited, your pulse fluttering, your heart speeding up.*

She hardly knew what the other side did, and during the songfest that followed the charades, sharing a songbook with Gavin, she felt even more unlike herself.

When their hands accidentally touched, a warm feeling radiated into her hand, up her arm. She fought against admitting it, but knew she'd missed this, too, since Peter's death—the sensual delight of touching and being touched.

"You young folks can finish off the game-playing," Jonas said. "I'm going to have more punch and another piece of cake. Nothing like Phoebe's devil's food cake." He grinned at Phoebe.

Serena watched her mother smile back and shake her head. Phoebe got to her feet. "I'm going to have some more of Mavis's potato salad."

She glanced at the woman. "I do wish you'd give me your recipe, Mavis. I'd dearly love to put it on the menu at the boarding house."

Mavis simpered and waggled her fingers at Phoebe. "Now, you know I can't do that. It's an old secret family recipe."

Serena struggled to hide a grin at Mavis's predictable response.

"Well, would you consider making it once a week and selling it to me to serve here?"

Serena blinked at this surprising offer from her mother.

Mavis lost her simper and looked surprised. "Why, I don't know, Phoebe. I've never thought about selling any of my cooking."

"Well, think about it and let me know. I'd give you a fair price and I know all of my boarders and dinner guests would enjoy it."

Why hadn't her mother talked this over with her? Was she trying to ease some of her work? Give herself more free time? Maybe that was a good sign, too, Serena decided. Maybe she wanted the free time so she could spend it with Jonas.

"Let's play Authors—with forfeits," one of the younger girls said.

A general groan arose. "No, not that!"

Fourteen-year-old Phyllis pulled her lip down. "It's not fair! We've done all the things you older people want— now let's do something *we* want."

Gavin smiled down at her. "That seems fair to me."

Serena felt a small shock along her nerve ends as her eyes followed the movements of his well-shaped mouth as he smiled and talked. She took a fortifying breath. This was silly. *She* was being silly. And she'd stop right this minute.

Phyllis gave Gavin an adoring return smile. "Only the unmarried ones—and that includes you." She turned and pointed at Serena and Alice. "And you two and Tom."

With another shock Serena realized the four of them, not counting the youngsters, were the only unmarried young people in the room. But not the only unmarried older ones.

"What about Lulabell and Zenobia?" She smiled at the two elderly maiden ladies.

Lulabell gasped. "Oh! We couldn't possibly do anything like that, could we, sister?"

Zenobia quickly shook her head. "No, of course not," she quavered.

"I was only teasing." Serena smiled again at getting the expected response. Resolutely keeping her gaze away from Gavin, she pushed back the thought that she was only doing this to keep her mind off him and how he was affecting her.

The older people took their refreshments to the parlor. Serena slipped into a chair at the cleared-off dining table next to Alice, relieved when Gavin sat down on Alice's other side.

For the next hour, they played the card game, and joined in the often hilarious "forfeits" required for the losers to stay in the game.

Finally, Gavin was the loser. Phyllis, the leader during this round, glanced around the circle, then gave him a mischievous look. "You have to kiss Serena," she announced.

Serena drew in her breath. She felt Alice stiffen. Gavin said nothing for a moment, then he nodded. "All right."

He pushed his chair back and rose, then turned to face Serena. He smiled his easy smile. "That doesn't sound like such an awful forfeit to me."

Everyone at the table except Serena and Alice laughed.

Serena felt a wave of red suffuse her face. She quickly rose. Might as well get this over with.

"Well, go ahead," Phyllis said gleefully, clapping her hands. "You have to give her a real kiss on the mouth."

Serena raised her head and looked at him. The teasing smile was still on his wide mouth, but some other emotion seemed to lurk in the depths of his dark eyes.

She couldn't read it. Was he wishing she was Alice? Was he thinking she was being silly and childish?

Serena tilted her head up a little. Gavin lowered his. His warm lips brushed hers lightly, and she gasped at the wave of feeling that surged through her body.

She knew he heard the gasp, she could see it in his eyes.

Instead of stepping back, for another moment the pressure of his mouth increased, and she could feel his lips moving on hers. Suddenly, wildly, she longed for him to put his arms around her and pull her into his embrace.

Then, he drew back, the teasing smile once more in place. "Was that such a horrible experience, Serena? You look like you've seen a ghost."

She managed to paste a smile on her mouth. "I guess I'll survive," she said, relieved her voice sounded cool and just slightly amused. She seated herself again.

Beside her, she still felt Alice's stiffness. They all picked up their cards and went on with the game.

Serena plucked cards from her hand, from the discard pile, wondering if anyone could see how Gavin's brief kiss had affected her.

That kiss had shaken her to the foundations of her soul. What was happening to her? She felt as if she were shedding layers of herself, not knowing what would be exposed next.

When Peter died, she'd buried part of herself with him, sure she could never love again, never *want* to love again.

Never even be *attracted* to another man again.

It appeared she'd been wrong.

Chapter Five

"Mama?" Serena tapped on Phoebe's bedroom door on Monday afternoon.

After a pause, Phoebe said, "Come in."

Serena wondered why her mother's voice sounded odd—sort of muffled. Just inside, she paused.

Now she understood the reason for her mother's muted voice. A towel around her shoulders, Phoebe sat in her armchair, her face completely covered with a white mask.

Serena stared. "What on earth is on your face?"

Phoebe shrugged. "Just egg whites." She sounded a little defensive.

"Egg whites? But Mama . . ." Serena stopped in mid-sentence.

Amazed, she realized her mother was giving herself a beauty treatment. Serena could remember her doing this years ago, before her father died. But not since.

The plan Gavin concocted must be working—at least on Phoebe's part. What other reason could her mother have for trying to improve her appearance when she hadn't bothered to for years? And so soon after the party where she and Jonas had seemed to have such a good time.

Where Gavin had given Serena that soul-stirring kiss.

Soul-stirring? How absurd! He'd only touched her lips with his for a few seconds. But just the same, it had made her feel . . .

Serena quickly turned off those thoughts.

"Go right ahead," she said hastily. "I didn't mean to disturb you. I was just going to the store to get a package of needles. Do you need anything?"

Phoebe didn't say anything for a few seconds, then she shook her head. She gave Serena a smile. "No. I can't think of a thing, dear. But you run along—enjoy yourself."

Serena frowned at her mother's slightly arch tone and choice of words. "I'm only going after needles, Mama. Not to pay a social call."

"Of course, dear." Phoebe's smile widened. "That new pink dress does look good on you."

It felt good, too. Just as it had Saturday night. Serena managed a shrug. "I might as well get some use out of it. I'll be back in a little while."

She quickly made her exit, ignoring the knowing gleam in her mother's eye.

During the walk to the store, she tried to justify the trip. She truly did need some needles and she also needed to talk to Gavin about further plans to get Jonas and Phoebe together. True, it had been his idea, but they'd been cut off by Jonas's return in the middle of their planning that first day. And hadn't found an opportunity since.

She was *not* doing this just for the chance to see Gavin alone, she assured herself firmly.

When she reached the store steps, the door opened and Alice Hastings came out onto the porch.

Serena picked up her long skirts and climbed the steps, forcing a smile. "Good afternoon, Alice."

Alice gave her a return smile that looked every bit as

forced. "Afternoon, Serena," she said. "I just remembered something I needed."

"So did I," Serena answered, going inside. She didn't believe Alice for a minute. The woman just wanted to see Gavin.

Why don't you stop pretending your reason for being here is any different? her mind asked—and this time it was harder to ignore it.

As always in the summer, the store was pleasantly cool and smelled of a blend of tobacco, kerosene, soap, and a variety of the other wares.

It was also empty—except for Gavin. In the winter, when the weather was too bad to go out, the store was usually crowded with fishermen sitting around the stove.

Serena felt a little breathless. Part of her wanted to turn around and leave and the other part wanted to stay. She kept on going. At the counter, she leaned over.

"Is your father out of earshot? Can we talk?" she whispered.

"Yes," Gavin answered in a normal tone. "He's upstairs looking around the storerooms. We've decided to rent one of them to the Oddfellow Lodge." He smiled at her. His usual, friendly smile.

Or was it a little different—a little more personal? *Oh, for heaven's sake,* she told herself. *Stop it!*

But her gaze lingered on his mouth, remembering the kiss. Could Gavin also be remembering?

Stop it! she told herself again. She gave him a return smile. Her usual, friendly one. "Don't suppose they'll be too noisy."

He shrugged. "Only at the monthly meetings."

He had such a nice voice—low-pitched and richly resonant. Why had she never noticed it before?

Why are you noticing it now? Get on with the reason you came.

She cleared her throat. "I—I just thought we'd better

discuss our next move. Since Mama beat us to it the last time."

"Yes, she did. I thought Phoebe looked very nice in her new dress. She and Pop seemed to have a lot to talk about."

Did you notice my dress? she asked him silently. *Or were you too busy admiring Alice? And why aren't you noticing it now?*

"Yes, I thought so, too," she answered, pushing down the disturbing thoughts. "If Mama keeps on having the parties, they'll be together once a month. That is, if your father continues to come."

"Oh, I'm sure he will," Gavin assured her.

Serena nodded briskly. "That's good, but it's not enough—we need something else in between. Of course, you and your father eat dinner with us six days a week, but Mama's always so busy running back and forth to the kitchen."

Gavin was leaning forward, close to her, looking at her in such an odd way. His eyes seemed to be fixed on her mouth as hers had been on his a few moments ago.

Serena felt breathless again. She knew she should move back from the counter a little. But she didn't. "So can you think of anything?" Her voice sounded breathless too, she noticed, dismayed.

They were directly facing each other, eye to eye . . . mouth to . . .

Gavin leaned a little closer. So did Serena. She couldn't move her gaze from his. Gavin seemed to be having the same problem.

"Serena," he said.

His voice was soft, yet at the same time, a little rough. The sound of it sent shivers down her back. Without conscious thought, she opened her mouth slightly and ran her tongue along her lower lip.

Gavin groaned. They were so close she felt his warm breath. Then, his lips were on hers, pressing softly. Serena returned the supple pressure.

His heart thumping, Gavin deepened the kiss. His arm slid around her neck, pulling her as close as he could with the counter between them.

Her lips were like velvet beneath his own; he could never get enough of them. He'd dreamed of this moment from the first time he'd seen her. The reality was so much better than the dream—or that party kiss.

"I love you," he whispered into her mouth. He felt her body stiffen, her lips become immobile. Then he realized what he'd said.

Damn it! It was too soon—had he ruined everything?

She drew back and he reluctantly moved his arm away and released her. Her eyes were wide with some kind of emotion—he couldn't tell what.

"I have to go," she said, almost whispering. She turned and hurried from the store.

Gavin stared after her, cursing himself for rushing things, for telling her how he felt. He hadn't planned to. It had just come out.

And he'd waited a whole year for her—it didn't seem rushed to him.

He felt his father's presence, dimly wondering how he'd come up behind him so silently.

"I'd say you're making pretty good progress," Jonas said.

Gavin whirled. "Were you watching?" he asked angrily.

Jonas shrugged. "Couldn't exactly help it. I was coming down the stairs and saw what was going on. Didn't want to make my presence known—afraid that would stop everything."

Gavin heaved a disgusted sigh. "It probably would have

been better if you'd interrupted before it started. Now I've scared her off."

Jonas laid a comforting hand on Gavin's shoulder. "Nope, don't think so. When a woman kisses like that, she's not one little bit scared."

Gavin stared at his father. "For a confirmed bachelor, you seem to know a lot about kissing."

Jonas looked a little embarrassed. "Said I wasn't the marrying kind. I didn't say I'd never courted a girl in my younger days."

Gavin suddenly remembered he was ten years old when Jonas adopted him. And Jonas had been twenty-five. Of course he could have had sweethearts before that.

"What happened, Pop? Did you get cold feet?"

Jonas frowned. "What if I did? Told you I knew I wasn't meant to marry."

Gavin decided to let well enough alone. He debated whether to tell Jonas the rest of what had just happened with Serena, then also decided against that. He didn't need his father telling him he'd been too hasty—he already knew that.

"Serena isn't like most women," he said instead. "She's lived like a nun for two years."

"Then maybe she's decided it's time to stop."

Gavin gave his father a wry grin. "I hope you're right."

"Sure I'm right. Told you she was waking up to you after you bussed her at the party."

I believe her mother may be waking up to you, too, Pop, he thought.

The front door opened. Both men glanced toward it. Phoebe stood framed in the opening for a second, then closed the door.

"Hot day out there," she said, smiling at both of them. A woven basket was hung over her arm.

Jonas cleared his throat. "Afternoon, Phoebe," he said.

His father's voice sounded a bit odd, Gavin thought, not quite its usual hearty boom.

Phoebe made her way to the counter, picking her steps around all the goods fighting for floor space.

She wore the pretty blue gown she'd had on at the party, and something looked different about her. Her hair was loosened a bit from its tidy bun, Gavin finally decided, giving her face a softer look; her cheeks looked faintly pink, her eyes bright.

Gavin gave his father a sideways glance. The older man was trying hard not to stare at Phoebe, but was losing the battle. Despite his own troubles, Gavin had to suppress a grin.

Now, if Jonas had the sense to move cautiously, and he couldn't imagine his father doing anything else, this match had a chance of running a smooth course to a happy ending.

A lot better chance than his with Serena.

A hard lump formed in his throat. Would his impulsive kiss and even more impulsive words a few minutes ago send her back to the shell she'd encased herself in since Peter's drowning?

He'd seen the signs. She'd been ready to emerge—but on her own terms. It was also possible that she'd needed the push of the kiss. After all, she had kissed him back.

But she hadn't been ready for his premature words of love.

"I seem to have run out of straight pins," Phoebe said. "I could use a package."

Gavin gave her a quick glance. She looked a little self-conscious. Would his father think it odd that Serena had claimed to need needles and now Phoebe needed pins?

"Pop, you get them—I have to bring in more coffee from the storeroom," Gavin said. He headed to the back, pretending he didn't see his father's frown.

He'd try to help this match along. If Serena *was* scared off for good, he'd feel a lot better if Jonas and Phoebe married. Since he wouldn't, *couldn't*, stay on this island if Serena was never going to be his.

Chapter Six

A wind gust buffeted Serena, who was crouching on the shore, clad in her oldest frock and boots. She staggered and her clam bucket, half full of the morning's harvest, fell over. The captive clams scattered over the mud flats that low tide made of the shore.

"Blast it!" she muttered, righting the pail and picking up the main ingredients for the boarding house's dinner fritters.

A gull swept low, calling raucously, no happier with the coming storm threat than Serena.

"Looks like we're going to get this one."

Gavin's voice. Serena's hand froze on her spade, tension blending with awareness, remembrance . . .

Slowly she lifted her head. His dark hair was windblown, his legs and feet, also encased in boots, braced, his brown eyes intent. She hadn't seen him—except briefly at dinner, of course, the last two days—since they'd kissed . . .

Since he'd told her he loved her.

A shiver went over her at that thought, which had been

in her mind almost constantly. She looked a fright and she wanted him to leave.

"Yes, I'm afraid so. I've got to finish before it gets any worse."

But instead of leaving, he walked over and squatted beside her. "I'll help."

Alarm hit her. He was much too close. They were almost touching. She wanted no more of that. It was too enjoyable . . . too tempting.

What's wrong with that, you ninny? some part of her mind told her. Lots of things were.

She didn't want to get involved with a man again. She couldn't! She'd promised Peter . . .

You're already involved, her mind told her.

All right, she admitted, maybe that was true, but it would go no further. She'd forget they'd ever kissed.

Forget that Gavin had said he loved her.

"You don't have a spade," she said, trying to ignore the tumult inside her and moving away a little.

Gavin grinned, brandishing a stick. "This will do." He proved it by plunging the stick into the soft mud and then triumphantly bringing out a clam. "See?"

Serena could think of no other argument, so she nodded and got back to work.

Another strong gust of wind hit them. Serena dropped her spade and tried to catch herself, but her shoulder bumped into Gavin's, making his hold slip on his newly-captured clam. Gavin made a grab for it but missed. The clam fell into her lap, mud and all.

"I'm sorry! Here let me get that off you." Gavin reached for the clam and brushed at the mud on her dress.

The fast-approaching storm had turned the day cool, but Gavin's fingers touching her thigh, even through her dress and petticoat, were anything but cold. She scrambled to her feet, not looking at him.

"I have enough. I'd better get back to the house. Mama is probably ready to come looking for me."

Gavin also stood. They reached for the pail at the same time. Gavin won. "I'll carry these for you."

She couldn't keep looking at the ground. She glanced at him, managing a smile. "You don't have to do that. It's not heavy."

He smiled back, something in his expression making her see he knew how his touch had affected her. "Heavy enough."

She wouldn't make a fool of herself by trying to wrest the pail out of his hands. "All right."

Gavin beside her, she walked down the shore, hurrying as much as possible in her too-big boots. Another gust of wind, sharpened with rain this time, hit them, buffeting them both. Gavin righted himself and turned to her.

"Are you all right?"

"Of course," she answered, trying to ignore the little thrill of pleasure that went through her at his words. It had been a long time since a man was concerned about her. Not since Peter . . .

An even stronger gust, driven by blinding rain, tore into them, catching them unawares. Serena staggered. Gavin dropped the pail and caught her by the shoulders, pulling her against him.

She gasped as rain pounded over them, her heart thumping as she felt Gavin's strong heartbeat beneath her ear. He was warm and his arms were so strong. It felt wonderful to be held like this. It had been so long since that had happened, too.

Not since Peter had held her that last day.

The warmth fled. Serena jerked away from Gavin's grasp, water plastering her hair to her head, streaming down both of them. "Let's get out of here!"

A muscle worked in his jaw. He stared at her for a long

moment, then nodded. "Yes." He quickly scooped the scattered clams into the bucket and picked it up again. Staggering against the force of the wind and rain, they hurried on and took the path that led to the main street of the village.

"Serena!"

The cry was almost whipped away by the storm, but Serena's head jerked up.

Phoebe ran toward them, the storm lashing at her, her clothes soaked and plastered against her. "I was so worried!" she almost shouted to get above the howling wind and rain. "Let's get inside! This is going to be a bad one."

She glanced at Gavin. "Close the store and you and Jonas come to the house. It's the stoutest-made building on the Island."

"I know. I'll try to persuade Pop. But I'll take these clams to your house first."

Phoebe plucked the pail out of his hand. "Nonsense. We're no weaklings. Go ahead! The bad weather bell is already ringing down at the wharf!"

Bent over, they labored on, the wind-driven rain stinging their backs. At the path's turning, Gavin headed right. Serena watched the strong muscles in his legs flex, remembering how it had felt to be in his arms, pressed closely against him.

She didn't realize she'd stopped walking and was standing, staring like a goose, in the raging storm until her mother's voice spoke sharply in her ear.

"Serena, stop woolgathering! Come on."

She started, and followed her mother. At last reaching the house, they saw Tom Rowland bringing in the porch rockers. The top shutters were also closed.

Phoebe tripped on the top step and Serena grabbed her as a wind gust almost knocked her to the ground.

Once under the shelter of the porch, they gasped with

relief. "Good for Tom," Phoebe said. "Not that we couldn't have done it ourselves."

They hurried inside behind Tom, who carried the last of the rockers, slamming the door against the storm. Phoebe smiled. "Thank you, Tom. Who'd have thought this could blow up so fast?"

Alice came out of the kitchen doorway and walked to where they all stood. "Tom and I carried in the rest of the wood from the back porch. It's not too cold now, but we'll need it for cooking."

Phoebe pushed her hair out of her eyes. "Thank you, Alice. You didn't have to do that."

"Yes, I did. We're all in this together," Alice answered.

Serena caught the worshipful gaze Tom gave Alice, who gave him an unaware, friendly smile in return.

Can't you see how he feels about you? she silently asked the young woman. *He's good-looking and a hard worker. He'd make you a very decent husband.*

She was instantly appalled at her thoughts. What Tom and Alice did was none of her business. She firmly pushed down the other thought trying to surface: maybe she'd like to get Alice paired off with Tom so she wouldn't have to worry about her flirting with Gavin.

Half an hour later, Serena and Phoebe had changed into dry clothes and everything was as snug and secure as the four of them could make it. The storm had worsened. Phoebe glanced out a front window, sheets of rain making it nearly impossible to see out.

"Why aren't Jonas and Gavin here?" she fretted. "That store building is too unsheltered. It's been damaged in many a storm."

"But it's still standing," Serena said. "They'll come here if it gets bad enough."

Phoebe gave her a sharp look. "It's already bad

enough.'' She turned back to the window, then exclaimed, ''Oh, praise be—here they come!''

She hurried to the front door, and the two oilskin-clad men entered on a rush of wild wind and rain.

''Thought you were going to be stubborn and not come!'' she told Jonas. ''Here, give me those wet things.''

She hung the oilskins on the hall tree, where they dripped onto a thick rug, while the men kicked their boots off.

''I may be stubborn, Phoebe, but I'm not a fool,'' Jonas said in his slow drawl. ''I was afraid if I didn't come now, I might have to miss dinner.''

Phoebe gave him a mock frown. ''If that's all you were worried about, then *that* makes you a fool. It's a wonder that building didn't come down around your ears.''

''Good Lord, Phoebe,'' Jonas protested. ''You know Gavin and I've got it in good shape now.''

''It's still old,'' Phoebe insisted stubbornly.

''So is this house,'' he said amiably, grinning at her.

Phoebe looked at him for a moment, then smiled back. ''You're right.''

Her mother and Jonas were exchanging a moment of closeness that reminded her of exchanges between her father and her mother, Serena thought, trying to feel happy about that and ignore her awareness that Gavin was standing close to her. Too close.

Despite her determination not to do so, she glanced at him. He had a very nice nose. Straight and long enough to be manly—but not *too* long.

''Clams make it okay?'' he asked lightly.

With a start, she came to herself, feeling her face reddening. ''Just fine. I was getting ready to make the fritters.''

''Oh, my, yes!'' Phoebe said. ''We're all snugged up— time to get on with dinner. We'll fix extra food in case some of the folks from down by the shore want to wait the storm out here."

They did. Within the next hour, a fisherman and his family of four and a bachelor fisherman came, seeking shelter. Inside the big, solidly built house, the storm didn't seem very threatening. Even the strongest gusts couldn't shake it.

The heavy wooden shutters kept the wind and rain from lashing at the windows and oil lamps gave a warm, comforting glow. Only an occasional thud as a tree branch fell caused moments of unease. But none of them hit the roof.

Serena had made the fritters go as far as she could, but still had to stretch the meal with an extra pan of cornbread and a big skillet of fried potatoes.

That didn't seem to bother anyone around the crowded table. By the time the meal was finished, the storm was tapering off.

Jonas pushed back his chair with a groan of satisfaction. "Hope there isn't much damage at the store. Don't think I'll be much good for a while."

Phoebe moved her own chair back and got up. "I'd better go to the attic to check the roof again."

Jonas got to his feet with surprising haste, considering his last remark. "I'll go with you."

Phoebe gave him a surprised look. Her cheeks pinkened a little. "You don't have to do that."

"I know I don't. I want to. Do me good to move around a bit."

Phoebe looked self-conscious. "Oh. Well, come on, then."

Serena watched them go, certain that Jonas wanted Phoebe's company more than the exercise he claimed to need. She carefully avoided meeting Gavin's glance. That way lay nothing but trouble.

The extra guests decided it was safe to leave and they

were anxious to see if their houses had been damaged. Much to Serena's relief, Gavin and Tom donned their oilskins and followed them outside to look around.

Clearing the table with Alice's help, Serena jerked her head up when she heard the attic door close loudly. A few moments later her mother came into the dining room alone, her mouth set.

Foreboding gripped Serena. "Where's Jonas?"

"Getting ready to go home, I imagine," she said sharply. "Why? What happened?"

"I don't need any man to tell me how to run my household. I've been doing quite well on my own for a number of years now."

Serena set down a stack of plates, glad that Alice was in the kitchen at the moment. "What in the world did he say?" she ventured.

"Only that I've been neglecting the entire house and it needs all kinds of repairs that I didn't have enough sense to see for myself."

Jonas appeared in the doorway, oilskins on and frowning. "That's not exactly what happened, Phoebe."

Serena heard the front door open and close and then Gavin appeared behind his father.

"I just said that it takes a man to see the things that need doing around a house," Jonas continued. "Such as rot in some of the attic framing—and roof shingles that need replacing. It's all very well to keep the paint gleaming, but—"

"There you go again!" Phoebe interrupted, her blue eyes snapping. "I'll have you know Serena and I worked many a fourteen-hour day to keep things going after Arthur died."

Glancing at Gavin, Serena saw his brows also draw together in a frown at Phoebe's vehement tone.

She glanced at Phoebe again. Her mother's face looked

pinched and tired. Serena felt a wave of sympathy roll over her.

Most women couldn't have kept everything together as her mother had done after nursing her husband through a long sickness, and then discovering he'd left them nothing but debts.

Of course the house needed work, but they'd kept up the basic repairs. Jonas didn't have to make such a slighting remark—as if women couldn't possibly manage as well as men.

She felt her own temper rising.

"We did a lot more than keep the paint gleaming," she told Jonas.

Jonas turned his frown on her. "What in the world is the matter with you two women? I'm just trying to talk sense and both of you are acting like hens with their feathers ruffled. 'Spect you'll peck me next."

Another wave of irritation rolled over Serena at this further evidence of his condescension. Jonas was showing the typical male attitude that she and her mother had been fighting ever since her father died. No one thought two women could make it by themselves.

Well, they'd proved they could! Serena walked over and stood beside her mother, her chin high. "I don't think you have to worry about that," she said coolly.

Gavin moved in front of his father. "This is getting out of hand."

Serena stared at him, realizing he was trying hard not to smile.

Why, he was *laughing* at them! Her indignation rose.

"You don't know what you're talking about. You weren't even here—you don't have any idea what we've gone through. How dare you stand there with that superior smile on your face!"

Gavin's incipient grin faded. "I expected *you* to be reasonable, Serena."

His words made Serena feel even more provoked. "Are you saying my mother and I aren't reasonable?"

Gavin sighed impatiently. "Not right now, anyway. Pop was only trying to help."

"It didn't sound like it to me. We're getting along just fine by ourselves, Gavin Mead!"

Gavin moved back a step until he stood beside his father as she stood by her mother. As if they were lined up, challenging one another.

Gavin shook his head and turned toward Jonas. "We'd better go home, Pop."

Serena watched them leave the room, heard the front door open and close, and her ire suddenly left her.

What in the world had all that been about?

She drew in her breath as she realized that in the last few minutes her mother had destroyed all the closeness that had been developing between her and Jonas.

Gavin was right. Things had gotten completely out of hand. There was no way Gavin and Jonas could have known how bad things had been. No one did. Her mother's pride had made sure of that.

And her mother would soon realize this, too, she told herself. Tomorrow, they could go to the store and apologize. Everything didn't have to be ruined.

Right now, her mother needed comforting. Serena put her arm around Phoebe. "You've been a tower of strength, Mama. Don't let—"

Startled, she felt her mother's shoulders shaking, knew she was crying. She hadn't seen her mother cry since her father's death.

"Oh, Serena, Jonas was right. I *didn't* notice those things. And maybe other things, too."

Phoebe gave Serena a quick glance. "That isn't why I

got angry. It had nothing to do with what he said. It was because . . .''

She paused, biting her lip. "I—I suddenly felt that Jonas was going to be there for me, take care of me, and for a minute it felt so good. Like I could lay down my burdens and rest.''

Serena turned to her mother, shocked to see tears in her eyes, rolling down her face. "Do you mean Jonas proposed to you?''

Phoebe shook her head. "Oh, no, of course not. But I felt . . . I could tell that things were heading that way.''

Bewilderment claimed Serena. "I don't understand, Mama.''

Phoebe swiped angrily at her wet face. "You wouldn't understand—you've never been married." She firmed her jaw and her gaze. "I can't let myself become dependent on a man again. I had no idea your father had all those debts. I thought we'd be well provided for. I pulled us out of that mess—with your help, too, of course. I didn't mean I did it alone.''

She paused again and took a deep breath. "I'm afraid even to think about marrying Jonas. Or anyone. Letting a man take over my life. I'll never do that again and I didn't realize it until a few minutes ago.''

Her mother's unexpected words struck Serena like stones. *You couldn't understand—you've never been married.*

Oh, but her mother was wrong. She could, did, understand very well. She'd never depended on Peter for her livelihood, but emotionally, she'd been completely dependent on him. When he died, she'd felt as if her heart had been torn out, that all her emotions were dead. And would stay dead forever.

Then had come this unexpected awakening. To her feelings—to the possibility of love. What her mother had realized a few minutes ago, Serena suddenly saw, too. With a clarity that scared her to death.

If she and Gavin married, she'd be dependent on him—just as she'd been with Peter.

Wasn't she jumping the gun? He'd kissed her only one time. A *real* kiss.

Yes, but he'd also told her he loved her.

Her heart contracted at that thought.

Did she love him, too? She'd thought of him as just a friend until a little while ago, but she *was* beginning to care for him . . . to love him.

And something could happen to him, just as it had to Peter. Life didn't come with any guarantees.

If she gave her newly awakening love, her heart, to Gavin and he died, too, she couldn't bear it.

Chapter Seven

Gavin watched his father morosely slice cheese onto the newly-built lunch counter, then reach into the big cracker tin on the counter top and grimace as he brought out a handful.

"Fish stew today at Phoebe's. And apple pie. Far cry from this," Jonas said.

It had been a week since the big blowup. The longest week Gavin—and, it appeared, his father, too—could ever remember.

The storm had caused little damage at the store—or their living quarters behind it. A few roof shingles blown off. One of the porch posts broken.

He wished the wind and rain had done more, Gavin thought. He wished they'd both had hard, exhausting work to keep their minds off what had happened.

"We could go over there and eat," he said.

Jonas slapped a cheese slice between two crackers and scowled at him. "Go back over there after Phoebe and

Serena practically ordered us out of the house? You know better than that."

Yes, he *did* know better. He also knew something else. And it was time he and his father talked about it.

"It's more than missing Phoebe's dinners that has you grousing around. You were just about ready to propose to her."

Jonas's scowl deepened. "Propose what? That I let her come over here and run the store, too?"

Why had he started this? Gavin wondered. He'd known it wouldn't be easy to get Jonas to admit he was growing to care for Phoebe.

"Stop it, Pop. You know what I mean. And you know Phoebe isn't a bossy woman."

"She sure as hell acted bossy the last time I saw her."

"No, she didn't. She was objecting to you criticizing how she took care of her house."

Jonas looked offended. "Wasn't doing anything of the sort. Just said she needed a man—" His voice broke off. He gave Gavin a sheepish look.

"I take it you weren't getting ready to volunteer for the job?"

"Don't start that again," Jonas warned.

Gavin sighed. "Phoebe and Serena got really upset, but I don't think it was about what you said—or what I said, either."

Jonas took a bite of cheese and cracker, washing it down with water from a tin cup.

"Since you're so smart today, then why don't you tell me what it *was* about?"

Gavin shrugged. "I don't know. We could go over there and try to find out."

Jonas snorted. "You go if you want. Not me."

"I plan to. I figure they've had enough time to cool off from whatever it was." He gave his father an intent look.

"I'm sure Phoebe was beginning to care for you. And I'd bet you this store she still does."

"Will you stop all the bull? You're getting to be as big a matchmaker as Phoebe."

Irritated at his father's legendary stubbornness, Gavin blurted, "Pop, that day Serena came in here a few weeks ago, it wasn't because she'd suddenly developed a yen for me."

As soon as the words were out, Gavin wished he'd kept his mouth shut.

"Then why in Sam Hill did you make me think she had?" Jonas demanded.

Gavin shrugged. "Never mind, it's not important," he said, trying to backtrack.

"If you think you can get away with not telling me now, you're sadly mistaken."

He should have known it wouldn't work. "All right, but you're not going to like this. I asked Serena to come. I asked her if she'd help me matchmake you and Phoebe."

"What are you talking about?"

"That day we walked on the beach, Serena had talked Phoebe into coming out because I asked her to—not because she wanted to see me."

Jonas's scowl was murderous. "You dreamed all that up yourself?"

Gavin knew he might as well lay it all out. "Yes, I did. I knew it would give me a chance to be with Serena."

"Why didn't you tell me the truth?"

"Because you wouldn't have gone with me—I know you, Pop. You wouldn't have gone to the party, either. You and Phoebe wouldn't have had all these cozy conversations in the store lately."

"So you're saying you wanted to help things along between me and Phoebe, too? Not just you and Serena?"

Gavin nodded. "Yep. And I still believe you two make a good pair."

"You're about as wrong as you can get. It's a good thing it blew up in your face. Just proves what I've always said. I'm not cut out to be a husband."

"I thought you said this misunderstanding was Serena and Phoebe's fault."

Jonas glared at Gavin. "It is—but that doesn't change the fact I had no business even thinking about getting married."

Gavin nodded. "Just what I thought. Then you admit you care about Phoebe."

"I don't admit anything to a son who's just said he tried to fool his own—"

The bell rang as the door opened. Gavin turned to see Alice enter.

"Enough of this," Jonas whispered hoarsely. "You tend to her. This one's pretty, too, and easier to get along with than the Crane women."

Jonas grabbed the remainder of his lunch and retired to their rooms in the back, leaving Gavin to face a smiling Alice.

"Good afternoon, Gavin. It's good to get some cooler fall weather, isn't it?"

Gavin managed a return smile. "Yes, it is." Alice was an attractive woman. Maybe some people would consider her better looking than Serena. But she didn't stir his blood, soften his heart, as Serena did.

No other woman ever had. No other woman ever would.

"I came to give you the boarding house order for the next month." Alice held out a piece of paper.

Shaken, Gavin took it. He should have realized this would happen. Since he and his father had ceased eating at the boarding house, it wasn't surprising that neither Phoebe nor Serena would come to the store.

That ridiculous argument wasn't going to blow over as he'd hoped and expected.

That meant, had to mean, there was more to this than appeared on the surface. Serena and Phoebe were sensible women. They were also easygoing and he'd never known them to hold a grudge.

"Everything all right at the Cranes'?" he asked, trying to make his voice casual, although he didn't know why he bothered. Alice had been in the kitchen the day of the argument. She must have heard it all.

She nodded. "Oh, yes. Not even so much as a cold among us," she said brightly.

She might have heard, but she wasn't going to let on that she had.

Her smile widened a little. Her gaze met his and lingered.

Alice would be more than willing to try to make him forget Serena. She'd shown that on numerous occasions. In fact, his merely friendly attentions to Alice at the party had bothered Serena—that had also been obvious.

"The moon will be almost full tonight," Alice said, her voice low and soft. "I thought I'd take a walk along the shore after supper."

That was as close to an invitation as she would come, Gavin thought. He looked at her another moment or two without answering.

"I know how you feel about Serena," Alice said, still in that soft, low voice. "But people get over things. Maybe if you spent some time with me . . ."

Her voice trailed off and he saw pink come to her cheeks at her boldness.

Gavin gave her a straight look. "That wouldn't be fair to you."

"I don't care," she said quickly. "We can just be friends if that's the way you want it."

A sudden urge to accept her invitation hit him. Maybe if Serena saw him with Alice it would shake her up enough so she'd tell him the real reason she and Phoebe got so angry that evening.

And if it didn't, then he'd march himself over there and demand some answers.

"Then, yes, I'd like to take a friendly stroll with you this evening, Alice."

She gave him a radiant smile. "I'll meet you—"

"I'll come to the front gate of the Crane house," he said firmly.

Alice's smile faded. "Oh, well, if you want to."

"I do. I suppose Phoebe wants the order by next week as usual?"

Alice looked blank for a moment, then nodded. "Yes, that will be fine. Well, I'll . . . see you this evening, then."

Gavin watched her go, wondering if he'd done the right thing. The door to their rooms opened and Jonas came out.

"Nothing slow about that girl," he said.

Gavin let out his breath. "I guess you had the door cracked? Or are you a mind reader now?"

"If you can figure out a trick like you did with Phoebe, then I've got a right to see what you're up to next."

"Did you decide what it was?"

Jonas nodded. "Yep. You're going to try to make Serena jealous. Alice knows it and she thinks it won't work and she'll get you in the end."

Gavin shook his head. "Pop, sometimes you confound me. Do *you* think it will work?"

Jonas gave him a bland look. "How should I know? I sure don't understand anything about women. I just found that out."

He picked up Phoebe's neatly written list and frowned at it. "Thought she'd have the gumption to at least come

to the store herself. Never thought Phoebe was the type
to hold a grud—''

Jonas's voice trailed off.

His father had also thought Phoebe would end the quar-
rel by coming to the store, Gavin realized.

Jonas, stubborn as a rock, wouldn't do anything to end
it either.

And *he* thought Serena would end it when she saw him
with Alice. That too might not work. His jaw set. The
difference was, he wouldn't sit here in this store, brooding
and miserable like his father.

If this didn't work, then he'd storm the citadel. He'd
held off so far, treating Serena as if she were made of glass.

Well, except for that one time when he'd kissed her.
And told her he loved her.

He should have done more of that. She was a lovely,
flesh-and-blood woman and he intended to have her for
his own if that was humanly possible. If not, he'd leave
this island he'd grown to love.

He'd have to.

Chapter Eight

The next night, Gavin stood in front of the big Crane house. He'd waited until now because he wanted to take Serena by surprise. Maybe her defenses would be down.

Agreeing to take that walk with Alice had been a mistake.

He'd met her in this exact spot, wondering if Serena watched from one of the windows. He'd also wondered if Alice had told her about the excursion.

The walk had been pleasant enough. The moon was almost full and Alice kept up a stream of sprightly chatter, careful to stay far enough away so there was no danger of them accidentally touching.

But her eyes told him she was ready for any overtures he might feel like making.

Which had been none. He couldn't even think of anything to say. All he could think about was how much he wished the woman he was walking beside under this moon was Serena. How much he missed her. How much he *wanted* her.

After a while, Alice fell silent, too. When they started

back, she stopped him well before they reached the Crane yard.

"You don't have to see me to the door," she said, something different in her eyes now, the invitation gone.

"Of course I will," he protested.

She shook her head. "No. You know I'll be perfectly safe." She gave him a look of regret. "Goodbye, Gavin. We won't have any more walks—or anything else."

He frowned, suddenly feeling ashamed of himself. "I'm sorry I was such bad company, Alice."

"Don't be. This is my fault. I know how you feel about Serena. I was foolish enough to think I could change that."

She'd leaned over and kissed him lightly on the cheek, then turned and, her shoulders erect, her head up, left him standing there.

If Serena had seen him with Alice, she might refuse even to talk to him. But he wouldn't take no for an answer—they were going to have this out.

Lamplight shone from Serena's upstairs front window. The rest of the house was dark. That must mean she was the only one still awake, just as he'd hoped.

The neighboring houses were dark. Good.

Knocking on the door and awakening the entire household would surely defeat his purpose. Gavin opened the gate, grateful the hinges didn't creak, and walked to the side of the house, under Serena's window. He drew out a handful of pebbles from his pocket and threw one of them at her window.

The pebble made a loud ping. Gavin held his breath in anticipation, but there was no movement from inside. He threw another, then several more with the same results.

Was she not in the room or had she gone to sleep with her lamp on? Or had she seen and heard him and chosen to ignore him? That seemed the most likely. After all, this wasn't exactly an orthodox way of coming courting.

So what did he do now? Go home defeated?

No! He'd had enough of that. He was going to change Serena Crane's mind no matter what it took. He studied the front of the house.

A thick growth of ivy covered the porch, including the railings. He could climb up that, get on the porch roof, then walk along the ledge to her window.

Surprisingly, his plan worked as easily as he'd envisioned it. But when he looked through Serena's window, he saw the room was empty. She must be downstairs after all. Doing what? Sitting in one of the darkened rooms?

But as he was shinnying down the vines, he saw a glimmer of white from the gazebo in the side yard and his pulse quickened. Could she be there? Could he really be that lucky?

The latticed gazebo hid as much as it revealed, so that he couldn't be certain Serena was inside until he reached the doorway. His heart leapt—she was there, seated on a bench, looking downward.

When his shadow blocked the moonlight, her head jerked up, her face startled.

"Gavin—is that you?"

Her soft, breathless voice swept over him like a familiar, beloved melody. He felt as if it had been a year since he'd heard her speak.

"Yes, it's me." He started to ask her if he could come in, then decided he couldn't risk her saying no. Instead, he stepped inside without permission.

She wore a white robe over what must be her nightdress. Her hair was loose, streaming down her back. It gleamed gold in the moonbeams shining through the latticework.

A rush of yearning filled him. She looked exactly as she always did in his dreams. Achingly beautiful. Infinitely desirable.

"Wh—what are you doing here?"

The time for holding back, letting her have all the time she needed, was past. That hadn't worked. Now he had to see if complete honesty would. He had no other choice.

"Trying to find you. Did you hear me throw the pebbles against your window? Did you hear me climb up there? Is that why you came out here? To get away from me?"

Serena's mouth fell open. Her face looked dumbstruck. Obviously, she hadn't heard or seen anything he'd done.

"You did all that?"

"Yes. And I'd do more to win you. I'd do *anything.*"

Serena's heart raced in her chest. Could this tall man standing before her, his dark hair tousled, his face set in determined lines, saying these bold, unbelievable things, be Gavin?

Oh, how she'd missed him! A dozen times a day she'd wanted to walk to the store, tell him she and Phoebe had overreacted and she was sorry.

But she hadn't. Instead, she'd told herself over and over it was best they not see each other again. Now she frantically tried to remember the reasons why.

"Did you hear me, Serena?"

She nodded. "Yes, I heard you."

"What do you have to say?" he demanded, his voice strong and forceful. "Do you still feel as you did that night of the storm? Do you still want to have nothing to do with me?"

He came farther inside until he stood very close to her. She could smell the fresh night air on him. She suddenly remembered how his heartbeat had sounded in her ears that day.

Serena swallowed. He was being painfully honest. She decided she must be the same. She would tell him the truth: That neither of the Crane women could ever be dependent on a man again—either emotionally or financially.

"I, uh, we . . ." Her voice trailed off. He was too close. She couldn't gather her wits. She moved along the seat, but he came, too.

"Serena? Can you tell me that now?"

Yes, she could. Of course she could. In just a moment, when her thoughts were clearer, when her senses stopped their clamoring.

He sat down beside her. He put his arm across her back, his hand curving around her shoulder. His warmth went all through her, further addling her thoughts. Despite all the reasons she shouldn't, she moved closer to him, until she was surrounded by his warmth, held tight against his chest.

A feeling of absolute rightness filled her. This was where she should be. Where she could stay forever.

No! It wasn't. She'd felt that way once before, in Peter's arms.

And she'd lost him.

Fear struck her. She tried to get up, but Gavin's strong arms held her fast.

"Let me go! Oh, let me go!"

"Not until you answer me," he said calmly, firmly. "Not until you tell me you don't want me ever to touch you again, hold you like this . . ."

She couldn't tell him that. Because she *did* want him to do these things. Her body throbbed with longing for him to kiss her.

Do more than kiss her.

Serena stopped fighting her feelings and surrendered to her desires. She twisted in Gavin's embrace enough to look up at him. His face was half-shadowed, but she could see the hunger in his dark eyes.

It fed her own. She gave a small, inarticulate cry and raised her hand to his face, stroking his high cheekbone, his firmly molded jaw. She felt him tense beneath her touch, then turn sideways on the bench so that they faced each other.

She opened her mouth to him, just as she had that day in the store. With a groan, he hungrily covered her lips with his own, drinking from her mouth as if he could never be filled.

Just as fervently, Serena returned his kisses, his caresses. He leaned her backward on the bench until she was lying down, kissing her neck, pulling the tie of her robe and gown open so he could reach her breasts.

Serena gasped at the first touch of his mouth on her breast, arched herself against his body, gasped again as she felt his hardened lower body against her.

Circling her nipple with his tongue, he teased it until once more she arched against him, wanting more. Wanting something she'd never had.

She unbuttoned his shirt, pulled it apart and ardently kissed his chest, running her fingers through the dark curls. He shivered beneath her touch, grasped her hand and held it tightly against him. "Don't stop," he whispered raggedly.

His words inflamed her. She found his own nipple and circled it with her tongue, teasing it, as he'd done.

Groaning, he moved her hand away and kissed her until she could barely breathe. But she didn't care. She didn't care about anything except these wonderful feelings. "Don't stop," she begged him as his hands left her breast.

"I won't," Gavin assured her hoarsely. He couldn't stop now if his life depended on it.

His hands moved down her body, found the edge of her robe and gown and pulled them up, his fingers sliding up her bare thigh until he reached that most secret part of her. She gasped as his fingers moved through the blond curls clustered there, then caressed the soft petals and finally slid inside.

She arched against him, her breathing fast and shallow, moaning softly.

He could stand it no longer. God, he didn't want to rush this, but he was about to explode. He raised himself a little, looked at her.

In the fitful moonlight, her blue eyes looked deep and dark, her full lips slightly apart.

"Don't stop," she said again, her light voice husky with desire. She leaned up and undid another few buttons on his shirt. She smiled, her whole expression inviting him.

He didn't need a second invitation.

Feverishly, they undressed each other, threw their discarded clothes in wild abandon on the wooden floor, until at last their naked bodies clung together, pressed together.

"Serena," Gavin whispered against her mouth. "You are the most beautiful woman in the world. I've wanted you since the first moment I saw you."

He felt as if they were moving in a dream. That in a moment he'd awaken and be alone in his bed, no sweet-fleshed woman under him, returning kiss for kiss, touch for touch.

"Don't talk," she whispered back, her face dreamy in the moonlight. "Just . . . love me."

A thrill went through him at her words—the words he'd wanted to hear for so long. "I will do that, my darling," he whispered back, kissing her so deeply he almost felt as if they were one person.

When he entered her, when he held her during the brief moment of pain, then when she relaxed and began moving with him, he knew they truly were one, as he'd always known they should be.

When she writhed beneath him, reaching her fulfillment, and a moment later, the waves of pleasure washed over him as well, he felt as if he could die happy here in her arms.

Serena slowly came back to herself, to the reality of the hard wooden bench beneath her, Gavin's weight on her body, to the full knowledge of what had just happened between them.

Oh, it had been so wonderful! She'd never dreamed lovemaking could be like this.

She and Peter had only exchanged kisses and caresses, although they'd wanted to go further. But of course they had to wait until marriage . . . and then that had been denied them when Peter had died.

Drowned in the storm.

Coldness went through her still-heated body. What had she done? She'd made love with Gavin, given herself to him.

Left herself vulnerable to losing him as she'd lost Peter.

Panic took hold of her. Frantically, she pushed at Gavin, trying to move out from under him.

"What's wrong?" he asked, smiling at her, his face relaxed and content, almost sleepy.

She stared at him. Oh, she'd made a terrible mistake!

"Let me get up!" she pleaded, again trying to slide out from under him.

Gavin's sleepy, contented expression faded. He rolled off her, giving her as much room as the narrow bench allowed. Instantly, she slid off and began gathering her scattered clothes.

"I'm not sorry this happened, Serena," Gavin said from behind her. "I love you. We belong together."

His words pierced her like arrows. She and Peter had told each other much the same things. Except for the part about making love, of course.

She couldn't take a chance on losing another man she loved. She couldn't stand another loss like that.

A *greater* loss, she finally admitted. Much greater. Her love for Peter had been first love, not fully developed. These feelings she had for Gavin were true, adult-woman emotions. Powerful . . . lasting.

She'd never be able to convince Gavin her fears were valid. If she admitted she loved him, he'd wear her down, and eventually persuade her they must marry. And she'd be too weak to withstand his *love*. And her own.

Only one thing would make him leave. Finish this before it was too late. Could she force herself to do it? Yes, she had to.

Quickly, she donned her gown and robe and turned to face him. He'd pulled his trousers back on and was buttoning his shirt.

Longing for him filled her. She didn't meet his eyes, she couldn't. "This was a mistake, I should never—"

"No, it *wasn't*," he said forcefully. "You'd never have admitted you love me if this hadn't happened."

He wasn't going to make it easy. She made herself meet his gaze. In the strips of moonlight filtering through the lattice, his dark eyes held her in their grip, weakening her resolve.

Desperately, she shored it up again. She had to. She could never make him a good, loving wife, as full of fears as she was. She wouldn't ruin his life. Both their lives.

"I haven't admitted I love you," she said, relieved her voice didn't show the weakness she felt inside. "Because I *don't* love you. I—I've only loved one man—Peter. A love like that only comes once in a lifetime."

Oh, how she lied! How she wanted to step forward, let him enfold her in his arms, hold her there sweetly safe forever.

But she didn't dare—because he couldn't keep her safe. She couldn't keep him safe. Any more than she'd been able to keep Peter safe.

His face changed, anger taking the place of the other emotions. He took a step forward. "I don't believe you. You couldn't have responded as you did if you didn't have some kind of feeling for me."

Serena gathered all the strength she had left. Somehow she managed to shrug.

"Of course I have feelings for you, Gavin. We—we've been good friends and wh—what we just shared was quite enjoyable. But it was still a mistake because it made you believe I love you."

He stepped forward again and grabbed her shoulders. "You're lying to me. Why are you lying to me?"

His hands burned into her flesh, even through her clothing. Made her weaken. Made her want to admit how right he was.

But she couldn't take the chance. She didn't have the courage. "I'm not lying. Why would I lie about this?"

"I don't know." His gaze probed hers. She turned her face away. In a moment he dropped his hands from her shoulders and stepped back.

"I've loved you since we moved here, and I thought I could make you love me. I was so sure I could. I guess I should be glad that at least I have sense enough to know when to quit. I'm leaving the Island."

His hard words seemed to penetrate her clothes, her skin, go all the way to her heart, because it felt bruised and sore.

He let go of her and stood back, his face as hard as his voice had been.

Serena stared at him, feeling that if she moved, she'd break into a million pieces.

Despair filled her. She'd done what she'd set out to do.

She'd made him believe she didn't love him, and never could.

And now she wouldn't even have the bittersweet pleasure of seeing him as they went about their daily life.

How could she live without him?

Chapter Nine

"Just about the last of the tomatoes," Serena said, plucking the remaining few from a straggly-looking vine and adding them to the partly-full basket beside her. "We'll soon be back to the canned vegetables."

"Yes." Phoebe straightened from her own task of gathering cucumbers, rubbing at a kink in her back.

The garden looked tired and old and sad in the October afternoon. *Like I feel*, Phoebe thought. Like she'd felt ever since that day of the storm a month ago when she'd last seen Jonas.

"We're finished here," Serena went on. "Guess we'd better get the room ready for the new boarder."

"Yes," Phoebe said again. "I'm sorry Jack lost his wife and decided to sell his house. But since he had to move I'm glad he's coming here. From all the signs, we'll be losing Tom and Alice. They'll be setting up housekeeping together before too long."

Her voice sounded as listless as she felt. It was strange how since that awful day, Serena had become the stronger one, the one who made the decisions. Especially since that's what the fight with Jonas had been about. She'd been unable to even think about trusting her life to another man.

Even Jonas, who was steady as a rock.

Arthur had seemed steady, too. She'd had no idea he was heavily in debt from bad investments. He'd never told her anything about business. He'd said she had enough to worry about, managing the household.

She'd vowed then she'd never again let herself and Serena be put into that position. Through hard, grueling work she'd gotten them out of the quagmire. Now they were comfortable and secure.

But somehow, she'd lost all her gumption, content to let Serena take the lead. *Maybe that's what getting old is all about.* She winced at that thought, but couldn't deny it.

Phoebe felt Serena's gaze and looked up to see her daughter staring at her intently. "You miss Jonas, don't you, Mama?"

Pain shot through Phoebe. She shrugged and looked away. "Of course I miss him."

The silence lengthened. Finally Serena said, "Maybe we . . . made a mistake. Maybe we shouldn't have sent Jonas and Gavin away."

The pain came again. "You'll have to decide for yourself about Gavin, but I didn't make a mistake sending Jonas away. Where I made the mistake was getting involved with him in the first place."

Phoebe heard Serena's sudden indrawn breath and glanced at her again. Serena's face was a picture of guilt and worry.

"What in the world is the matter, child? It isn't your fault this happened. It's mine for spending so much time with Jonas because I was trying to get you and Gavin together."

Serena grimaced. "That's where you're wrong, Mama. This whole thing started because Gavin talked me into trying to match you and Jonas up."

Jolted, Phoebe stared at her. "Do you mean from that first day when we all walked together?"

"Yes." Serena nodded grimly. "I'm sorry. I should have minded my own business. But I kept telling myself it was for your own good. That you needed someone. That you were lonely."

"Exactly the same things I felt about you. How in the world could I have been so dense not to see it?"

"Because you wanted so much for Gavin and me to fall in love," Serena said. She glanced at her mother again. "And maybe because you were ready to love again."

"No, I wasn't," Phoebe denied. "I may have thought so, but I was mistaken. I'll never be ready. I can't take that chance. I—I'm too much of a coward."

"You? A coward? Mama, you're the strongest, bravest woman I know."

Phoebe smiled wryly. "No, I'm not. But it can't be helped now. I'm too old to change my ways." She gave Serena a penetrating look. "But you're not too old to change. And you sound to me as if you're sorry you let Gavin leave the Island."

"I couldn't marry him. I couldn't make him any kind of a wife if I was afraid all the time, constantly worrying about something happening to him."

"Gavin wasn't a fisherman like Peter," Phoebe said, pointing out the obvious. "He wasn't apt to get drowned going about his daily work."

"There are lots of other ways to die besides drowning." Serena shook her head. "Oh, there's no use talking about this. Both of us gave up the men we love because we were afraid."

"Put like that, we sound like a couple of fools, don't we?" Phoebe asked after a moment.

The two women stared at each other, then Serena picked up the basket of tomatoes. "Yes, we do."

Phoebe picked up the cucumbers, gloom settling even deeper on her as she and Serena walked to the house.

Reaching the back porch, Phoebe saw Alice, who'd been to the store to place their monthly order, hurrying around from the front, a worried look on her face.

"What's wrong?" Phoebe asked.

"Jonas is in bed with a fever. I went back to talk to him and he looks very ill."

Fear shot through Phoebe. "Who's tending to him?"

"No one, not really. Billy said the doctor had been in twice today. Billy was trying to run the store and take care of Jonas, too, but he wasn't doing a very good job of either."

Phoebe untied her apron and took it off. "Of course not. He's only sixteen or so."

She glanced at Serena. "Can you tend to the dinner today? And getting Jack settled into his room?"

"Of course," Serena said.

"I'll be glad to help," Alice quickly put in.

"Oh, I hate to ask you to do this on Saturday. You need your days off from school."

"I don't mind, Mrs. Crane."

Phoebe gave her a relieved smile. "All right then, if you're sure. Thank you, Alice. You're a dear."

Phoebe handed Serena her apron and smoothed down her dress. "I'll go get the medical supplies and some of that soup from yesterday."

Heading down the lane toward the store five minutes later, Phoebe realized how briskly she was walking, how much vigor she suddenly seemed to have.

"Naturally, a body can pull herself together for an emergency," she said aloud.

Emergency. She didn't like the way that sounded. Maybe Alice was exaggerating Jonas's condition. Still, if the doctor had been there twice today . . . Phoebe picked up her pace, her basket swinging from her arm.

Behind her, in the front yard, Alice and Serena watched her go. "That's the most energy Mama has shown for a month," Serena said.

"Yes, it is," Alice agreed. "I do hope Mr. Mead will be all right."

"Oh, so do I, Alice. He's just got to be!" Serena answered with a worried sigh.

Walking to the house beside Alice, she realized she hoped something else. That Phoebe's hurrying to Jonas's side meant more than just a neighbor helping another neighbor out during sickness. Despite all that had happened, Serena still felt sure her mother and Jonas belonged together. Her mother's fears weren't rational, they were emotional, and the only way they could be overcome was by making a leap of faith.

By taking a chance on Jonas. Plunging into love and marriage again with hope and courage.

Serena opened the front door and walked into the old house that had sheltered her since she was born.

All these things she'd just thought also applied to herself. Her own fears weren't rational, either. She well knew that.

Gavin had given her a chance to take that same leap of faith—and she'd turned him down. Bitter regret filled her. She *had* been a fool and now it was too late to do anything about it.

Or maybe it wasn't.

Gavin needed to know about his father's illness. Jonas had told Alice that Gavin was living on the mainland in Delta Point, the closest town to the Island.

"After dinner, I'd better go down to the store and see

if Mama or Billy need help," she said to Alice. "And to send word to Gavin."

Alice nodded. "Yes, I believe you should. You go ahead—I'll take care of getting the new boarder settled in."

"Oh, I couldn't ask you to do that," Serena protested. "I planned to wait until Jack got here."

"You go ahead. Tom and I were just going to sit on the porch and talk anyway."

Serena smiled her gratitude. "Thank you, Alice."

Alice smiled back with real friendliness. "People have to help each other out when there's trouble. Especially when you live in a small place like this island."

"That's true," Serena agreed.

And Crane Island was the only place she ever wanted to live. Now that he'd gotten away, how would Gavin feel about the tiny place where he'd lived only a little more than a year? Would he ever want to come back here? Hadn't he told her the Island didn't have much to offer him?

She faced her greatest fear. Would he want to come back to *her* after the way she'd treated him? There was every reason to think he might very well not.

All she could do was hope.

Jonas felt as if someone had built a fire all around him. His mouth and throat were so dry he couldn't swallow. He flung his arms out from under the smothering weight on top of him, muttering and thrashing wildly.

"It's all right, Jonas. It's all right."

His arms were held down gently yet firmly. The soothing female voice seemed to come from a long way off. It sounded familiar . . . and something else. He wanted her to keep on talking. His brow furrowed. Who was it?

He struggled to open his eyes, but like his body, they seemed to be weighted down, heavy. Finally he managed to open them a slit, enough to make out the blurred image of a woman standing over him.

He heard her draw her breath in sharply. "You're awake. Oh, praise be! You're better."

"Better?" he growled. "What do you mean? I never get sick."

"Well, you've been sick this time, Jonas Mead, no mistake about it."

Phoebe. That was Phoebe's voice. A feeling of comfort and . . . something else went through him. "Can't be. I never even get a cold. Don't hold with coddling myself."

"You could do with some coddling," Phoebe said, her voice losing some of its soothing quality, gaining a little sharpness. She pulled the quilt he'd pushed off back over his arms, tucking it around his neck.

"Damnation, woman! Take that cover off me. I'm burning up!"

"Yes, you are, but your fever has broken and you're sweating buckets. Uncover yourself now and you'll take a chill and get pneumonia for sure."

He tried to glare at her, but could still open his eyes only a slit. "Who made you my keeper?"

She put both hands on her hips and glared right back at him. "I guess I appointed myself to that thankless job. I can't imagine why."

"Neither can I," Jonas grumbled. But he left the quilt on. "Think I could have a drink of water? Or will that give me pneumonia, too?"

When she turned back she held a glass of water. "Can you lift your head a little? Otherwise, you won't get much of this down."

"Of course I can lift my head. I could get up if you'd take this blasted cover off me."

To prove it, he tried to jerk himself upright. Instantly, a sharp pain shot through his head and his senses swam. A wave of weakness traveled through him, making him tremble. He heard a clunk, then Phoebe's hands had slipped under the quilt, to his shoulders, steadying him.

"Oh, Jonas, you stubborn man. Here, just rest a second, then I'll hold your head up so you can have your water."

Her voice had lost its sharpness and gone back to the soothing warmth. Her hands on his shoulders were comforting. More than comforting, somehow. Closing his eyes again, all his irritation gone, he basked in the sensations she was creating inside him.

"Jonas? Are you all right?"

Anxiety was in her voice now, mingled with the softness. He liked that, too.

Reluctantly, afraid she'd turn sharp again and move away, he nodded. "Yes."

"Thank God! You don't know what a time you gave us. And how worried we've been about you."

Us? He struggled to open his eyes again and managed a little wider slit this time. "Is Gavin here?"

Phoebe bit her lip and then shook her head. "No, not yet. Serena sent him a message and I'm sure he'll be here soon."

Disappointment filled him. He closed his eyes again, sagging in the bed.

"Jonas! Will you stop that? Here, sit up and drink your water."

Her hand was on the back of his neck, tugging him forward. Funny, hot as he was, her warm hand still felt good on his bare flesh.

"Here, take a sip of this."

He felt the cool glass against his mouth, felt the welcome trickle of water slide over his tongue, down his throat. He swallowed and eagerly waited for more.

She let him drink again, then withdrew the glass. "That's enough for now. Don't want you getting sick again and losing all of it."

Now, she'd take her hand away. He didn't want her to. He slid one of his hands out from under the confining quilt and caught one of her wrists.

"Don't go. Stay with me." He lifted his eyelids again, relieved he could get his eyes nearly all the way open now. He looked up at her.

Her mouth was open, her eyes wide.

"I've missed you. I've missed you so dang much," he told her, surprising himself, not knowing he was going to say the words until they were out.

He wasn't sorry, though. He wasn't sorry at all.

Phoebe closed her mouth, then her lips curved upward in a smile. "I've missed you, too," she said softly.

"You have?" He smiled back at her. "From the way you talked that day of the storm I didn't think you were ever going to speak to me again."

Phoebe disengaged his grip on her wrist, laid his hand on his chest, then put her hand on top of his, squeezing gently.

"I—I said a lot of things I didn't mean. I acted like a fool."

"No more than me." He returned the squeeze. "I didn't even try to find out why you jumped all over me. I knew it wasn't for what I said."

"You're right—it wasn't. I—I was afraid. That's why I said those things."

Jonas gave her a disbelieving stare. "You? Afraid? Of what?"

Her expression changed. She moved her hand from his, laid him back on the bed, then stepped back. "Never mind. I'm glad we can be friends again," she finished primly.

Phoebe's touch gone, he felt bereft. "What I had in

mind for us to be was a lot closer than friendship." He blinked, surprised at himself again. Had he actually said that?

She blushed rosily. "You don't mean that. It's just your fever talking."

"I do mean it and I should have said it sooner. And you just said my fever had broken."

"But you're still sick and weak. You don't know what you're saying."

He frowned at her, his patience wearing thin. "Phoebe Crane, I am entirely in my right mind and I certainly *do* know what I'm saying."

He paused, then doubt swept over him.

"If you don't feel anything for me except friendship, then say so. I can take it."

Phoebe stared at him for a few moments, then a radiant smile broke over her face.

"Both of us are getting too old for all this pussyfooting around. Yes, Jonas, I'd like us to be more than friends."

Relief swept over him. "You had me worried for a minute. What was all that about you being scared?"

"I'll tell you when you're feeling better."

After a moment, he nodded. "All right. Guess maybe I'm not up to a whole lot of talking yet. But I want to say one more thing. You're a fine-looking woman. And I should have told you that a long time ago, too."

Again, rosiness pinkened her cheeks. "Thank you, Jonas. And you're a fine-looking man—at least when you get over this illness you will be." She grinned at him. "You'd better get some more sleep. When you wake up the next time, I'll have some chicken soup ready."

"Have you been taking care of me all by yourself?" he finally thought to ask.

"No, Serena and Alice have been spelling me."

He frowned again. "How long have I been sick?"

"Nearly a week."

"And you said someone sent word to Gavin?"

"Yes, but don't you worry. He'd left Delta Point, but was expected back soon. I'm sure he'll be here by tonight."

Profound tiredness overtook him. He nodded and closed his eyes and turned over on his side.

Phoebe stood watching him, allowing the frown she'd held back to furrow her brow.

She hadn't told Jonas everything. True, Gavin had left the mainland town, but no one knew where he was or when he'd return.

Or even *if* he would.

She heard a rustle behind her and turned to see Serena standing in the doorway. Her worried expression mirrored Phoebe's uneasiness.

"Thank God Jonas is better," Serena said in low tones.

"Yes," Phoebe whispered back. She left the bedroom, going into the front storeroom, Serena following.

"Now we can talk without Jonas hearing and getting worried. You haven't heard anything from Gavin?"

"No." Serena tilted her chin with a determined look. "If we don't hear by tomorrow, I'm going over to Delta Point and see if I can find out anything about where he went."

Phoebe nodded her agreement. "I think you should." She paused, then went on, "And once Gavin's back on the Island—don't you let him get away again."

Serena's eyes widened. "Mama! How can you say things like that?" Then she gave a rueful half-smile. "I don't intend to. Unless it's already too late for us."

"I don't think so. Gavin truly loves you."

Serena's smile faded. "But I drove him away."

"I drove Jonas away, too, and just a few minutes ago, we . . . well, we agreed we . . . cared for each other."

"Mama! How wonderful." Serena moved to her mother and hugged her. "I'm so happy for you."

"Now, you go on home and get some rest," Phoebe said. "I'll help Billy with the store and keep an eye on Jonas."

Phoebe walked to the doorway and looked at Jonas. He slept soundly for the first time in days, with no tossing and turning.

"All right. I'm going to make some chicken soup anyway. Jonas needs it to regain his strength, now that he feels like eating again."

Serena put her hands on her hips and gave her mother a mock-frown. *"I'll* fix the soup here. I'll go and get everything to do it with now. And when I come back, you are going home and rest."

Phoebe suddenly felt tired enough to sleep on her feet. But the weariness was a contented kind. Finally, all was right between her and Jonas. During those hours when she feared for his life, she'd realized how much she cared for him and how little her other fears meant to her, set alongside the thought of losing him.

"Go ahead. I'll wait here."

Watching her daughter leave, her step determined, Phoebe's heart ached for her. She didn't feel nearly as sure as she'd sounded a few moments ago. Gavin surely wouldn't have gone far without telling his father. Serena could no doubt find him, and he'd come back to the Island to see Jonas.

But that didn't mean he'd stay.

Chapter Ten

"Hear your Pa is took bad. Guess that's why you're comin' back to the Island."

A gust of wind blew Roy Scott's last words away, but Gavin understood. Worry and impatience filled him. He longed to take the oars away from the man, row harder and faster. But since it was Roy's boat, he couldn't do that.

"Yes. I've been gone—just got back to Delta Point a little while ago. And the message was three days old. Do you know how Pop is now?"

His arms straining, Roy shook his head. "Nope. Was in to the store day afore yesterday and Serena told me he was holdin' his own. She looked mighty worried, though."

Serena? All his feelings for her flooded over him. He pushed them back. He had no time for that now. And besides, he knew how she felt about him. She'd made that very clear.

"The note just said he had a fever. Do you know anything else?"

Another gust rocked the boat. Roy struggled to keep it under control.

"You were lucky to catch me. Should have headed back a lot earlier. Gonna be a blow, looks like. No, don't know anything else. Gettin' on to time for the winter fevers, though. Some of 'em can be bad."

Gavin knew that—and Jonas wasn't a young man. Fear and self-reproach hit him again.

He shouldn't have left Delta Point before going back to the Island to see Jonas. But his father had never been seriously ill before—how could he have known this would happen?

He'd wanted to find work elsewhere. Baltimore was the nearest city to Delta Point, but although jobs were to be had, he hadn't been able to stand the city. He longed for his island life with a hunger that drove him back to Delta Point. The store-clerk job he'd been offered there would have to do. He knew he could work up to manager before too long.

And he could see Crane Island from his room. Even if he couldn't live there anymore, couldn't stand to see Serena every day and know he'd never have her.

They were getting close now. Impatience seized Gavin again. "Why don't you let me row? I'm fresh and you've worked all day."

Roy glanced up, then nodded. "Fine with me."

Gavin slid along the board seat, then moved up to the one Roy occupied. He grasped the oars, Roy half-stood to switch seats, and a vicious gust swept over the small boat.

Before Gavin could react or try to grab him, Roy fell over the side into the choppy bay. In a moment the boat drifted away from him.

"Help! I can't swim!" Roy's frightened wail blew on the wind as a wave swept over him. Splashing frantically, he went under.

There was no time to try to maneuver the boat close enough for Roy to grasp—he was probably too panicky anyway. Only one thing left to do. Gavin peeled off his coat and dove overboard, searching for Roy in the murky water. Finally, his lungs bursting, his hands found Roy's coat, and tugged. Roy turned and grabbed at Gavin, almost pulling him under, too.

Gavin barely managed to keep his head up. Good thing Roy was a small man! He was so scared he didn't know what he was doing and he'd have them both drowned if Gavin wasn't careful.

Another huge wave rolled over them, sucking them under. Grimly, Gavin tried to hang on, but Roy slipped out of his grasp, disappearing in the turbid water.

This time it took Gavin longer to find him. When he finally did, and brought his dead weight to the surface, Roy was sputtering and coughing, but still fighting. Knowing he had no choice, Gavin gave him a sharp blow to the neck which instantly made him go limp.

The waves had taken the boat too far away. Gavin knew he couldn't reach it with his burden. He had to try to make it to shore. Clutching Roy's unconscious form, Gavin struck out for the Island, thanking God it wasn't very far.

But by the time he reached the wharf, after fighting the rough water all the way, he'd used up all his strength. A man saw them and yelled at someone else, who came running out of one of the fish shacks. Willing hands pulled Gavin and Roy out of the water onto the boards of the wharf.

"He's swallowed a lot of water," Gavin gasped, "and I had to knock him out. Turn him over, get the water out. Here, let me . . ."

"You just lay there and get your strength back. Let us do that, Gavin," one of the men said. "You're near-drowned yourself."

Gavin started to protest, but a wave of weakness went over him. He closed his eyes and rolled to his side.

A bug-eyed boy watched the furor, then turned and ran toward the village. Reaching the main street, he headed for the store and burst inside.

"Roy and Gavin is down at the wharf drowned!" he yelled.

Serena's eyes widened, her hands clutching the edge of the counter.

"Johnny, what are you talking about?" she asked, her voice shaking as she hurried out into the room.

"It's true," the boy shrilled. "I was just down there. Saw it with my own eyes."

Phoebe appeared in the doorway from the back, horror and shock on her face. "Serena, wait!" she called.

Serena was already halfway to the door. "I can't, Mama," she flung over her shoulder.

She passed by the boy and kept on running. The wind gusted, tearing at her hair and flinging her skirts around. She paid no attention.

"Please, God, don't let this be true!" she prayed, her breath coming in gasps, a stitch in her side not slowing her down. "You can't be this cruel!"

Sobbing, gasping for breath, at last she came out onto the wharf. Several men were gathered on the far end, bent over two other men who were lying down, covered with blankets.

A wind gust rocked her on her feet, but she was scarcely aware of it.

Terrible fear leapt in her chest, almost smothering her as she ran to the group. Roy Scott and Gavin lay on the wharf planks, unmoving, their eyes closed.

The boy had been right, then. They were dead.

Gavin was dead!

Sorrow and despair filled her. Serena dropped to her

knees. She flung her arms around his neck, feeling the coldness of his body. She laid her head on his chest, sobs tearing out of her.

"I love you so much," she said, her words little more than gasps. "I lied to you that night. I was afraid to let myself love you. I feared I'd lose you as I lost Peter. And now I have. The damned bay has got you, too!" she wailed.

A hand touched her head, smoothed down her hair. She tried to fling it off. "Go away! Leave me alone!"

"I don't think I have the energy to do that," a voice said close to her ear.

A very familiar voice.

She suddenly became aware that she felt a vibration from the chest she lay upon. A heart beating.

Serena jerked her head up. Gavin's hand fell away at her movement. He still lay flat on his back, but now his eyes were open, staring at her.

Joy leapt through her. She fell upon him, kissing his mouth, his eyes, his nose. "You're alive! Oh, God, thank you, thank you!"

His arms came around her, pressing her closer. "Did you mean what you just said . . . about loving me?"

"Yes," she whispered, her tears now from happiness. She sat up, looking down into his face. "I meant every word. I was a cowardly fool to let you go. If you're finished with me, I can't blame you."

Gavin pushed himself to a sitting position. "Then *I'd* be the fool. I'll never let you go again."

His arms pulled her close, and he kissed her long and deeply. Serena kissed him back, putting all her love into it.

Finally, Gavin moved back a little. "Pop—how is he?"

Serena heard the anxiety in his voice, and rushed to ease his fears. "He's much better. His fever has broken and he's keeping Mama busy bringing him soup."

A wide smile curved Gavin's mouth. "I take it Phoebe and Pop are back on speaking terms?"

Serena smiled. "More than speaking terms. Quite a bit more."

An explosion of coughing erupted nearby, abruptly making Serena aware that she knelt on the damp boards of the wharf, with men all around her. Men who were giving her bright-eyed, interested looks.

In a moment she realized why. Oh, Lord. She'd proclaimed her love for Gavin for everyone to hear.

She didn't care. She didn't care if the whole world heard her. Serena smiled sweetly at the men, who gave her sheepish grins in return. Glancing at the one doing the coughing, she saw it was Roy.

He stopped coughing and looked over at Gavin. "Guess you saved my life," he said. "Don't remember much about it, but I'm much obliged."

Gavin nodded. "Afraid your boat may be lost."

"Might find it tomorrow, if the storm's not too bad. Anyway, a feller can get another boat." Roy grinned weakly. "Can't get another life, though."

Serena sighed in relief. "Nobody drowned, then. What happened?"

Briefly, Gavin explained, then pushed himself to his feet, letting the blanket fall away. "Let's go home."

There was such a depth of feeling in the way he said "home," it brought a lump to Serena's throat. "Can you make the walk?"

"Need some help, Gavin?" one of the men asked. "We'll be glad to give you a shoulder. Or send for a wagon."

Gavin walked a few steps, then shook his head. "I'll do fine."

Serena moved over beside him. "Do you want my shoulder?"

He grinned at her. "I want a lot more than your shoulder, but I guess that will have to wait a while."

Serena frowned at him, then smiled. "Hush! Do you want everyone to hear you?"

His grin widened. "Don't think it would matter. Everyone's already heard enough—they can't wait to get home to tell their wives."

Serena's frown smoothed out. "You're right. Lean on me, and I'll take you home."

They walked in silence for a while. The wind had died down—for the moment, anyway. Maybe it wasn't just the lull before the storm.

"Do you ever plan to leave the Island? Live somewhere else?" he asked.

Serena gave him a surprised look. "No, of course not. Why do you want to know?" Then her face changed, tightened. "Do you want to go back to the mainland?"

"God forbid!" he said fervently. "I want to live here the rest of my life and marry you and raise a houseful of children who will love this place as much as we do."

She let out a sigh of relief. "You had me worried for a minute. Of course, I'd go anywhere with you."

He squeezed her shoulder. "But aren't you glad you won't have to?"

"Yes," she admitted. "Did you think when we began planning to pair off Jonas and Phoebe that it would end like this?"

He stopped walking and slid his arm from her shoulder. "Of course. Or at least I *hoped* it would. Why do you think I dreamed up the plan?"

She looked at him for a moment, then smiled. "I see I've been a fool in more ways than one."

He smiled back, then drew her to him. "I wanted you from the first moment I saw you. But you'd retreated from the world."

"And I started coming back that day of Margaret's wedding. I actually *saw* you that day. As if I'd never seen you before."

She looked up at him, silently giving thanks for this second chance. "Can you ever forgive me for what I said to you that night in the gazebo?"

His smile faded and he released her, then gave her a solemn look. "Probably in about a hundred years."

She gave him a wary glance. Was he joking? He must be, but still . . . she'd done a dreadful thing.

"Is there anything I can do to shorten that?" she asked, keeping her face serious, too.

He nodded. "Yes. You can kiss me ten thousand times. That might do the trick. And the first kiss will be . . . about now!"

He pulled her to him again and covered her lips with his own. Serena opened her mouth to him, opened her heart and soul to him, and kissed him back.

Now that the blanket was gone, she felt dampness seeping into the front of her dress from Gavin's soaking clothes. They needed to hurry on back to the store so he could change. However, the evening wasn't too chilly and Gavin wasn't shivering.

A few more minutes wouldn't hurt . . . the kiss went on and on.

"Mr. Mead," a voice said into the silence. "Are you sure you don't need any help? You ain't got very far toward the store, and I'm supposed to run back and tell the men if you're all right."

Serena and Gavin broke apart, both breathing hard. Johnny Drake, the boy who'd come bursting into the store, stood there, looking expectant.

Gavin gave him a wry smile. He reached into his pocket and took out a coin and flipped it toward the boy, who easily caught it.

"Go tell them we're doing fine."

Johnny grinned at them both. "I'll sure do that." He headed back toward the wharf.

Gavin turned to Serena, took her hand in his, gazed deeply into her eyes. "Would you say we're doing just fine, my future wife?"

She felt their souls meeting in that gaze.

"Yes, my future husband—we are."

His Mother's Gauntlet

Martha Hix

DEDICATED TO THE MEMORY
of the last Princess of Wales
Diana

Prologue

God's Year 1294

"What in God's name has happened now?" the king sought to know, while trying without success, as usual, to hide his lisp.

"The Welsh have burned Caernarfon Castle."

King Edward, grinding his teeth, scowled at the messenger, a varlet in service to the Marcher border lord Gilbert de Clare. "Caernarfon?" the king repeated. "Where my heir was born, ten years past. Where I would invest him with the title of Prince of Wales. Damn the scurrilous Welsh!"

His long legs striding across the Moorish carpet, his gait belying his five and fifty years, England's monarch grabbed a chalice of wine, downing it in one gulp. "Did the de Granvilles take part in the uprising?"

Ralph de Monthermer audaciously approached his king. "They—"

"Answer not!" King Edward's fingers clamped the messenger's throat. He squeezed until eyes bulged, cheeks flashed crimson, and spittle seeped from a corner of liver-fat lips. "I know their minds. And won't hear it voiced."

Eduardo, kill the messenger not. As if from her Westminster tomb, gentle yet shrewd Queen Eleanor had admonished Edward. He let go and stepped back. He needed a wife's gentling.

"Why should I concern myself over Wales?" he asked no one in particular, especially not de Monthermer. "I was outwitted by Philip the Fair. I should not have offered to exchange Gascony for his sister's hand." Philip unfairly had kept both the duchy and his sister.

"What about William Wallace in Scotland?"

"Fermez la bouche," the king roared. "And mind your place. Else, I'll finish on your throat."

"May I beg your highness's leave?"

"Go."

Time, Ralph de Monthermer wasted not.

The king fell to reflection. He'd thought Wales—Cymru, the natives called it—had submitted after the death of their overlord prince, Llywelyn ap Gruffudd, in 1282. Yet princes such as Morgan ap Maredudd and Madog ap Llywelyn had fought on, when they could collect arrows, maces, and men of war. Damn those dogs!

Southern Wales, on the other hand and for the most part, had been a crown holding since the time of William the Conqueror. Save for pockets of princedoms. To dig pockets, Edward had sent trusted cousins. What had happened to Breckbryn? Where did it go wrong?

King Edward called for a page's assistance. "Fetch the letter from my cousin in Breckbryn."

The page knew which one. He dug in the casket where the king kept letter rolls from the more favored of his relatives, then presented a parchment. "This one, your highness?"

"What other, you idiot!" Edward unfurled the two-year-old letter, reading:

"My dear monarch, King of England, Duke of Gascony, beloved by all and most dearly by his cousin,

I seek to inscribe this in the language of your commonfolk, since I know you mastered the local tongue, and I wish to impress you. Write, cousin, either in the patois of your *vassals, or in* la langue propre à notre coeurs. *I, too, as you know, am a student of life and will try to translate to our French.*

William of Granville has reached the castle in the Welsh princedom of Breckbryn, and bids you a Pipe Roll.

Castle Breckbryn is a hilltop citadel surrounded by Lord Gilbert de Clare's Glamorgan. The castle is raised on a rocky crag above the river Rhymney to the west, with vales to the other directions. A steep look-down, I might add!

Despite rumors to the contrary, the natives seem not to have propensity for eating, drinking, or being merry. In truth, they are a warring lot, epitomized by the Maid of Breckbryn, Cordelya Howel.

You are no doubt aware of the princess and her late father, Howel ap Rhodri, since she is of faint relation to the descending line of England through her mother, although her highness would be strapped to a siege engine and catapulted into England itself ere admit her ties.

The Welsh, I gather, lack pride of lineage where ties outside this peculiar land are concerned.

By the by, how are your children? Naturally, I know all of your Joanna. 'But what is a daughter?' I can almost hear you say. Merely a pawn. Sons are the future.

Pray, is little Edward progressing well with tutelage at the joust, or is your heir still fond of dolls?"

King Edward lowered the letter, biting down, catching the tip of his tongue. Enjoying the pain. He had caught his cousin's barb, albeit it hurt little compared to the gist of the question.

He poured another chalice of wine and took another long quaff. The king, rather than distress over his heir or on the problems with Unfair Philip—or with the rebel William Wallace in Scotland!—lifted parchment anew.

"Castle Breckbryn is remote, just as William seeks. The stronghold seems impregnable. Woe be unto the soldiers who try to breach the ditch gaps. Or to lug battering rams or trebuchets up the steep incline apparently carved out by legionnaires of Rome and fortified by primitives, when iron came into fashion. More recent builders have improved on the stronghold's theme, replacing timber with siltstone and grit.

A quite secure outer ward is terraced below the keep. It surrounds all sides of the inner ward, save for the impassible approach from the cliff to the river.

Within the outer ward is a stone abbey. Will and I distrust the abbot. The man squandered what was left of the treasury and mocks his churchly honors. We shall be glad to have done with him.

The natives say plenty abounded before 'Longshanks' began to exert absolute authority to the north. God save your absolute authority, my dear long-shanked cousin. May He be kinder to you than He was to ours in Jerusalem. That, naturally, is a discussion for another time and place.

Breckbryn is quite large by local standards, typically Welsh. Meaning, not typical. You will find the usual appurtenances of a good bailey. Cistern. Cellars. Stables, mews, kennels, sties. Cobbler's hut. Bakeries and a meadhouse. All found lacking.

There are two towers. One is D-shaped, conforming to

*others favored by the natives, and holds the armory. The
western keep is Norman in its rectangular construction,
with a great hall, a chapel, the lord's chamber, and the
lady's solar within. The latter comes complete with a tub
for bathing. In that the princess gives off the aroma of herbs
and flowers—methinks she avails herself of the tub.*

    *Devious describes the builders of Breckbryn. One drain—
quite a maze!—covers an escape route."*

Edward scowled at the trailing of handwriting and a
blotch of ink that took up too much of the parchment.

*"Must dash this off to you, Ned. We have encountered a
problem.*

        *For William of Granville, Knight of Cyprus and
        Jerusalem, I am your cousin both of blood and
        heart, L—"*

King Edward tossed the letter aside. What had happened
in Breckbryn to consequence Caernarfon in the north . . . ?
He knew, for certes. It was enough to make a mighty king
cry.

Chapter One

Breckbryn Castle in the South of Wales
May Day, 1292

There are times when every woman longs for the sooth-ing, sweet strains of a lullaby from her mother. There are moments for Mam's scolding. Or for her advice. There are incidences when a woman yearns to cuddle her moth-er's soft bosom and wail, if not scream, "Save me!" and be fed on the milk of protection in those dear arms.

Down through the ages in Wales, it was said, *"Modryb dda."* A good aunt is a second mother. Cordelya Howel—Princess of Breckbryn, also styled Maid of the same by those in the surrounding Marcher border lordship of Glamorgan—had laid her mother to rest and had no aunts. To say naught of losing her father and only brother, when they had joined revolts against English authority.

Advice or scolds, lullabies or protection? Impossible. This, however, would have been an excellent morning for wailing and screaming. The principalities of Wales had

been falling into the greedy hands of King Edward Longshanks, with Breckbryn one of the last still blessed with
relative liberty.

Freedom now threatened.

"Lady Cordelya, 'tis time to announce our imminent
marriage," the invader to her home and heart, a knave-
knight in service to Longshanks, said in the tongue of his
king's court. "Let us remove to the great hall to break our
fasts."

Cordelya Howel had no stomach for humble pie.

I must send word to Morgan ap Maredudd,, must beg his aid.
It would take days, though, for the Welsh prince to reach
Breckbryn from his camp in the Black Mountains.

Her limbs shook with desperation as she peered through
the window of the lady's solar, gazing across the bailey to
the D-tower, where the fighting men of Breckbryn had
once been housed, along with their armaments. Foreign
invaders had emptied their carts into the armory there.

It was all she could do not to throw herself from the
window.

For calm, she looked beyond the keep, seeing misted
and magnificent green hills.

"Niece, do not stand there ignoring your knight-husband."

Bereft of even her uncle's support, she pivoted to Uncle
Cyfeiliog. Wearing an abbot's habit of simple fustian, yea
though wearing a valuable signet ring, he stood next to
the lord of Glamorgan.

The knave-knight who would force her hand crowded
into her line of vision. He towered above Cordelya, his
stance arrogant.

Sir William de Granville had what she imagined to be
the Saracen look to him, swarthy and dangerous. Saracens.
Always, she'd held romantic fancies of Crusades and of

slaying the infidel. She, however, didn't mind Sir William's appearance. It was his English blood she despised.

How should she fight his threat? It was a princess's place, as it was for ladies and women alike, even in untamed Wales, to bear children, run households, and keep as quiet about it as possible, lest she bring upon herself the wrath of God and chroniclers.

Yet . . . surely the Lord God who'd given Saint David—Dewi Sant—to Wales would understand. She must save herself. For Breckbryn!

No mean feat.

At vespers last eventide, her corpulent uncle had ordered both drawbridges lowered to allow the retinues from England and Glamorgan inside the castle walls. Breckbryn's only line of defense had been breached.

Sir William offered an arm. "Let us attend our people, Lady Cordelya. We will eat, drink, and make merry."

Had she but a chance, she would have tainted the ale that the invaders now swilled in the great hall below.

Alas, her uncle had locked her in chamber, upon the first sight of the upward advent of usurpers. At least the abbot had not sent her to the dungeon. Small favor. Paltry minutes had passed since the bar had been lifted this dawn for the entrance of these three men—three too many men—into her chamber.

" 'Tis not a Welsh custom, a meal at daybreak," she said in the knight's tongue. *Please don't let my voice quake.* "My people will notice this breach, will think ill of you for it."

The lord of Glamorgan, a stocky Marcher baron of eight and forty, stepped to Sir William's side. Gilbert de Clare, called Red Gilbert or simply The Red for his fiery shock of hair, scowled. "Where is the hospitality Welsh households are so famed for? Your larder has not been imposed upon. The morn's cockles and cheese are gifts from my villeins, as well as the seaweed for laverbread. Sir William himself brings wine and fruit, and further bounty beyond reason."

"My monks supplied the ale," Uncle Cyfeiliog announced with the pride he should be showing Breckbryn. Like many of the native sons, he was short of stature and pitch black of pate, although his head held the tonsure of ecclesiastical honor. He brought shame on Breckbryn.

Vying for the sentimental, she said to Red Gilbert, "Where is the gallantry you English are so fond of boasting?"

His freckles stood out beneath his blanching face.

"Niece! Take heed whom you address with sharp tongue."

Forsooth, few would dare shame the great Gilbert de Clare. Theirs was an unusual relationship, though, one of faint blood ties and that of a friendship of sorts with his young countess. "Lord Gilbert, you treated me fairly, after my brother Martyn went to the Lord God. I ne'er thought you would betray me." A terrible ache knifed her chest. "It grieves me deeply, your fostering this marriage."

The Red squinted toward the ceiling, flexed his fingers. When he turned his eyes to her again, she looked upon the pale hardness he usually saved for others. "Take yourself to the great hall, Cordelya, to your proper seat at the dais."

Uncle Cyfeiliog piously folded his arms, tucking fingers to elbows beneath habit sleeves. "Be not petulant, niece."

"Bid us welcome," Sir William said, straightening to an even grander height. "Let us do get on with it."

Eyeing each of these churls in turn, she feared her knees would fold. If only Morgan ap Maredudd were closer by. How could she borrow time before his saving grace? *Save yourself!*

How?

What would dead Mam have said at a moment such as this? *Conduct yourself with the dignity befitting your rank, and 'twould not hurt to hang the liver of a wild boar above the archway to the great hall, to ward off evil spirits.*

There were no wild boars about, simply boors.

Ignoring the knave-knight's proffered arm, Cordelya jerked up a brow at The Red. *Be as a man, Cordelya. Give no quarter.*

"Red Gilbert, you overstep your bounds. You made a treaty with my brother, forsooth. 'Tis quite specific. You are not to arrive at these gates to do ill, either in words or by deed. In that you have done so, you beg war."

She turned to the abbot. It was a fact he tossed dice with wayfarers, and whored women. He thought naught of cruelty to others. Why, he acted as English as any born east of Offa's Wall. But he was her familial hope. "Uncle, I pray your support."

"Sir William offers a good match, niece. Give him the benefit of study."

Should she? She eyed the foreigner to the Welsh hills and vales, heretofore unknown to her. Who was he truly?

Sir William de Granville appeared seven or eight years older than Cordelya; she'd passed youthful a set of years ago. Sun-darkened of flesh, black of eyes and well-curled hair, he had clothed himself casually, his coat of armor having no doubt been left in his appropriated quarters. Fine hose and a soft tunic draped his shape well. Boots of Spanish leather rose to his thighs. For a mere nobleman, he dressed rich, a Toledo sword with jeweled hilt buckled at his narrow waist. Mayhap he hailed from wealth. Breckbryn cried for wealth.

Mayhap he had stolen his sword.

Only impoverished, landless knights, her mother had said, were sent by Longshanks to claim land from orphaned damsels. Until now, as far as Cordelya knew, the pickings had been selected from the wood-mice heiresses of their own country.

Sir William stepped closer, near enough so that when he spoke, he wafted pleasant breath. As well, he smelled clean. Sweat and wild garlic usually clung to men hereabouts.

"Demoiselle," he said, his voice melodic in its flow, "you appear on the verge of wild uproar."

"How perceptive. I yearn to rage and roar, and to brandish a broadsword at my enemies."

"Niece! Take care with curses, else you'll answer to the Almighty. And to *me.*"

Sir William roared over his broad shoulder, "Leave her be, man!"

Such was not a trait of the abbot's, leaving aught be. "Sir, I tutored her to stay silent, unless she could find something of a gentle nature to say."

"With the unsettling events of the past decade, I had scant to speak about," she said to the knight, not mentioning that when she had spoken, too often her uncle took exception and locked her in the dungeon.

For some odd reason, maychance in appreciation for Sir William's defense of her, she explained, "I am undone. Quite so. You would be, too, were our places switched."

"Aye." Sir William lifted her fingers, brushing his lips along her knuckles. " 'Tis a shame we could meet not under more pleasant circumstances. I ache to show you courtly love befitting your purple blood, then help you enjoy the red of it."

She hid a grin, saying in Welsh, "Would you now, exquisite usurper?" A trace of her grin slipped. "To your favor your breath is fresh, your lips gentle. And you fill your hose nicely. If only I could find comfort in small favors."

Sir William looked blankly at her. Obviously he did not understand the language of the land he would steal.

Gilbert de Clare laughed.

Uncle Cyfeiliog made the sign of the cross, saying, "She is usually modest of presence."

Frowning, the knight swung round to loom over the abbot. "I give you leave to let me form my own opinions. Go, man! Princess Cordelya and I will join you in the great hall forthwith. After she adjusts to the notion of marriage."

His tonsure in danger of slipping, Cyfeiliog ap Rhodri shook with fury. "I am still the male head of this household."

"Out with you!" the knight roared, pointing to the doorway. "Take yourself to the food, Abbot."

"I'll join you, Cyfeiliog," said the lord. " 'Tis better if we allow Sir William and Cordelya to talk alone."

"Such would compromise her virtue," the abbot sputtered.

"Out!" Sir William and Red Gilbert both snarled.

Uncle Cyfeiliog scurried out the doorway, Red Gilbert strutting behind him. Fur flew as Cordelya's corgi raced round chaussures, entering the solar from the opened door to the hallway.

"Woof." A bulldog—jowls swinging from side to side, slobber going this way and that from his undershot jaw, his claws stirring the rushes for purchase—bounded behind the dwarf bitch. He chased sweet little Isabelle under the bed.

"Leave her be!" Cordelya screamed, her hands flapping.

Left to his own devices, that dog would pass along English pests and a litter of mutts! As would his master. "Sir William, control your dog."

One whistle; the bulldog obeyed.

The knight moved to the chair before the cold hearth. Mam's favorite chair, where Princess Eleri had tutored and cuddled her only daughter. *Mam, I need your help!*

Cordelya paced like the caged animal she was, and had been since losing her brother. She went by this window and that, she eyed the furnishings, the wall hangings, all frayed by age and poverty. Even the bathing tub had dents.

Sprawling into that precious seat, extending legs even longer than his king's, Sir William made an unusual presence in the small chair. A knight too large in a place too small.

"Lew," he commanded. "Come, lad."

The bulldog, panting, thunked his belly to the rushes next to his master, while Isabelle . . . To add insult to Cordelya's injury, the corgi slunk from beneath the bed, pranced across the solar, and jumped onto the usurper's lap.

She licked Sir William's shaven chin.

One broad hand, scored by scars, stroked the furred neck. "What is your name, sweeting?" Sir William crooned to the corgi, who wiggled her tail and curled as if to toast before a fire.

"Her name is Isabelle."

"A quite lofty name for a bitch."

"Again, may I comment on your perception," Cordelya said, galled, knowing full well what he meant but wondering if he would catch her meaning. Perchance not. "You English favor the name Isabelle. I insult it."

It wasn't the truth, but it made for a sullying story, and she almost chuckled.

A slow yet wide grin lifted his lips. His teeth appeared undisturbed by rot. His head of raven-black, shoulder-length hair tilted. "May I take it you have a wry sense of humor?"

This was neither the time nor place to worry about naming patterns, nor the possible mixing of bloodlines, at least in canines. Cordelya stepped toward him. "Am I to take it that you of the knighthood are bound to chivalry?"

"You are correct."

"Then you won't mind my asking . . ." Mayhap if she

could coerce Sir William into recognizing the incongru-
ousness of their union and the imbalance of their match,
he'd simply move on.

Bald questions being unwise, given the armies within
the inner ward, she sought something of worth in him,
apart from his sightly appearance and pleasant breath, in
case escape eluded her. "What, sir, do you bring to this
marriage?"

"Peace for Breckbryn."

"And your king is a kindly and gentle leader. Please
don't try to deceive me, Sir William. I have suffered enough
insult. What honors do you bring me?"

"Nary a scrap to impress a scornful princess." He made
a smacking sound at Isabelle, as if to kiss her. "That I
impress you, though, is of little consequence. I am here
by edict of the king, and here I shall stay."

"You have nothing of property to offer Breckbryn?"

He tickled beneath Isabelle's chin. The corgi's tongue
lolled, her head drooping in delirium. Sir William looked
gravely into Cordelya's eyes. "I bring you my skills as a
warrior who'll foster peace in this curious land, although
I would have no fighting hereabouts. I bring this to you
by my oath."

His rank sincerity startled her, but not for long. "And
what else?"

He shrugged. "Alas, I am but a third son."

"You English and your laws of inheritance. Estates
should be divided amongst sons, as they are here in Wales."

Cordelya whipped about, heading to the window seat,
where she plopped down. The mist had cleared, giving
her an unfettered view of lovely Cymru, beautiful Wales.

Precious Breckbryn. Hers. None other's. Certainly not
Uncle Cyfeiliog's nor this knight's.

"By all that is sacred to chivalry, you must let go this
wild claim to Breckbryn. Pray, seek an inheritance else-

where, sir. This is Wales, I am Welsh, and I live by the laws of my ancestor, King Hywel Good. No Welshwoman is ev'r forced into marriage. I will not be the first.''

Sir William set Isabelle to her paws, rose to stand on booted feet, and crossed to the window. His palms flattening on each side of Cordelya's hips, he leaned toward her. His voice steady, he said, ''I recognize your plight as brutal. Howbeit—''

A gnawing caught Sir William's regard. Glowering downward, he ordered, ''Stop that, Lew! Enough with the fleas.''

With the toe of his boot he urged Lew to cease abusing a loin and to move aside. The bulldog, to Cordelya's distress, decided to abuse Isabelle. There would be puppies.

Sir William, his lips twisting, glanced at the pair of covenants, then said, ''If we have the devil's luck, we'll be presented with a fine basket of babes.'' He winked at Cordelya. ''Many times it takes the mixing of breeds to form strength.''

''Only in dogs.''

Dark eyes softer now, as if showing sadness, he lifted her chin with the crook of a finger. '' 'Tis unfortunate you were not born in the great age of Welsh princes. Circumstance would have afforded you the benefits of Welsh laws and the hot breath of Welsh warriors. Alas, the great age has passed. For you, for . . . for—'' He stepped back. ''The great age has passed.''

She wondered about his faltering of speech. What did he mean? It was as if he had suffered a disappointment.

He said, ''You must accept the inevitable, demoiselle. Your overlord is dead. The Statute of Rhuddlan is fixed, and all must learn to live by English laws.''

Forsooth Llywelyn ap Gruffudd, highest of the princes of Wales, had fallen with her father at Ifron Bridge, near Builth, a decade past. In those years, the English king had

busied his men to the north, and had left Breckbryn be.
Until now.

It was time for Cordelya to take a firm stand. *Mam in
heaven, help me.* "Red Gilbert will come to his senses about
our treaty," she pointed out, hoping against hope. "We
live quietly as neighbors. I trade wool and mead for his
cheese and beef. I don't disturb his peace, and he does
likewise. He won't desert me, not truly, at the hour of
reckoning."

"I would not count on Gilbert de Clare, were I you. The
earl was most agreeable to escort my troops to Breckbryn."

"By all that is holy—why? And why does Longshanks
stick his nose into Breckbryn's affairs?"

Sir William straightened to pat her shoulder as if she
were a child. "Do you not know the affairs of Lord Gilbert?
King Edward is vexed, doesn't trust him."

For the better part of a year she'd not strayed from
within her wards, keeping mostly to her private chapel.
Devotions, prayers for a fine Welsh prince to arrive and
return Breckbryn to its former glory . . . and dreaming of
the glory of holy pilgrimage—these were her pastimes.

Said the de Granville knight, "Lord Gilbert made private
war against the Marcher lord of Brecon, Humphrey de
Bohun, over the rights to Morlais Castle. Both barons were
imprisoned at the king's order, and are newly released."

Stunned, Cordelya pressed her spine against the window
seat's wall until the stone ate into her back. "How can that
be? Red Gilbert is Longshanks's son-in-law."

"King Edward has had enough Marcher impertinence.
The Lord of Glamorgan has too long enjoyed free rein.
Those days, like the majestic days of your princes, are
over."

"Absurd."

For two centuries the de Clares of Normandy had occupied a goodly portion of south Wales, by the grace of the

English crown. Like other lords of the borderlands, Red Gilbert had ignored royal writs, had made his own laws and decisions. The Red had built or improved a string of castles extending even beyond the border at Offa's Wall to protect his demi-realm.

As a young man, fresh to his titles, he'd even taken London from Longshanks's father, and kept it two months. He'd been instrumental in forcing Henry III to adhere to the Magna Charta signed by his father in 1215. He'd fought Simon de Montfort and left the martyred Earl of Leicester dead at Evesham field.

Along the way, Gilbert de Clare married the niece of one English king and the daughter of the next.

Gilbert de Clare. Eighth Earl of Gloucester, ninth Earl of Clare, lord of Gwynllwg and Caerleon and Usk, not to mention Glamorgan. No longer young. Made to suffer an insult that would bring any man to shame, much less the richest and most powerful baron in the English realm.

"Longshanks has further abused Lord Gilbert," Cordelya said, "by ordering him to press our marriage."

"Aye."

"Poor Red Gilbert, twice cursed," she whispered in Welsh, not wanting to voice weakness to the enemy. "My heart goes out to him."

"Lady Cordelya, do not speak to me in the unfathomable language of the Celts. I find it rude."

"I beg pardon, sir." Hah!

"We have but the future. 'Tis our choice to make the worst of our situation, or the best of it. Which do you choose?"

Red Gilbert in disgrace, the best of the great princes now dead, enemies inside her keep. Hers was not a position of strength. Yet Welsh, pride died hard, and Cordelya Howel was years from death, although she did see the shadow of it.

The great age had indeed passed for Gilbert de Clare. *If . . .*

Cordelya bit down on the glorious smile that suddenly threatened to beam. If the Lord of Glamorgan approached the still waters of his own making, his losses could bring momentous opportunities for the remaining princes . . .

Sir William chucked her chin. "Enough with Lord Gilbert. Our people have waited long enough for our appearance." The knave-knight's brow beetled when she moved nary an inch. "Downstairs, Cordelya. To the great hall. Now."

"Know my heart and know it true, Sir William." Cordelya raised her chin. "I would choose to pick the bones of a sewer rat, ere I would break bread with you."

Chapter Two

Strains of Welsh harp gave the illusion of peace to the great hall. Food bearers and alewenches wove through the rows of trestle tables, serving guests and locals. It was a rather quiet group for a large collection of peasants and men-of-arms, William de Granville noticed. The quiet of hostility.

Those of Breckbryn had separated from William's men and Gilbert de Clare's to show disrespect. And in fear of the unknown. They knew ere being told, changes were hereabout.

He had expected a different reception. King Edward had sold the holding for a pittance, and had led William and his captain of arms to believe this remote fragment of the realm, where Arthur and Lancelot had come to legend, would welcome William to the tranquillity he so desperately required.

Winning the trust of these Welsh was of great import.

Winning the forgiveness of their princess was an imminent task.

On the platform holding the lord's table, William was seated betwixt his captain on the right and on his left, the fair-haired princess of the castle. Others of rank also ate at this prominent board. Lord Gilbert, forsooth, beyond Lady Cordelya. And the abbot. Ah, the fat abbot. In one breath unctuous, the next brutal, Cyfeiliog ap Rhodri had been paid off and would be sent away for the sake of harmony.

Harmony with the princess might be the most difficult task at Breckbryn.

"What a cat you are," William whispered to her, remembering the lengths it had taken to coerce Lady Cordelya to the great hall, the scratch on his cheek attesting to her feline claws.

He peeled a Spanish orange, and used thumb and two fingers to offer a section to her. " 'Tis not sewer rat, puss, yet you might find this tasty."

"My only hunger is for your blood, you beast."

"Mayhap I am beastly. But you refused to budge until I threatened to beat you soundly."

Haughty as a palace cat, vindictive as Baibars of the Mohammedans, she refused both to touch her food or to bring her blue gaze to the dark of William's. "Lay one hand on me, sir knight, and you would be wise to have your food thereafter tasted and your back covered with armor."

He chuckled. *Here, kitty, kitty.* Never would he raise a hand to her. To say as much would give an advantage. Many things he would leave unsaid.

"Quite a lovely she-cat are you. Your eyes remind me of a haughty wee flycatcher of oriental breed I once beheld. Some said she'd wandered from the camp of Kublai Khan." William sliced a wedge of Caerphilly cheese and centered it in his ladybride's trencher of laverbread. "Her eyes were blue as the cloudless sky, when the sun is at its greatest celestial sphere. Like yours.''

"I don't know of any Khan and I believe you not about blue-eyed cats.'' Lady Cordelya glared up from her untouched fare, turning that furious feline gaze toward William. "Leave me alone.'' She added in Welsh, "You scare me with your mixture of blandishments and violence.''

Better she should fear him, if she could love him not. Yet he believed her capable of love. While Lady Cordelya might not show it, might not speak it in common tongue, expressing herself in Welsh, she displayed a kitten's purr.

And she purred above a tantalizing bosom.

"Puss, we could profit from acquaintance, as I profit from your flowered scent.'' He ran his finger along her sleeve. "On your graceful form this robe is as regal as velvet.'' He eyed her barbette and snood. "Fetching, your hair not hidden by a wimple. A lovely color of pale gold tresses, yours.'' Never again would he touch a woman dark of coloring. He had done too much of thus. "Do you have Viking blood in your proud Welsh veins, puss?''

Her knee thwacked against his. "Leave me alone, else I shall scream. Loudly.''

"I am but trying to make up for our tiff in your solar.''

"Stop, or I shall stab you with this cheese knife,'' she whispered.

"Think on screaming and stabbing and poisoning, demoiselle. My men outnumber your peasants.'' William turned back to a tankard of ale.

She grumbled under her breath.

It was better, relative silence. Admiration for her appearance could wait. William hadn't enjoyed the argument that had finally gotten the Maid of Breckbryn to the great hall for the morning meal, and would have her smiling and merry, were he given a choice.

Fractious women suited him not.

He had known enough fighting, and the idea of battling the fairer sex was deplored from the western to the eastern edges of the earth. For shame, the issue of Breckbryn coming between him and his ladybride. He would have enjoyed a simple game of wooing the blue-eyed kitty.

Nevertheless, he would do as he must in the issue of princess against knight.

William eyed the Glamorganers and the force that rode under his own command. He then studied the people of this tattered princedom. Old men, women, children. Winning their fealty was more important than the good humor of their princess. Lady Cordelya, William would deal with in good time. He wished not to leech sap from weakened twigs of Welsh trees.

He rose. "Friends . . ."

Eating the sour fare of humble pie, Cordelya clenched her teeth as Sir William stood to speak to her people. If only she had the bows, arrows, and men to fight him. She did not. The young men of Breckbryn had fought to the death to prevent moments such as this, and if she argued in front of Breckbryn, her people would fight for her. To the death.

Morgan ap Mareduff and his followers must do the fighting.

Covertly, she eyed young Adam, a keeper of the gate. He could be trusted to carry word to Morgan. And she had an alternative, in case . . .

". . . 'Tis my duty to wed the Maid of Breckbryn forthwith, by decree of King Edward." Sir William paused to allow reaction.

Glynis's fingers stilled on harp strings. Breckbryners spoke heatedly, quickly, frantically amongst themselves, not liking what they heard, yea using the Welsh language to do it.

Sir William, she knew, didn't understand the slurs. He continued to smile pleasantly.

Meanwhile, Uncle Cyfeiliog behaved as if he had not a care beyond the pleasures of a full belly and a subsequent good belch.

Red Gilbert, for certes, understood. The lord of Glamorgan sat mute. Considering his situation with Longshanks, Cordelya wondered if she might yet have an ally in The Red.

"You have chosen to seat yourselves away from your guests," Sir William said to her people. "May you learn to accept me and my men as your protectors. Then as your own."

"Here, here." Red Gilbert lifted his tankard of ale, but lacked zest.

"Don't do this," she whispered to him.

Red Gilbert uttered, "Accept your destiny, lass. And you would do well to behave in your former manner."

"I find I am freshly discovering myself. Placid no longer suits me, since it gains naught." Taking liberty, she laid her hand on the baron's forearm. "Lord Gilbert, if you would be asked to swear before our Heavenly Father, you would admit this match is loathsome. Some alliances are not meant to be."

A long moment passed before he said, "True." No doubt he thought back on his ill-fated first marriage, yet he recovered mettle. "Albeit, some alliances are God's gift. We know not these things till after marriage. Once Sir William has trained you to his lance, you shall be happy." The Red sipped from his tankard, refusing to meet her eyes. "Think on it, lass. Your lord husband will rank, and you shall be free of . . ." He motioned his head toward Uncle Cyfeiliog. "That."

Her eyes rounded. Mayhap the cloud had a silver lining. If only she could be rid of her uncle!

The Red winked. "And you need never again rely on mere pillow dreams of voluptuous adventures with a Crusader."

She gasped. More fool she, to think he could be swayed. And what a silly fool she was to trust his countess with her most private secrets. *Joan and her flapping mouth.* Even a fool knew when to shut up. Thus, Cordelya said no more.

The captain of rock-gathers, Caradoc, rose on what she knew to be crippled feet. "Wales for the Welsh!"

Breckbryners, in agreement with Caradoc, roared in support. They appeared ready to upend tables in general mayhem.

Red Gilbert shot to stand, banging his fist twice for quiet. "You behave as lack-wits! Use reason for once. Accept your fate. Go forward in prosperity!"

Cordelya tugged on his arm. "My lord, for the sake of Saint Dewi, hush! You make matters worse."

The abbot-uncle selected yet another wedge of yellow cheese from a foodbearer's tray and said nonchalantly, "Sir William, you may have to send her to the dungeon."

As if that could hurt her. The dungeon was her second solar.

Sir William's captain of arms—Sir Loyce, was he?—stood. The captain wore a coat of mail. Time had silvered his hair and brows and lined his handsome face, but naught had thickened his twig-wide frame.

In a voice both effete and bold, he said, "There will be no manhandling of womenfolk, not as long as I'm captain of this garrison."

Sir Loyce's commander groaned.

"Thank you, sir," Cordelya said to the captain, appreciating chivalry, even if it did come from English. "You would make a good Welshman."

The swineman's wife, Dirce, called out, "That's tellin' 'im, milady!"

Sir Loyce said to the crowd, "We will become Welsh, and be better for it, in the end. Sir William prays peace."

"Sit down, auntie," shouted the wheelwright. "We'll not be listening to a girlie-man!"

Sir Loyce did appear somewhat effeminate.

"Aye!" Sion, guard of the battlements, surged upward with such speed he jostled those who shared the bench with him. "Be gone, English!" His voice broke in a show of his few years.

"To arms, men," shouted the toothless meadmaster, Taffy.

Breckbryners scrambled. Englishmen and those from Glamorgan reached for weapons of choice. Sir William shouted for calm.

Fear, like sparks from flint, fired Cordelya's spine. She wished not for this knave-knight as husband. She could easily sick up her empty stomach at the thought of Breckbryn falling to invaders. Something must be done, though. Until Morgan ap Maredudd could reach here, she must purchase time.

"Silence!" On quivering limbs she got to her feet. "I beg you, one and all, let us welcome our friends from Glamorgan and England. I have long been in need of a husband to help me bear the great burden of Breckbryn."

The hall went deathly quiet.

"Sir William de Granville is a fine knight of great skills and fighting prowess." Surely Longshanks would not have knighted him, were Sir William weak-limbed. For certes, he appeared strong. "And he prays peace." Somehow she managed to smile at the knave-knight whose chest puffed like a peacock she had once beheld at a Caerphilly fair.

"I would to entertain the notion of marriage between the houses of Breckbryn and Granville. I pray the Lord Gilbert's and Sir William's indulgence that I might have a fortnight to think on this match."

From the corner of her eye, she noted a flash of irritation cross the usurper-knight's face. Uncle Cyfeiliog's lips hardened. Red Gilbert spilled ale.

The odd-looking Sir Loyce scratched a shock of stubbed, near-to-white hair. "A reasonable request, her highness's"

"I should murder you in your sleep," Sir William whispered, then muttered under his breath, "Women." He popped a chunk of laverbread into his mouth, chewing it slowly. Once he'd washed the bread down with another swallow of foam-topped ale, he said, "You will not checkmate me."

She would have sworn he added, "I've had enough of that."

"We shall see, sir." She turned to The Red. "I beg you, Lord Gilbert. Return to your castle at Caerphilly. I will present myself there, a fortnight from this day, to place my hand in Sir William's." Or ride at the head of a fighting force to avenge their broken truce.

An archer from the Glamorgan retinue called out, "She'll not make good of her word. Ne'er trust a bloody Welsher's word!"

The abbot pried open a cockleshell.

"Enough!" Red Gilbert's freckles stood out. "The Princess Cordelya has asked for a fortnight, and a fortnight she shall have. She is accorded this courtesy as a lady of rank, as ruler of Breckbryn, and—it should not be forgotten!—my cousin through her late mother. To your coursers, men." He turned to Cordelya. "We shall be past your outer gate by noontide."

On a sigh of relief she sketched a curtsy of gratitude at the baron.

Red Gilbert rode over the lowered gate, along with his train, yea what he left behind? Cordelya Howel found it most irksome and galling: Sir William and the full contingent of Granville forces.

Later that day William de Granville, with Sir Loyce's assistance and Lew following along, went about recording the castle holdings. They would finish the roll by nightfall, he pledged. King Edward would have a timely report.

After being turned from the lady's solar—Lady Cordelya had chosen to sequester herself after Lord Gilbert's departure and had archly refused to hand over her ring of keys— William walked the halls, his keen eyes missing nary a drain or pigeonhole. And, thanks to his captain's talents at lockpicking, he discovered a secret or two.

He and his party descended to the bailey that lacked able-bodied peasants and crofters, and no warriors. Most of the young men had sacrificed their lives in northern Wales.

"A waste," he commented to the captain. He knew well of wastes.

Breckbryn had suffered. While the pastures beyond the curtain walls held an adequate number of sheep and the odd cow or two, the buildings within the bailey were in need of repair. William further noted the lackings in the buttery and storehouses. Mews were empty, pens for swine and fowl nearly so. Even the armory, he knew from earlier inspection, had lacked the arms of defense.

He took pride in knowing that a caravan was on its way to fill these voids. He looked forward to showing Lady Cordelya the gifts of plenty.

At the dungeon, located in the ground floor of the

D-tower, William opened the oubliette and gasped. "Captain, have someone change the rushes. This place is an abomination."

Lew thereafter relieved himself on a small cache of stones piled near the staircase to the parapet. Undoubtedly those few missiles awaited carrying up to the machicolations that overhung the curtain wall.

"I warrant the lady would have dropped rocks on our heads with abandon," William said to the knight known as Loyce. "Had she the chance."

"Leave it to a man, in this case her uncle, to find a way to stop her."

"Damned false of the abbot, locking her away. Then again, 'twas for the best. Ladies, uh, most ladies are useless in battle."

"Glad you corrected that." The captain, quill in one hand and parchment in the other, marched with a stoppered horn of ink swaying from the belt of a wafer-thin waist. "I would not trust the abbot with Lew's life, and am most pleased we shall shield our pretty princess from his designs and thieveries."

"He will be gone to Asia Minor soon enough."

"Acre would have been a fine place to send ol' Cyf."

"Captain, Jerusalem is no joking matter."

"My apologies, Will. I used bad taste."

Lew chose that moment to chase a stray pig. William, having enough to deal with already, became fed up with the bulldog's escapades. He caught the errant Lew and set him inside the kennel. "There. Now. On with the survey."

"Battlements next, Will?" asked the captain.

William had already begun the climb to the upper wall. Striding along the allude, he took a moment to gaze at the view below. The castle stood atop the highest peak in these surrounds. He knew the Irish Sea and the land of

Eire lay to the west, yet it was as if he could see to the end of the world. As far from the East as possible.

"Peaceful, be it not, Captain? May Breckbryn always stay this way."

Leave it to his captain to make the worst of it. "Since the era of the Romans, who just happen to have built the road we used for our approach, there has not been peace in this land. Too bad we did not know this when we picked Breckbryn as yours. And we thought rebellion would be limited to the north of here—hah! Well, worry not. I will fight, if it comes to it."

"I know." The captain was single-minded as a Saracen in disputes, had fought for years for William and his causes. There was no finer warrior than this.

William wandered down the walkway to eye the river that ran beneath the steep ridge to the west. "At least we won't have to concern ourselves with enemies arriving by water. The Rhymney's bedrock defies navigation."

"Not by pike or salmon. My, I savor the idea of a salmon dinner."

"Set a squad to fishing then. The lads should enjoy the task. But first make haste writing your report."

The captain set parchment on the shelf of a murder hole, then dipped a quill. A graceful hand wrote the notation with care. "There. 'Tis done."

William gazed at the whole of the castle. "Order the parapet walls well defended. Double the guards. No, triple the watch. The portcullis at either drawbridge must not be lowered or raised unless I am at the gate. I don't trust the Welsh, and most assuredly don't trust Lady Cordelya not to summon them."

"Your wish is my command." The captain's thin and silvered eyebrows drew closer over a sharp nose. "Tell me, Will. What do you think of your ladybride?"

He fell to contemplation, clicking his tongue. "Poor

Cordelya, last of the Welsh princesses. Too proud to accept it."

"The chroniclers warn of women as the embodiment of Eve. Methinks—"

"History is lies agreed upon, as you well know from the so-called romance of Crusade."

The captain carried on, as if uninterrupted. "Methinks the chroniclers know not of Cordelya Howel. Methinks she is the embodiment of your own mother."

"Be that so, Captain?" he teased.

Those graceful yet aging fingers rolled parchment. "What do you think of your ladybride, beyond pity?"

"She is naive. Knows naught beyond Breckbryn and Glamorgan, and scant of the latter. How little she knows. Pray she stays that way. I want not a worldly wife, such as my father had. I refuse to spend my life being harped on, picked at, or led by the nose hairs."

The inkhorn undulated, precursory to a flashing of green eyes that had cowed the mighty Baibars of the Mohammedans. "You'll not gentle a lady with roughness, Will."

William wished not to comfit his captain further. "Could we center on the future? Please."

The inkhorn grew steadier. The fight had not drawn the last blood, though. "You were boorish with Princess Cordelya this day. Hah! I did love it when she bested you, gaining time before the nuptials. And look at that scratch on your cheek. Well deserved, your wound. Be that as it may, I am ashamed of you. The blood of Moors and Gauls flows in your veins. Why do you not show it? You were too much spoiled by harem girls."

"Enough, Captain. Attend to your survey, and I shall attend my romantic soul."

William stomped down the allude, meaning to descend the staircase, but movement in the gatehouse's direction caught his eye. "Damn! I'll not put up with this." He hurried down the stairs. "She is to blame for this," he shouted to his captain, no more than two steps above him. "Cordelya did this!"

Chapter Three

It was done, the deed. Now Cordelya could do aught but pray her plea would reach the Black Mountains safely. By the grace of God, through a miracle of Saint Dewi, Morgan would arrive to assist her in saving Breckbryn from the encroaching Sir William.

And pray she did. Altar candles burned in the chapel. Her quivering knees pressed to cobbles, her shaking hands mashed together in supplication, she'd reached the paternoster, when . . .

"Your highness? Pardon. Sir William bids you to the lord's chamber to join with him in the enjoyment of mead. At once."

Sir Loyce's peculiar voice had made Cordelya jump, guilt having her on edge. The ring of keys at her waist jingled, yet she collected herself to say, "I am at my devotions. I will be with him later."

"Were I you, your highness, I'd save the devotion."

"He should learn I am not to be ordered about, as if I were his slavering Lew. Apart from thus, I find it quite

nervy, your master's disturbing my late father's chamber."
That the locks were picked came not as a surprise. "Tell
Sir William to get out. I shall join him in the great hall."

Cordelya turned back to prayer.

A finger tapped her shoulder. "You've got a nice little
chapel here, your highness. Should Sir William order the
less gentle of his men to escort you upstairs, 'twould be a
shame, seeing the cross desecrated or that fine alabaster
relic toppled. It is to Saint David, the one you call Dewi,
is it not?"

"For certes."

"Must be comfort, having your chapel on the same floor
as your own solar. Some of the men have never seen a
lady's chamber, much less a bathing tub. It could get ugly."

"Go away!"

"Perchance you don't know. We fought in Jerusalem.
Many of the lads were coarse to begin with, some being
criminals given the choice between goal or Crusade. The,
um, how shall I put this? The Saracen influence did not
further their manners."

Freshly from Jerusalem? Saracen influence? As always,
any mention of holy wars piqued Cordelya's interest. She
shuddered, though. Criminals were sent to the Holy Land?
Never had she heard such. Woe, she never heard enough.
Scant news of pilgrims or their progress ever reached the
gates of Breckbryn.

"Sir William rode to the white cross?" she asked.

Sir Loyce nodded. "He rode as a knight, dubbed as a
lad."

"Is he one of those criminals?"

"Of course not," the captain answered defensively.
"Although he is not without sin."

Cordelya made the sign of the cross and swept from the
chapel, the captain at her hems. "I had no idea Sir William
was a pilgrim. This shines a whole new light on him."

"Does it now?"

Up the staircase Cordelya went, climbing to the lord's chamber, but hesitating at the cracked-open door. Not since her mother's death had she entered this sanctuary.

It was as it had always been at evensong. Candles, fire-light. Princess Eleri's touches were everywhere in the large chamber, from the embroidered tapestries to the caskets that sat here and there, holding ornaments and tokens of remembrance. As in the olden days, logs burned in the hearth and bed-curtains were drawn. The chamber remained the same.

With one odious exception.

The ill-mannered clod Sir William bothered not to stand upon her entrance. Arrogant as a monarch, there he sat in Princess Eleri's chair. Curled in the larger chair, the one Howel ap Rhodri had favored, Isabelle snored with contentment.

"Where is Lew?" Cordelya asked tightly, trying to keep a civil tongue in her head.

"Banished."

"You have even gained my bitch's favor." Civility's thin thread snapped. "Is there naught end to your bids to vex me?"

His black gaze on Cordelya, Sir William sipped from one of two goblets that had been arranged on the coffer betwixt the two chairs. He shifted his lower portion, and filled one beaker from a pitcher, saying to Sir Loyce, "Wait outside, Captain."

On a bow the captain stepped back and left.

"You may sit down, Cordelya."

Affronted at his imperious attitude and invasion of sacred privacy, she said, "And where, pray tell, would I sit? On your lap, or with Isabelle?"

"I would be honored to pull another chair forward."

From the cold look on his face, she doubted much would

honor him, save for letting loose with a throttle to someone's person. What was the matter with him?

"Never you mind." She went to her dear and departed *tat's* chair, lifted the rear legs of it, and sent a traitorous bitch to the floor. "May we discuss your insolence, sir? I should like to know what you are doing in the lord's chamber, and what makes you think you have the right to be here."

"Fair enough. I do seek fairness." He got from his deceptively relaxed position and ambled to the bed. Ambled? Swaggered.

He threw back the curtains.

To yank the ear of a huddled and bound figure.

"Dewi Sant," Cordelya whispered, shaking, too poleaxed with discovery even to make the sign of the trinity. Adam!

Sir William shoved the young gatesman to the rushes.

Isabelle, in great fits of barking, now circled the trussed Adam, as if he were foreign and unwanted.

"Get away from him, you!" Cordelya screamed to Isabelle, then, rushing forward, turned her fury on the knave-knight. "Leave him alone. He is an innocent! A child."

The run from his eyes mixing with that from his nose, Adam begged, "Have mercy, milord!"

"Why should I?"

"Brute!" Cordelya scrambled to unwind ropes. "Adam, poor dear." Picking the knots free, she pulled the boy close to her breast and asked frantically, "Are you all right?"

Isabelle cocked her head, as if to wonder what the scuffle was about.

Sir William answered for the scared boy. "He suffers not. If one were to deduct wounded pride and thwarted purpose." On a craning of torso he looked toward the door. "Sir Loyce, enter," he shouted. "Take this prisoner to the dungeon."

"No!" Cordelya stepped in front of Adam, protecting him. Praying Ieuan had escaped and was on his way with word to Morgan, she compelled an even tone. " 'Tis a scary place, the dungeon, unfit for even the Eng—Do not order him there, Sir William, I beseech you."

"You should have thought of that ere you tried to send him to the prince Morgan."

"Then punish me, not this child," Cordelya argued, but already Sir Loyce and a burly soldier had maneuvered round her and were shoving Adam out the door.

Sir William dusted his hands once the prisoner was on his way. "Never send a lad to do a knight's work, Cordelya."

Her shoulders shook with anger. "Tyrant."

"Nay. I am Breckbryn's champion. Had I known you wished to invite your kinsman in the mountains to our wedding celebration, I would have sent heralds to fetch him."

What? Cordelya's mind worked. Why had Adam mentioned celebration? Well, he was a clever lad. "Do that, sir. Do fetch Morgan ap Maredudd. He should be with me during my period of reflection on the marriage. I should warn you, though. I don't look kindly upon your gaoling Adam. I am angry enough to scratch your eyes out over it."

"Meow, meow." Sir William poured a goblet of mead. "For you, my dear puss."

She knocked it from his hand. "Knave."

He filled another beaker and took a long quaff.

"Would that you choke on it, loosing your bladder on your codpiece."

"Noticed my codpiece, have you? I didn't think 'twas displayed 'neath my tunic." The breadth of his chest expanded. "Your eyes are exceedingly keen."

"Would they were as keen as your conceit."

"True." He pranced over to the curtained bed, where

poor Adam had huddled. Lying back on the pillows, nestling into the wolf-fur throw, he crossed one ankle over the
other, then balanced the goblet on his accursed codpiece.
"Come here."

"I'm not accustomed to the nuances of your voice. Do
you refer to me, or to Isabelle?"

"You."

"And if I don't?"

"Then I shall sic your Isabelle on you." He drained the
mead down his sun-toasted throat, then set the goblet away.
Whistled.

Even before someone fast of tongue could have said
"Longshanks," the obsequious corgi had gained the lord's
bed and was in Sir William's thickly sinewed arms.

Isabelle, one eye closing, lolled her tongue when Sir
William's fingers ruffed brown-and-white fur and dug into
the sweet spot on her neck. "Urf."

A devilish grin formed on knightly lips that were neither
too thick nor too thin. "I would have you this lovable."

"That faithless bitch deserves to be filled with Lew's
pups. May she whelp a dozen. Two dozen."

"Lew would be most agreeable, I am sure."

"You would be. You have certainly made yourselves at
home. I do not appreciate your interloping, Sir William."

"Call me William. Or Will. I prefer William."

"I'll call you naught. Give me my Isabelle." Cordelya
huffed over the rushes, her course set for the corgi.

The bitch raised hackles, bared her fangs, growling.

"You hush. Remember where your loyalties lie." Cordelya grabbed for Isabelle.

Within the split of a second and a swirl of her veil, Sir
William had Cordelya toppled to the bed, his warm, hard
body above hers and pressed to it.

Isabelle howled from next to them, her mistress's barbette now covering her head. Cordelya's hair had tumbled free. And her attacker wound a handful around his wrist.

"Lovely," he commented.

"Get off me, knave-knight." She shoved futilely at his armor-hard chest. "You insult my person and virtue, and disturb my peace and my bitch's."

"Insults to your virtue are moot, puss-bride." He then buried both hands in her unbound locks, near her scalp. "As for Isabelle, she may have to be sent to the kennels to join Lew, if she cannot be disturbed."

"You've a quick solution to everything, do you not?"

"Aye."

One of his hands cruised over Cordelya's bosom, moved downward to count her ribs, his thumb wedging into the pit of her arm as he clasped her shoulder. His lips pressed to hers. The whole of him pressed closely, hotly.

He tasted of honey from the mead. He smelled fresh, as if he'd aired in sunshine. *I am as bad as Isabelle, delighting in his qualities.* He then whispered her name against her ear, once he had finished with a kiss that went from deliciously gentle, almost reverent, to torrid.

"How can you be gentle?" she asked as he rolled to the side, bringing her with him.

"Would you prefer I not?"

"Oh, I complain not—you simply surprise me. One moment you're a churlish knave, sending a poor child to the dungeon—"

"Worry not for Adam. I called for the rushes changed, and Sir Loyce has ordered a hot meal. Woe, no sewer rat. If Adam were afforded a bedtime story of brave Welsh princes or demoiselles in distress, forsooth he would sleep like a babe in arms. Now . . . what is the rest of your complaint?"

Distrusting such claims, she went on. "You tossed me

to this bed, yet the next moment you were kissing me as if I were holy, then most unholy. You are baffling, sir.''

It was then she remembered that he was a knight of the white cross, which would explain a good bit. Adam might not be in such pathetic fettle after all.

Sir William traced his thumb along her lower lip. ''A wise person told me I would win you with kindness.''

''I thought the issue of winning my sympathies was secondary to securing your hold on Breckbryn.''

''There is that. This castle may not be as fine nor as new as Lord Gilbert's at Caerphilly. Few are. Yours is splendid.''

She was taken aback at the compliment.

Warm lips kissed her shoulder. ''You are splendid.''

''I would that my castle knows its former riches,'' she admitted, weakened by the feminine passions that defied reason.

''How was it, when all was fair at Breckbryn?''

Oddly, she would rather know his kisses than to break the spell with remembrance. She must stop behaving as Isabelle. '' 'Twas a simple yet sublime life, ere the youthful men went north to join Welsh resistance. Our children picked chunks of coal from cleaves in the *mynydd*. In the mountain,'' she translated. ''The men toiled at fishing or the grazing of livestock. The women tended fields, or hives for making mead, or—women do as women have always done.'' Cordelya sighed. ''Some matters never change in Wales.''

''You find it irksome, womanly duties? Does the tending of men or babies while making sweet music from your throat or harp interest you not?''

''Playing the harp is not one of my talents.''

He smiled; it was a look that must have won a few hearts between England and Jerusalem, and back. Isabelle enjoyed it. Barbette still tilted atop her head of long nose, she hopped on his hip to perch and pant.

He said, "I am eight and twenty, not a young man."

Eight years Cordelya's senior.

"I am battle-worn, too," he added. "I would enjoy evenings filled with . . ." He reached to pet Isabelle as if to show emphasis. "Fine little bitches."

"Then scour market towns for litters of corgis."

" 'Tis time for me to beget sweet-natured daughters and excellent sons. Will take a ladywife for that. I long to be kept well fed, well lodged, well warmed, and well bedded."

What part am I to enjoy? "You seek meek obedience. Now that I have tasted free tongue, I enjoy not holding it. You and I would never suit. Surely there are many heiresses of amenable nature who would appreciate the talents of your broadsword. Find one. Elsewhere."

"King Edward made my choice. You are it."

Where were the miracles of Saint Dewi? Why did she never know a simple bit of mercy?

Sir William tickled her earlobe. "I wonder if your venerated King Hywel Good considered tart tongues when he was writing laws to free his womenfolk from arranged marriages. A king should think through his decisions."

"So should a knight. I could make you quite unhappy."

"We shall see. But I warn you. I have beheld the pit of hell in Saracen eyes. Would take much to top that."

Saracens. As always, a rush of interest bulged her marrow. She yearned to know everything about Crusades and Crusaders. What would be wrong with indulging herself?

Ieuan was on his way. The keep had retired for the night. But Adam—she could do no more at the moment to save him from what she had suffered many times; 'twould not kill him, even at its worst, although the dungeon carried no recommendations. She needed this one evening to cure curiosity.

Furthermore, 'twas to all's favor, making peace with the usurper.

First, though ... "Get down, Isabelle," Cordelya demanded to the yet-hovering corgi, gaining nary a response.

"Down."

At last the faithless bitch complied, to Sir William's order alone.

The air suddenly freshened.

Cordelya wiggled. Thus brought her into the tuck of his arms. Yet she moved not, allowing her senses to chart how it felt to be held next to a knightly form. 'Twas not an altogether unpleasant feeling. A knight, English yet a pilgrim. Maychance he was not beyond hope. Most assuredly, God favored him.

Snuggling her cheek against his wide shoulder, she looked into his eyes, eyes lit by candles, fanning flames in her spirit. "Sir, about your crusade ... What was it like in Jerusalem?"

"Hot."

"I don't mean the climate," she said, noting a tensing of his thews. "What was it like, crossing swords with Saracens?"

"What makes you ask?"

"I dream of arriving in the Holy Land, armored myself, scaling walls to wield a sword in the name of Christ the Lord."

He exhaled and patted her arm. "I had such dreams myself."

"You acted on yours. Woe be it, princesses, ladies, and womenfolk are kept from Crusade. The most I can hope for are pilgrimages to St. David's Church, or to the well of his sainted mother, Non. Two pilgrimages equal one to Rome, my *mam* said. Yea, there is no pilgrimage to equal the one to Jerusalem."

"Many have died to that aim."

"To die in the Holy Land is my most cherished dream."

She closed her eyes, her admissions flowing swiftly, like holy knights felling one Saracen after another. "I pillow-dream. I imagine marriage to a Welsh pilgrim, a prince. This blessed campaigner would hold me in his arms, tantalizing me with tales of Christian zeal." If only Sir William were Welsh ... Still, he had proved himself pious and righteous, and had paved his way to heaven by seeking Christ's Sepulchre. "Even now, sharing such communion with you, my bones heat with passionate cravings. 'Tis the holiest of holy, to gain Christ the Lord's tomb and pray over it. To die for thus would be an honor."

"More with the passionate cravings, puss. I fancy such."

"I should imagine my voluptuous cravings will be quite strong, once my prince comes along."

"Interesting. Do go on with your oratory, but ..." Sir William swallowed, his brow furrowing. "Let us put your romanticism to rest. Your Welsh princes are given not to Crusade. Nor are your villeins."

"Freemen. We have no villeins in free Wales. King Hywel's laws forbid slavery. Yea I won't argue Welsh lack of interest in Crusades. Our men must fight to keep our lands."

Cordelya fiddled with the material of the knight's tunic, noticing a jagged scar beneath his collarbone. "Were you injured in Jerusalem?"

Silence fell for long moments ere he answered. "I was much wounded in Jerusalem, but I took this scar as a lad."

"I would truly love to hear your Jerusalem adventures."

He ran his palm over the rise of her derrière. "The night of our wedding, you will have your answers."

"That is extortion."

"Aye."

"I refuse to become prey to it. Could you not, as a gallant knight"—she lifted a finger and thumb to indicate a small amount—"tell me just a little bit?"

"Nay. 'Twill be your wedding gift."

Suddenly she yearned for marriage, a concept she quickly put away. "Do you forget? I have a fortnight to decide."

"You seek to decide nothing, puss." He studied a lock of her hair. "You stall for time, so you can send for your wild-haired cousin in the mountains."

"Speaking of that, about Adam . . . Set him free, sir."

"Please set him free, *William.*"

Humble pie began to taste familiar. She said, "Please set him free, William."

"Well done. Let us take a moonlit stroll to the dungeon tower. Come, puss. Your boy awaits freedom."

Cordelya sat upright and brushed the sleeves of her underrobe. Wise, motherly advice from the past whispered for her to leave well enough alone. Like Uncle Cyfeiliog, though, Cordelya was loath to let go. "How do you know Adam won't try again to go for Morgan?"

"I do not, do I?"

Sir William swung his feet to the rushes. When she flicked her hair over a shoulder and clasped her barbette to set her coif to rights, he said, "You do not need that this night. We shall walk with your hair free. We shall walk and talk. Be warned, though, puss. I know you better than you think I do."

"You would wish."

He ran a fingernail along his strong jaw, a smirk filling his features. "Shall we first have a look at the false door in the chapel?"

The escape tunnel. Discovered. Cordelya shuddered, desperation and panic setting in, the walls of her impregnable castle closing about her.

Sir William loomed over her. "To the chapel, Cordelya. You have much explaining ahead."

"Wherever do you mean?" she feinted.

"You know what you have done. You've been found out. And you, my dear puss, have played into a trap. For your boy Adam, for the matter of the chapel—"

"If you have—if you've disturbed Ieuan, I will kill you," she shouted in a blind fury.

Sir William's face was a stony mask. "So it's 'Ieuan,' is it? How quaint. Would you care to watch as I drop Ieuan's contents from a machicolation?"

"You beast! Vicious, bloodthirsty, land-stealing churl! You are the devil's own. I *will* kill you."

Sir William rose on the toes of his boots, bouncing once and cramming fists against his waist. "Just try it."

From the coffer where he had abandoned the goblet, she grabbed the beaker and arced her arm. Swung hard. The goblet hit its mark. His temple. The big knight folded.

She covered her mouth in horror, gawking at the huddled heap. The flesh at his temple hadn't been broken. Why didn't he move? Why didn't he *breathe*?

Cordelya lurched forward to feel Sir William's pulse. There was aught. To give him air, she tugged his legs and arms, stretching him out. Blew in his face. Tapped his wrist. He was dead!

"God in heaven help me," she wailed, praying to the saints, and especially Dewi and Non. "I have killed King Edward's knight." The implications were many. The worst? "I have slain God's pilgrim."

Chapter Four

"You've killed my son!"

"Your son?" Cordelya asked, bemused. "You are his father?"

"Be gone with you, evil chit!" There in the lord's chamber, Sir Loyce stood in front of Sir William's remains, guarding it with words and threats. Behind the captain, Isabelle tried to lick life into the departed's face. "Hide yourself, princess," Cordelya was warned, "lest I hoist you upon a trebuchet and send you sailing to your own death."

Cordelya was half a head taller and a great many years younger than the wiry captain, yea she feared not this returned Crusader. She had killed one of God's pilgrims. Her soul could burn no hotter in hell if she killed another.

A shard of realization went through her. To be as callous as an infidel was not her way. She used reason. "We have no trebuchets at Breckbryn, Sir Loyce, as surely you know. Unlike you English, we search not for war."

"I'm not English. I am of Angoulême, but that is not

important. You killed my son. And I will have an eye for an eye."

"Angoulême, England. Little difference. I have killed your son, but as lady of this keep I am responsible for arrangements for Christian burial. Fetch my uncle and a quartet of his monks. We must move the body to the abbey."

"You fetch your uncle. I will tend my . . . my youngest, my dearest son."

It was then that the hard armor of Sir Loyce's face went soft and tears sprang. Facial lines deepened. The captain threw himself upon Sir William's body, and fell to mournful wails.

Isabelle stiffened her neck to howl.

And Cordelya felt a tear spill. She didn't want to care about invaders. If only Sir William hadn't been so fierce, so threatening. If only his captain weren't so overwrought. If only Cordelya could undo her sin. "I am sorry, Sir Loyce. I will answer to the Almighty, but I pray your forgiveness, too."

As if the captain hadn't heard her, he beat a fist upon Sir William's chest. Over and over again. "It shouldn't have happened like this! Not now, not here. Not after all he suffered. Will, my Will!"

"Mother, please. Stop. You're killing me. And do not air my dirty linen."

What?

Was Cordelya witnessing a resurrection of the dead? She gawked at the now-grinning face of the knave-knight, then pressed her palms together. "Thank you, Lord God. Praise be to Jesú. Bless you, Holy Mother. Thank you, Dewi Sant, for this miracle."

Wait a moment. Mother? What had Sir William meant by *Mother*?

Accompanied by a fit of hysterical laughter, Cordelya untangled the web. "You are his mother!"

Holding her sides, she stumbled from the lord's chamber. She barely noted Isabelle reaffirming her loyalty by trotting at her hems. Somewhere in the stew of her head Cordelya knew she must set Ieuan and Adam free, must rally her people to strike while William was weak.

Isabelle flashed by, her loyalties with the invaders, running for the kennel and Lew.

Cordelya passed an English guard posted at the doorway from the keep. "Can you imagine that? He took his mother on Crusade!"

"Everyone will know. Your men may revolt. Oh, Will! I should take a switch to your ankles for playing dead."

Feigning death was an element William had learned during his two-year escape to the Ilkhanids on the Euphrates. Mohammedans, he'd come to learn, had spawned the great mind of Omar Khayyam and others of equal genius. William had learned too much.

Of himself, he knew he must perform many good deeds before Judgment Day.

Would that he could disregard the pain from Cordelya's having crowned him with a goblet.

And that he might keep his most shameful secret from her.

Said he, "I took full enjoyment from Delya's ministrations, ere . . . Well, captain, let us not pick the nits from our actions. We are both to blame."

The captain, known in France as Dame Lois de Granville, ran a hand down her face. "All these many years you have kept my cover. Even our cousins Henry and Ned humored me. If we are found out, 'twill bring ridicule on Ned's crown."

Henry. A year ago this month, the King of Cyprus and Jerusalem's crown had been knocked from his young head, moments ere a Mamluke had sliced Henry's head from his neck.

William's own head reeled. His gizzard roiled. How could he ever tell innocent, naive Cordelya such tales? She must never know the truth about jihad.

"Ned will be furious," Sir Loyce yammered, bringing William back to the situation at hand.

"King Edward seeks a quiet outpost to provide taxes and vassals. He wants sweat, not souls. I assure you, *maman*, titters and mockery will not phase King Edward."

"But I let you down . . . and in front of that contemptible, vengeful princess. She of this paltry place. Princess—bah! She's not worthy of the title. I cannot believe I was foolish enough to speak with Cousin Ned about her."

"Captain, stop pacing and quiet yourself. We have gotten out of worse spots than this. And don't curse the lady who will become your daughter by law. It pains me much worse than my aching head."

"As we speak she no doubt incites mayhem below."

"There you go, worrying unduly. Guards are in place, in every important post. The worst damage she could do would be to tattle on you. We may lose some men—so what?" William picked rush stems from his clothes and struggled to feet that seemed to sink in quicksand.

"The princess has a mighty arm. I would wager she could flail a mace with the best of them." He grinned, despite the pain at his temple and the threat of upsurge from his gizzard. "Mayhap the two of you could form a dread army of women. You are a fine-matched pair."

A smirk of pride lifted those wrinkled lips. *"C'est possible."*

"Take yourself away, Captain. Find the princess. Do what you must to smooth the hackles of her fur. I fear I am not up to the . . . up to the taahhhskkk . . ."

The lord's chamber blackening, images of Cordelya wavering in and out of his mind's eye, William fainted.

A rat jumped from a perch and skittered over the rushes, just as the first rays of dawn bled through wall-slits of the dungeon. The light, scant though it was, and the squeak of that rodent awakened Cordelya.

She tossed aside the cover that had been provided by her gaolers and got from her pallet. On the other side of the dungeon, she saw Adam still sleeping. Three nights ago, when her keys had been yanked from her waist by a guardsman and her person had been tossed in the cell, she had found the lad eating a bowl of rabbit stew, a tankard of ale beside him.

The rushes indeed had been changed, had been sprinkled with mint and thyme. Such had not tempted the rat, for Cordelya knew the beastie well. The meantime collection of food leavings had piqued his small nostrils.

With wee canny eyes, a high-pitched squeak, and twitching whiskers, the rat stared at her.

"You are Satan's night creatures, your kind carrying plague," Cordelya said. "Yet I find you oddly intriguing. I pray you find no reason to leave." Everyone knew that when the last rat left a dwelling, it would collapse.

Breckbryn must not collapse.

And she took a modicum of delight. Nowhere to be found within this gaol was Ieuan. He had escaped, a thrice of lovely days ago. Had it been a ruse, Sir William's claim?

Apparently so.

William. Half from Angoulême. What other secrets did he harbor?

The scrape of metal against metal from the doorway drew her attention.

Sir Loyce—or whatever the woman had been christened,

if the woman had ever been christened—entered the confines. Her manly voice in place, she said, "I bring food to break your fast."

Cordelya decided not to disabuse the captain of her assumption of a Welsh lady eating at dawn. By now she had decided to stop shunning the captain's attempts at conciliation. There had been two yesterday, three the day ere, as well as one the night of Sir William's comeuppance.

Why Cordelya's change in attitude?

Yesterday—*think not on that.*

Last eventide, when vesper bells had tolled from Breckbryn Abbey and Adam had savored the last bites of supper bread, she had accepted her plight. Until Morgan's arrival she must be patient. "Do come in, Captain."

"Wot?" The lad sat up to scratch his head and rub his eyes. "Who be here?"

"We have a guest, Adam."

"You may take your leave," the captain said to Adam. She held a tray in hand. "I grant your pardon."

"Wot's going on? I'm t' leave afore having some o' those eggs and *caws?*" He smiled at the captain. "I am hungered for eggs and cheese, sire."

First Isabelle, now the gatekeeper. What was Breckbryn coming to? "Just leave, Adam."

He left, the bar to the door falling into place after him.

William's mother set the tray down. "I've been told your uncle as locked you in the dungeon many times."

" 'Tis a good way to keep me silent."

"You should have slit his throat. No woman should countenance brutality. But what were your choices? You've been a prisoner in your own castle far too long."

Strange words from a gaoler. Much too concerned about the knave-knight, Cordelya wished not for a debate on gaols or gaolers. "Why has Sir William not been here?"

"Hungry?" asked the captain on winged brow.

"Actually, nay. Sir Loyce . . . I shan't call you that. What is your name?"

"Sir Loyce, or simply Loyce, will do. For near to twenty years I've been known as that. I answer to it readily."

"As you wish . . . Sir Loyce. 'Tis time for reason. As women, surely we can haggle peace."

The captain set the tray down, taking a peeled egg within her hand to juggle it once. Fingers closed around the sphere. "Catch."

On instinct, Cordelya's arms extended and she caught the egg.

"My Will," the captain said, "is the chick of my egg, if that is a proper comparison and I cannot see why not. You have boiled him whole."

"I beg your pardon?"

"My son lies dying."

The pain in the woman's eyes was real enough, although . . . "Another of his hoaxes, perchance?"

"I think not. Your blow struck his head. Many times death follows a blow such as his. He fainted after you bid your leave. He is yet unaware."

Cordelya blanched. "Pray the Lord God and our own Dewi, may Sir William survive."

She wished his life for a number of reasons. As a Christian. As a curious wretch who yearned to gain knowledge from his experiences. As a woman who, before he retaliated, had enjoyed their communion. Mostly he must live so that his men would have no reason to avenge his death.

"We cannot allow him to die, Sir Loyce. Let me help save him. Yea, I am not learned in the skills of a leech. My mother—she died some years ere, you see—healed the sick and wounded of Breckbryn. But I took note of her remedies. A red curtain for the sickbed. A poultice of fresh, fat puppy skins applied to bruises. An elixir of fish-liver oil."

"Red curtains? Puppy poultices? What offal. The liver oil might have properties . . ." The gaunt planes of Sir Loyce's face tightened in agony, and she crossed her arms to dig fingers into the meager meat of her arms. "I have called up everything I learned in the land of the sultans to save Will. Naught worked."

"What would it hurt to try the curtain or the—"

"We must plan for his passing. We must ease his mind so he can pass to Our Lord in peace, if Our Lord will take him. Go to him, Princess. Caress his hand and brow. Say kind words to Will. He would appreciate a nicety."

Was this some sort of trickery? "You said he is unaware. My words would be wasted."

"A wise prophet—a physician of broad mind and wisdom—made a study of the dying. He believes our thoughts stay with us, even when others believe we are not cognizant. He says the mind is the last to pass away." A pause. "Whether 'tis true, I am not smart enough to know."

"Where did you meet this prophet?"

"While fighting my way across the Judean Desert. No fight has pained me as much as the one I now face." Sir Loyce dabbed a finger beneath a weeping eye. "I beg you, your highness. Say a few words over my baby."

"What should I say?"

"Speak from your heart, not from your regal head."

Hoping she was up to the task of tenderness, knowing she must for his sake as well as Breckbryn's, Cordelya nodded. "I shall go to William."

William could neither move nor speak. He knew that his brain had bled. It had taken a mighty effort on his part to tap the cosmos for the power to cauterize his wound. He would live; he knew this well. Now his sapped body had to catch up with the healing.

"William?"

Cordelya. She'd called him William. Not sir, not churl, not knave-knight. Not devil's own. William. *I like that.*

"Please do not die."

I thought my death would please you.

"Who'll tell me stories of Crusades, if you go away?" The mattress dipped as she sat beside him, her sweet bouquet wafting. "I suppose I could ask Sir Loyce, but 'twouldn't be the same. I have no interest in lying in her arms to learn the secrets of the Templars."

You will never know my secrets.

Forget Crusades, Cordelya. They are at end.

"Your arms are quite nice. So strong. As are your dark, dangerous features. You intrigue me, William. I regret hitting you. Truly. But I thought you had captured Ieuan."

Ieuan again. Strange tag for a casket of treasure. Poor Cordelya. Yours is a paltry cache, not enough to trade for half-sober soldiers to pull the weight of a used trebuchet. Be my kitten, puss, and I shall fill your coffers with whatever you like, whatever you need.

"Ieuan has surely reached Prince Morgan by now."

Ieuan? Ah, so Ieuan is a man. Hmm. Wish I had known that.

"When you die, your men will be incensed to withstand Morgan's attack. They are well-prepared for siege. Yesterday, I heard a fierce racket. On my way here I saw the source of it. Many canvas-covered carts arrived. So many, so much. You have laid in a fine battle larder."

I bring you fineries and food.

William heard a sigh of surrender, then she said, "Pity, you won't be at the helm of your command. What delight you would take at besting the Welsh."

Nay, puss. The killing of man does not please me.

She touched his hand, squeezing it. "If only brutality did not fit you as if it were a fine coat of mail. If only you'd arrived saying, 'Cordelya, I am foreign but I have no wish to fight you and yours. I will harm nary a Welsh head.'"

I never intended to raise Welsh heads on pikestaffs.

"If only you weren't King Edward's own, we might have had a happy marriage, such as my parents knew."

If only I could speak.

"I . . . well, 'tis neither here nor there. I refuse to watch my people, or Morgan's, die. I must stop Morgan ap Maredudd." The mattress moved as she stood. "Good-bye, sir."

Dare not leave me, Delya!

Lips touched his. Sweet lips. Soft, feminine. Precious. Oh, that he could put his arms around her, that he could return the kiss and deepen it. That he could be as tender a lover as she wished. Or as wild.

Kiss me deeper. Please!

One part of him showed definite signs of life. His faithful warhorse of lust reared his head.

She took her lips away, aggrieving William at the loss. "May the gates be as pearly as we are taught to believe," she whispered. "Rest in peace."

On a swish of robes Cordelya made her exit.

Damn!

Chapter Five

"How many lives do you have?"

"Now, puss, I meant not to raise your hackles by refusing to die, much less by charging to your rescue."

"Rescue is not what I need," Cordelya tossed back, strangely relieved to see William in this wane of afternoon. My, what a sight for the eyes. Her mouth watered at it.

Nose guard shoved high on the conical helmet to show his smug grin, William wore a suit of mail. His white surcoat had been embroidered to herald the symbol of Wales. The dragon.

He pulled off one gauntlet, hooking the glove to a destrier's saddle. "Brave of you, shinnying down the curtain wall on a rope of linens in the dark of night. Not simply one wall, but both of Breckbryn's."

"I had no other choice. The escape tunnel was guarded, the only way out being over the walls at midnight. By no means could I have taken a palfrey to carry me away. I journeyed afoot."

"I stand in awe."

"You stand arrogant, as always."

Actually, he did not stand at all. Astride a sturdy and broad Andalusian destrier fitted with gold-decorated trapper, Sir William dominated this cluster of trees and gorse in the foot of a hill located northeast of the village Senghenydd, where Cordelya had made camp for the night.

"You do justice to the garb of a peasant," the knave-knight mentioned, perusing the simple clothes the mead-master's daughter had loaned her.

"Cease with your leering."

"Is yours any way to greet your champion?" A rare white dove flew down to perch upon his shoulder.

"You will not be my knight-husband, unless you were to concede many points. I cannot see you in a mode of concession."

"Delya, Delya, Delya—"

"Do not shorten my name. It offends me."

The dove flew away.

"You would rather I call you 'puss?'" William taunted.

"I would prefer you called me naught."

"Fair enough, Naught."

"Oh, for the sake of Saint Dewi! Call me as you wish. I care not."

"I prefer puss. Or Delya." William alit the courser. The rowels of his spurs pinged as he walked toward her. "I am famished. Have you anything to eat?"

"Little. And what I have, I would not share."

Fruitlessly and for four days, she had searched on foot for her Welsh kinsmen, hearing stories that Morgan had gone this way or that, all of which having indicated he left the Black Mountains weeks earlier, on a course to the south.

Ieuan, she had learned, had been taken captive by the Marcher lord of Brecon, Humphrey de Bohun.

Frustrating.

Such a dilemma she had been in. Not knowing whether to return to Breckbryn Castle to face a murder charge, or to run fast for Caerphilly to throw herself on Lord Gilbert's mercy, she had chosen The Red. Had she not been interrupted, she would have reached his castle on the morrow.

At least she wouldn't face a charge of murder. *I am glad you didn't die,* she thought while eyeing William.

She had no wish to escape him. Good or evil, he was her destiny, she realized. Somehow she had to work with what God, and King Edward, had given her.

"I have but half of a roasted pigeon that a goodwife spared me," Cordelya announced. "You may have it."

"Nay, thank you. I would not take from your mouth."

"Yea from my purse, you thought not twice." Upon gathering her supplies for the journey, she'd noticed her horde tampered with. Tampered with? Confiscated. "You thought Ieuan was my casket of silver and pennies, did you not?"

"Aye."

"I want it returned."

"The coffer awaits you in the lord's chamber at Breckbryn."

Cordelya, trampling upon wild garlic, went to lean against the trunk of an oak. "How do I know I can trust you? You have not earned my trust as yet. Yea though I am willing to give you a chance."

"Give me a chance? Delya, step down from the high horse of your opinion. I am the lord of our household. I will give the orders. And it should be pointed out, you have done naught to earn *my* trust."

"Well, 'tis plain we do not suit."

"Is that so?" He approached her, his finger trailing up her raised chin. "At my bedside you said if I would swear never to bring harm on the Welsh, we could match."

"You heard what I said?" She slapped his hand away.

"Naturally."

"Oooh. You vex me. How many forms of trickery do you have in your cache?"

"A few. You vex me as well, Cordelya. While I have to admire your fighting spirit, for it reminds me of my mother's, and she is to be admired, I find your quarrelsomeness utterly tiresome."

"I am what I am."

"What you need, puss, is gentling to the bit."

"Cats are not harnessed."

"A fact that troubles me. After careful consideration, I have decided . . . well, we shall discuss my decision later. For now, worry not over my gizzard or yours. I bring food."

Devil's own—he had to know she'd been without much, save for the pigeon, since her flight.

William stuck thumb and forefinger between his front teeth, turned halfway away on a squeak of chain, and whistled. Lowering his arm, he said, "Welcome my companions."

Twigs snapped as two mounted figures emerged from the woods of oak and ash, with a thrice of well-loaded-down squires to their rear. Uncle Cyfeiliog rode his usual mount, a gelding. And that had to be Sir Loyce astride the palfrey of white.

Lew, his stocky shoulders holding a form-fitted cloak of steel, rode before Sir Loyce's breastplate. The bulldog licked his chops, shook his large head, and—Cordelya would have sworn—grinned.

"Woof!"

Flying as if he were some oversized bird, Lew shot through the air, landing on Cordelya's chest. Sending her to a nest of wild garlic.

His claws jabbed her chest and thighs. A cropped tail shook his hindquarters, literally. Limpid eyes gazed happily into her astonishment. He snorted through his wrinkled muzzle, spraying, at the same moment his long tongue snaked out to graze the underside of her chin. "Woof."

She couldn't help but laugh. "Someone is happy to see me."

"Count me amongst your admirers, Delya. I would do as Lew, if I thought you would allow me."

Uncle Cyfeiliog made the sign of the cross. "Conduct yourself with dignity, niece."

The other armored figure threw visor back, indeed showing the face of Sir Loyce. "Godspeed, Princess."

"And to you, sir." Stroking Lew's neck and trying to quiet his zeal, she looked up at the knight who most held her interest. "I should hope if you welcomed me as your dog does, you would not spray me with your enthusiasm."

Uncle Cyfeiliog's mouth dropped, then tightened. Yea, William and his captain laughed. The squires chuckled too.

The knave-knight said, "I cannot warrant my actions. I am most enthusiastic to find you unharmed. And I do believe you might end up being sprayed with something of mine."

Cordelya blushed.

William set Lew aside to offer a hand. "Shall we break bread together, puss?"

The devil forced her to say, "Is the fare roast of rodent?"

"Never give up, do you?" Armored legs planted wide, arms raised to the heavens, William went from buoyant to hamstrung. "I am weary. I have suffered. I have been forced from my deathbed to charge after a demoiselle. As yet my bones ache with weakness, and my captain has poured horns and horns of revolting fish-liver oil down my gizzard. A quarter of my men have deserted my service, after learning my captain binds her breasts. Why can I find no peace?"

Cordelya knew that some had deserted. She had witnessed their flight. Men were men, no matter their race or rank; they viewed women as unfit for warring or decision-making, and would desert rather than accept. No wonder Sir Loyce had thrown off the mantle and bound her breasts.

To her son's favor, he had accepted his mother as captain, and that should be remembered. 'Twas something to admire in Sir William de Granville. Beyond hope, he was not.

Cordelya grinned, considering the possibilities.

One hand still raised to the heavens, William beat a fist against the surcoat that covered his chain-protected chest. "Why does Cordelya never *give up!*"

She could neither give up, nor give in to the challenges of womanhood.

From the nursery Lois de Granville, born of the ruling class, had been trained to make a fortuitous marriage and to become a proper ladymother. Her temperament had not been favored by princely houses, though. She refused to become the bride of Christ. After much searching, a match was found for the prickliest from a family of beauties.

At the age of twelve she was brought to the domed cathedral of St. Peter in the walled city of Angoulême, and led to the altar to meet a husband not as highborn as her parents would have chosen. But the heir to the *seigneur* of the Normandy seaport city of Granville had professed not to mind her spirit or lack of feminine graces. She did, after all, bring a large coffer to enrich the Granville holdings.

As was common in marriages of children, two years went by ere Curtice de Granville, little more than a child himself, had installed her in Granville and claimed husbandly rights. She had enjoyed the husbandly rights, for Curtice carried Moorish heat and Gallic romance in his veins.

More's the pity, though. Not long after reaching Granville, he demanded she even her temper. She tried. But grew weary of saying, *"Oui, mari.* No, husband." Thus, she quit saying it. Had spoken her mind. Which had displeased Curtice. Having by then gained the *seigneurie* from his dyspeptic old goat of a father, Curtice had tried to rule as if by divine right.

Too often the *comtesse* had chided her less-noble lord, saying, "And who, sir, died and left you *roi?"*

Still, they had reared three fine sons, William being the last born. During which the countess had carried forth with the duties of châtelaine, and seeing to the making of gold. She had earned the ransom of a hundred kings, from shipping, from trading, from being more clever than men.

Then Curtice had fallen to wasting disease.

Even now, a score of years after his death, Sir Loyce grieved for her *roi du coeur.*

She longed to give Curtice another instruction or two, for the sake of olden times, then end up abed with him . . . for the best part of the times.

If truth were known, though, Dame Lois de Granville enjoyed the benefits of answering to no one, save for herself and king, and the joys of manly guise and title. Perchance it had been folly, her decision a year into her widowhood to sail with her landless son, then of nine years, to visit her cousin's palace on Cyprus. She sailed with the intent of journeying on, to the church of the Holy Sepulchre.

What would have unfolded for her and William, had she not?

Best to disregard what might have been.

She regarded the moment. Sun dying over a Welsh mountain to the west, Sir Loyce, eschewing help from the pink-cheeked squires, attended her palfrey. She hauled the saddle to a spot outside William's tent of Saracen design—Sir Loyce herself had sent the striped canvas tent from the Holy Land before the fall to al-Ashraf Khalil's Mamlukes. Another issue not to think on.

"Madam, why do you do the work of men?" the abbot asked her, sidling up. "You should know your place."

Cyfeiliog, who had learned the truth about the captain's gender, eyed her with unseemly interest. The abbot did not wear well with Sir Loyce.

A shame, having to bring him along. But there had been no recourse. He was the stoutest at Breckbryn and could ride, knew the hills and dales of the area, and had insisted. The ill wind also blew good, though. The nearer to have done with him.

"You have crumbs on your frock." She went round him, rather than acknowledge those small, ratlike eyes. "Squires, fetch water for the mounts."

Returned to the palfrey's caparison, she folded the trapping and gave a look at her son. He and the princess sat stools of campaign, eating from horns of plenty. William was frowning.

Lew, Sir Loyce noted, had roosted on haunches before Lady Cordelya, his forepaws waving to beg a bite. The princess dropped a hunk of bread. The bulldog caught it with the swiftness of an eastern cat after a fly.

"Such a fine lad you are," Cordelya complimented, patting Lew's head. "You must be fed well. I will see to it."

A few days earlier Sir Loyce had been furious enough to kill the young princess, but she had forgiveness in her heart and would see her son happily wed. Albeit, Sir Loyce saw history repeating itself. *May they never argue sans a good making-up.*

"You left Breckbryn," William said to Cordelya, "ere you could inspect your newly supplied larders."

She turned her pretty eyes to him, thick lashes batting. "And that means?"

"Means you should be thrashed for half-killing your lord, then for leaving him dead!" Cyf's beringed forefinger shook at his niece.

"Leave her alone," William shouted, echoing his captain's sentiments. "Go elsewhere, abbot."

"Help me with these trappings," Sir Loyce ordered the abbot.

"I am not your serving boy, madam." Cyf's belly shook, at last disturbing the breadcrumbs that were shelved upon it.

"Fine. Come over here, and let's share a wineskin, and you may entertain me with tales of your piety."

That, naturally, interested the abbot.

She heard the princess say, "Pardon. I long for a walk."

"I will join you." They set off for the woods, William's voice drifting to camp as he said, "We have much to discuss."

"Go with them, madam," the abbot demanded. "Anything could happen. It's unseemly. The marriage contract is not yet valid."

"Your hypocrisy amazes me, Cyf. I've heard tales. You are a satyr. And I know you're greedy and cruel." Sir Loyce went about the tidying up. "I should have locked you in the dungeon to give you a taste of your own meanness."

"Locked me away? Would you like that, madam? Would you have enjoyed locking me in irons with your own hands?" Cyfeiliog hovered too close to the captain. "You need a man to make a true woman out of you."

"Better men than you have tried." She elbowed him out of the way. "You've served your usefulness, Abbot. We are near Senghenydd. We can make our way onward. Be gone at first light."

"Why should I leave? You paid my debts, and I would like to have at your *religious* education. Take off that coat of mail and let's see what you've got for teats."

She tossed a wineskin to him. "Suck that, abbot. You'll get more out of it. And don't think for a moment you are not leaving Wales."

"Who are you to tell me what to do? Women do not rule Britannia. And none orders me about."

She lifted her hand. "See this? I wear an iron glove. I earned it. And I have bought the right to order you about."

"You buy too much. I know you have money for that scoundrel Morgan ap Maredudd's fight. I know you plot against Gilbert the Red."

Sir Loyce's mouth yanked into a devious smile. "And there's nothing you can do about it, is there, Cyf?"

"I will tell Lord Gilbert." Cyf surged to his feet, the stool tumbling behind him, his belly quivering like a great platterful of boiled eels. "I will tell him you lowered the drawbridge while your son lay ill. I know you met with Morgan ap Maredudd and a northern prince. One of my monks followed you, heard every word. You promised gold for a Welsh attack on Caerphilly. I will tell Lord Gilbert," he repeated.

"I don't think you'll say a word. The marks waiting in your account with the Cardiff moneychanger would be forfeited. Do not tarry reaching the port. My ship awaits you. It sails on the tide for Asia Minor."

"No Armenia."

As he tipped the wineskin to fat lips and gulped, she said, "Don't drink too much of that, Cyf. Else, you won't feel up to the morrow's journey to the port of Cardiff."

"What I feel up to is thus." He gave his jewels a jiggle. "What are you up to, madam? A farewell toss?"

He was long and she'd long been without. "Allow me to show you, Abbot."

Chapter Six

"William, did you hear that?"

"Aye. Do not let that shriek trouble you, puss. Probably a beast is being butchered."

"At night?" She clutched her arms, chilled. " 'Tis dark. Too dark. We must turn back to our camp. I am frightened."

"Do you not hear the rush of water? We are near a stream of good size. Let us sit on the bank and discuss our situation, away from big ears. Worry not. I will protect you. Let me take your hand, puss, and guide you."

Before he could, something popped in the dark from a gorse bush. Cordelya jumped. Screamed. Sir William grabbed her, whirling her to him.

"Shhh. 'Tis nothing to fear. A simple hare, disturbed from his rest. I promised your safety, and you shall be unharmed. By my oath, I swear devoted protection. Take pity. Reward me with your trust."

On the verge of tears, her teeth chattering, Cordelya pressed her face to the leather gusset at his chest; he had shucked chains of armor and for that she was glad. His arms closed round her, gentleness to his embrace. Gentleness and solicitude. She feared naught, especially this knight.

Her hands went around his back, moving up to his shoulders. He smelled of wild garlic, as she surely did as well, although 'twas a pleasant aroma on William de Granville.

He groaned, then whispered her name. "May I kiss you?"

"You may."

He kissed her deeply, in the manner in which she had only heard whispered about in the bakehouse or in the great hall, when the peasants had consumed too much ale. He had slipped his tongue into her mouth.

She enjoyed it.

There was no taste of garlic on his tongue.

And then, all of a sudden, he lifted her into his arms and was carrying her to the stream, placing her on the bank, folding down beside her. There were fewer trees here, more starlight, and his features were bathed in argentine splendor.

She wanted him most fiercely.

Yea, the matter of Breckbryn must be settled.

"William," she said as he rolled her into the crook of his arm, flattening his palm on her derrière, "will you promise never to bear arms against the Welsh?"

"What if they should attack me or mine?"

"They would not. As long as nary an English knight or earl draws a lance in the king's stead, there will be no trouble."

"I come in peace. Now allow me to come in your piece."

"What do you mean?" she asked, befuddled.

"Never mind, innocent one." He undid the bindings of her head mantle to slip a hand into her hair. "On my oath I have already promised my loyalty to you. You must trust me. The Granville forces are now of Breckbryn. No Breckbryner will rise against the Welsh. Thereto I pledge you my troth.''

"Oh, William! We must both praise God on this joyous occasion. Kiss me. For once there will be an alliance of—''

He drowned her words in the swift currents of a kiss.

This time the kiss was even more bold. His lips afterward moved to her cheek, to her ear, and behind it. His fingers delved beneath the bodice of the meaddaughter's frock. His lips traced a path along Cordelya's collarbone and down to the rise of one breast. Voluptuous passion slew the chill in her bones.

"Oh! What are you doing?" she asked.

"I'm going to suckle your breast."

"Is that done? I did not know such was done betwixt men and women, much less with knights or ladies.''

"What is your age, puss?"

"Twenty."

"Old enough to have had a son near ready for fostering, yet you know not the least aspect of getting a son. Such a shame, so much of your life wasted. We shall make up for it.''

She had reached the age to dry on a vine without having been wed. But would not be mocked for it. "I was affianced in the cradle. To a prince. He was run through on Ifron Bridge, near Builth, on the same day our overlord prince, Llywelyn ap Gruffudd, breathed his last.'' The day her own father had gone to eternal salvation. "But . . . oh—oh, my! Your lips—''

"Quit talking," William ordered, his mouth full.

By now her fingers had wound into his shoulder-length curls, and were tugging with excitement. She yearned to pull the knight within her. Her body writhed against the tautness of his. Uninformed she might be, desirous she was, and she would have the rest of their lives to mine the mountain of his experiences, yet . . . her curiosity must be appeased. Now.

"I do not believe begetting sons takes suckling a lady's breast. 'Tis not done in animals, why would it in mankind?"

William lifted lips to her ear, his hand closing over her exposed breast. "My innocent puss, 'tis your right as a higher form of animal to enjoy the pleasures of lovemaking. I have shown you but a part of what can be enjoyed."

"Higher form of animal? You speak sacrilege, William."

"Let me rephrase my statement." Yet for a moment he said naught, then . . . "As a woman, highborn or not, of the family of animals or not, you can enjoy what your lord does to you. And he should do all in his power to please you."

"Where were you taught such? Wild rutting is for serving wenches and lowborns. My mother said so."

"I am sure your late mother taught you many valuable lessons, puss. But when you lie with me, I must demand you leave dear *maman* to rest in her heavenly haven."

Considering that William's hand gathered her hems and caressed her inner thigh, Cordelya found nary an argument.

Yet . . .

Much more of thus, and she would be despoiled. "I do not think marriages of alliance are much different in Wales than they are in your England. 'Tis demanded I stay untouched until vows are exchanged."

"I am not English. I am Norman. Born in Normandy. I should have made that clear earlier."

"Makes no difference. The ruling class of England is Norman. English, Norman. 'Tis all the same. But you are a good knight, indulgent of your mother. A good knight does not defile a lady. I know you are good. You rode to the white cross."

Ere this evensong ended, would he indulge her in more tales of Crusade? The mere thought left her wanton of reason. "Tell me true." She nuzzled closer, her fingernail tracing the dragon's tail. "Did you ride or sail to Jerusalem?"

"Crusade, Crusade, Crusade. All I hear is your obsession. What do you know of Crusade?"

" 'Tis the greatest journey one can make, ere the final journey to Saint Peter's heavenly gates. There was once a Norman fletcher in my *tat's* service. Robert had been an adventurous soul and went from Pembroke to join the second crusade of saintly King Louis of France. Robert had many tales of glory to tell. I sat rapt on a stump as he carved arrows, listening to every bit of it. He even had wondrous tales to tell of your king—then a princeling, of course—joining King Louis's battle."

"Puss, King Edward did not join with Louis IX. The King of France died of plague in Carthage, as did the majority of his legions. Edward and his consort did reach Jerusalem. In fact, Lord Gilbert's countess was born there, but Edward near lost his life to an assassin's dagger."

The part to center on? "Princess Joan was born in Acre? She never said a word. How cruel of her. She knows my dreams."

Cordelya had learned more in two evenings of snuggling than she had ever learned amid the sawdust of arrow-making or the company of a king's daughter. "Queen Eleanor went on pilgrimage. Imagine that. I never knew ladies were allowed. Well, save for your mother. She seems quite an exception to rules."

"Ladies, women, and children alike went to the Holy

Land. Not to fight the Saracen, forsooth, but to turn Jerusalem into a Christian kingdom of true believers.''

"I should like to do that! Take me there. Show me the way. Let us pray at the tomb of Jesú.''

William's arms tightened about her; he kissed her forehead. "And what, my puss, would you have done with Breckbryn while you chased the Holy Sepulchre?''

Her excitement went away. "As it has been pointed out to me, o'er and again, Breckbryn is beyond my control. Albeit, I would like a voice. Could we not rule as joint heads of the principali—William! Cease this instant!''

His fingers were delving way too deeply into her feminine secrets. While she longed to let him do as he would, she was a princess. "We must save my maidenhead for the wedding night. Uncle Cyfeiliog, as my surviving male relative, will seek proof our marriage is valid. Surely your . . . Surely Sir Loyce will expect the same. I have decided to become your ladybride. Shall we ride on the morrow to Caerphilly for the nuptials?''

She expected her knight to give a great whoop of joy; her feelings hurt when he did not. Perchance he was too overwhelmed with emotion to speak.

"William? William, have you naught to say?''

"I sense there is more you have yet to say.''

"Once we are bound in the eyes of the Lord God, and our vows consummated, we must launch a Crusade.''

He untangled himself from her and pushed to a seated position on the ground. "How would we find this effort, pray tell? 'Twill take more than the pennies and silver in your treasury, demoiselle. Crusades have made paupers out of kings.''

"The Lord God will show us the way. We will make haste to Jerusalem. You. Your mother, if she wishes. And I.''

"Nay. You know my mind. Quiet evenings, children, a sweet bitch to stroke.''

"I know you want sons and daughters, but, William, indulge me. Naught would bring more peace or happiness to my heart than to ride to the cross."

"May I point out, you were this night spooked by a mere hare? Give up your romantic notions, demoiselle. Use your head. Crusades are hell lived on earth."

Given his general propensity to deny her any request, Cordelya silently chided herself for having expected William to concede on a moment's notice. "I do get ahead of myself, sir. We must first marry, then think to the future."

He stood, paced. Grabbed a pebble and sent it forcefully in the rushing stream. And then William returned to hulk over Cordelya. "There won't be any exchange of vows. I will not have you for my ladybride."

William would not take her to ladybride? "Fine!"

A sennight ago, even a day earlier, his refusal might have overjoyed Cordelya. She was not overjoyed. Offended, most definitely taken aback, she hurt. "You are unpleasant, William. Mean. Despicable and devious." Yet some part of her —the part that had no name, but squeezed her heart— recalled how tender he could be.

"I know," he murmured.

Her dignity gathered, she followed him from the stream as they wended from the darkened forest, making certain to give no screams in the night, not even when a creature, mayhap a fox, darted into her path.

As soon as she saw light from the campfire, she went no further. "William." She spoke false to protect herself and her heart, saying, "It pleases me, as I know it pleases you, that we have at last come to agreement. I bear you no grudge. For certes, as soon as we return to Breckbryn, I shall order a banquet to bid you and your men farewell."

Why did she have the urge to cry at the thought of losing him?

He halted, turned, underbrush crunching beneath his feet. "You misunderstand. I will not be leaving Breckbryn. I mean to have you as my concubine."

"Concubine? What is that?" She had a vague idea of this strange word, but . . . She readied for pitched battle. "What *exactly* is a concubine?"

"They are found in the East, in the harems of the sultans of the Mohammedans. Sultans take many concubines, nary a one of wifely status, although the first might be considered of rank. You will be my first. Perhaps the last."

Cordelya's right eye ticked. "Whore. *Putain.* How do you know of these women?"

"Have you ever seen me frocked as a monk?"

"So, sir. 'Twas not for the glory of Christ the Lord that you journeyed to the East." Whereas she had been hurting, she now felt the sink of disappointment at the tarnish on his armor. "You went to lower your hose."

"If you as much as breathe the word *crusade*, I shall—"

"Worry not, knave. 'Twould be sacrilege."

"Will you become my concubine?"

"Ne'er!" She lifted her nose to such a height that a flying pest was near sucked into her nostril. Batting at the nuisance, she said, "What greater insult could you mete me, not only as a princess but also as a lady of piety?"

"You would be happier as a courtesan. Some ladies are not meant for marriage, and you, like my mother, are not. I thought you would be pleased at having your burden lifted."

I am going to arm myself with a dagger. I am going to plunge it in his black heart until I am certain he has lived the last of his lives. Then I will crave that cold heart from his chest and feed it to the dogs. But first I must find my dagger.

Rather than give in to hysteria, which he undoubtedly

sought, she forced reason. "If you wish an amenable lady-bride, then by all means, do find one."

Such wanton words might challenge him into a quick marriage, but . . . she would have enjoyed seeing his expression, but his tone of voice gave away his surprise. He asked, "Then you are agreeable to becoming my concubine?"

"Once you are well-wed and well-bedded, I shall invite you to my solar," she lied. "But nary a moment beforehand."

"Why wait?"

"Surely, sir, you would not wish to *insult* me by demanding my favors. That would be rape. Even your supporter Red Gilbert would not look on that favorably."

"Delya . . . I—"

"On the subject of Lord Gilbert, may I suggest you look to Castle Caerphilly for your wood-mouse? His two daughters from his first marriage could be summoned from exile. Alice de Lusignan's daughters. You could take your choice. Given the disgrace on their heads—did you know their father annulled his marriage to Alice?—I am sure they would be most agreeable to marrying a knight of the cross, even a knave fallen to harems."

"No Lusignans for me."

Cordelya almost chuckled, so preposterous was this traffic in the honorable estate of matrimony. "I cannot blame you there. Poor Red Gilbert did rue the day he married a Lusignan."

"What is wrong with the Lusignans?"

"Better put, what is right with the Lusignans?" Cordelya knew she should say nary a word to William. She should present a cold shoulder and not allow it to warm, yea she did have that problem with letting go. "My mother told me Red Gilbert's first ladywife was a conniving foreigner. Alice de Lusignan treated The Red coldly, yet she was quite cozy with her half-uncle, the past English king, *and* with his son. Your present king.''

''You don't say?''

''I do. And I heard worse. When The Red planned his attack on London, his own ladywife went to King Henry and betrayed the confidence. After the fray of London was at end, to Red Gilbert's advantage, he packed Alice and their daughters off. Had the marriage annulled. Who could blame him? He was greatly cuckold.''

''Your mother's memory reached far. Those rumors went round while you were still but a gleam in Princess Eleri's eyes.''

''You must not have spent much time in England, William, if you do not know of other Lusignans. They are such pompous goats, snatching honors and land, and causing mayhem wherever they go. Why, even that scoundrel, William of Lusignan, who calls himself Valence, managed to wrest an earldom for himself. Pembroke.''

''Now I understand. You don't fancy a foreigner taking one of the Marcher lordships.''

''There is that.''

''Delya, we have enough trouble without borrowing Lord Gilbert's. But I would like to point out that the Lusignans rightly, and with dignity, hold titles in many lands. Jerusalem's last king was of that house. He was martyred to the cross's cause.''

Now that her tirade was spent, Cordelya remembered the cold shoulder. ''I have no wish to discuss the sacrifices of any Lusignan . Good eventide, William.''

Cordelya rushed round him, running toward camp. She barely noticed that the squires and her uncle were missing.

'Twas then that she heard a mighty male bellow from behind her. She pivoted toward it, but soon made fast for camp. A fetid stench was rolling toward her.

"I have been sprayed by a polecat," the knave-knight shouted into the night. "God's blood! I am ruined!"

Perhaps not forever, but William would be unfit for anyone's companionship for days on end. Cordelya gave forth gales of joyous laughter. "Serves you right."

Chapter Seven

"Phew." Sir Loyce held her nose.

Even Lew had retreated.

Cordelya, with many questions to ask, fanned the morning air. "You have banished your son to the woods, yea his scent still wafts."

Chains rattling with her efforts, Sir Loyce tugged on an iron stake, bringing the tent down. "Will! Go to the stream and bathe yourself," she shouted. "Leave your clothes where they will lie and dress from that bundle I tossed you."

Cordelya called to the stink's direction. "If you show your face, I shall curse your soul to Hades!"

"His stink is bad, but not that bad."

If only you knew, sir.

When Cordelya had returned to camp the past night, she had not been of a mind to mention William's despicable offer. She had wondered at certain absences, but the captain had been too engaged with keeping a stinking son at bay to answer.

"Where is my uncle?" Cordelya stepped up to have her answers. "What have you done with him?"

"Nothing that he didn't ask for himself." Arms akimbo, the captain grinned. "He was trussed for ill behavior, then strapped to his mount and led away by the squires. He is banished. Forever cast away to the farthest reaches of Christendom."

"Good. I despise him." The most glorious feeling started in Cordelya's entrails and spread throughout her limbs. Birds had never sung so sweetly, the sky had never been this clear. She grabbed the captain's gloved hands. "I want to dance. I would to sing. May we rejoice as we should have on May Day?"

As if girls, the two women danced and sang with joy till they fell in a heap on the ground, Sir William's courser and the captain's palfrey eyeing the pair as if they were hell's horses come to take them away.

"I am famished to break my fast." Cordelya turned her head to grin at the captain. "Have you anything left to eat?"

"Not a scrap. But I shall treat you to a delicious feast in Caerphilly. Naturally we cannot arrive at Lord Gilbert's gate until William is fresh of scent. We'll find an alehouse that serves meals. Would that please you?"

"I could eat every bite in Wales!"

Sir Loyce patted Cordelya's hand. "If it's a banquet you want, Princess, it's a banquet you'll have."

"You are most gracious." A pause. "Would that . . ." She pressed her lips together, feeling sudden guilt at decrying her own kin. "Sir Loyce, what is my uncle's fate?"

"He has agreed to accept the post of Bishop of Armenia."

"I do not know of Armenia."

"It's beyond the Holy Land, deep in Asia Minor."

"Captain, how is it he was offered this post?"

"I bought it for him."

"How can you, Sir Loyce, buy such as a bishopric?"

"I am the richest woman in Christendom. And also the most vengeful when crossed." Sir Loyce creaked to stand, then lent a hand to help Cordelya to her feet. "I go to any lengths for my family's happiness. And I have indebted many to my ends."

"Whatever do you mean?"

Sir Loyce was quiet a moment. "I would like to leave it at, I look to the future."

Cordelya nodded, stunned at what she had heard. Some heartbeats later she asked, "Why was I picked for William?"

"You aren't rich. You may not be of a powerful ruling family. You are a fine choice. I have had my ears open about you since William and I first landed in England."

Partly flattered, Cordelya asked, "What did you hear about *me*?"

"That you were most agreeable. And beautiful. You are quite beautiful. My son is fond of fair-haired ladies. And I have always longed for a daughter with hair like purest honey."

"You have learned I am not at all agreeable."

"That is one fly in the honey."

Grinning with guilt, Cordelya lifted her palms in a gesture of naught-can-be-helped. "Impressions are most assuredly wrong at times. I thought William landless and penniless."

"He is not penniless. He needs a title above knight, as far to the western edge of the earth as possible. Frankly, I had no interest to look to Ireland. Those of Eire are too unruly, not of my tastes at all. And surely not to William's. What he needs, dear daughter, is kindness and care."

"Then he should be kind and caring. He is hateful."

"Daughter . . . William has spent most of his life in the lands of the Saracens. They do not think as we do. Being amidst much influence can twist one's thinking, if not steal one's soul. But he can be saved. By the right ladywife.''

"Lost soul? Sir Loyce, surely 'tis not so. Crusading is the most holy quest.''

"If one is not torn asunder by jihad.''

"Would you explain that to me? What is jihad, and what did it do to William? Does it have something to do with harems? He speaks as though he knows well of concubines.'' Concubines!

"That, my dear daughter, is for William to tell you." Sir Loyce took her hand. "I beg you, ladydaughter. Allow William to accustom to you. He'll be a fine husband. And I think you will become the most agreeable daughter.''

Daughter? "I am not your . . ." Cordelya closed her mouth. The captain might not have birthed her, yet a bond was growing betwixt them. 'Twas not awful, being called daughter by a brave and powerful lady. She fancied it.

"I will ne'er be your daughter, sir, and for that I am aggrieved. You see, William would have me for concubine.''

Sir Loyce gave a hitch to the chains that had slipped down her lack of hips and eyed the woods. She shouted, "William de Granville, come forth!''

It took several shouts ere he stepped into the clearing, keeping to the edge. The sight of him roused a giggle in Cordelya, for hairy shins poked from beneath a monk's habit.

"Son, there will be no harems at Breckbryn.''

His face hardened—Cordelya could tell, even from a distance. Fists clenched, he shouted, "I am not some pup to order about, Mother *dear.*''

Sir Loyce patted Cordelya's shoulder. "He'll give up the foolish notion of concubinage. He needs you, as you need him. Be strong, daughter. And make him suffer for insulting you.''

Cordelya had the sudden urge to be gathered to Sir

Loyce's flat, mail-chained chest. Yet she had been given motherly comfort. For certes no one would ever replace Princess Eleri, and she knew naught of mothers of sons, yea . . .

"*Modryb dda.* Glory be to God, and to the Son, and to the Holy Ghost. Ave Maria! Dewi Sant has blessed me with a miracle." Cordelya curtsied—curtsied deeply and with reverence—to William's mother. All she now required was William's love and devotion. And pilgrim's progress to gain heaven. "World without end, amen. I have found my second mother."

Second mother? William would be further damned! He would face Judgment Day unrepentant, ere he would take Cordelya Howel to ladywife. Forsooth, he hadn't meant to make her his concubine. His had been a move to force her to stop training him to a lead.

"Phew." Cordelya held her nose. "His bath helped not."

Damned if he would now even take that wench to whore. He lied to himself.

"We ride for Caerphilly," Sir Loyce said. "Lord Gilbert expects a wedding, and we'll give him one."

William ignored the captain. He knew what she planned beyond saddling him to a wild mare, and knew there was no stopping her. Why stop her? She had done as she pleased, and always would.

He stomped out of the woods to mount his courser. Khayyam's eyes bulged, his nostrils flared, and as he gave a great whinny of fright at his master's stench, the courser reared on hind legs and drove his hooves into William's chest.

Old wounds burned as William fell to the ground.

"William!"

"Leave him to his pain, daughter. He should think on it."

Hours later William gave a flick of reins and tasted bile. He guided a despicable mount toward Senghenydd. His mother and Cordelya had earlier gone about, leading Khayyam away, returning with his plough horse and a mare for Cordelya. At least the dull gelding hadn't reared at his stink.

William knew he would be left outside the village's palisades to fend for himself, a veritable leper.

The gloating Cordelya rode a stone's throw to his right. Lew was at her side, her far side. Lew the deserter. William hunched his fustian-draped shoulders, hating the feel of a monk's frock. Naught could bolster his mood.

Ridiculed and set against, he knew his face was hardened into a frown. Many times in his life he had known humiliation and shame. This was not the worst, but he was much offended.

Cordelya laughed. "I wonder if the perfume of polecat will be with you forever?"

"You are vindictive," he muttered loud enough for her ears.

Nasty as the foulest of Mamlukes, she threw back her head to laugh. "Ah, and I taste the sweet nectar of it."

William returned his gaze to the rutted road. *"Chut."*

"I will not hush. I do believe God sent the polecat to punish you for asking a princess to be your whore."

I was but testing you. I sought your surrender. 'Tis all. I would willingly have you for ladywife, if only you would be less like my mother.

Cordelya, Princess of Breckbryn, he understood fully, would never be anything but her aggravating self. Yet . . . savage that he was, he yearned more than ever to strip her to the most base, and drive the black knight of his lust into her comely body.

Hmm.

Maychance he could docile her with passion.

"More's the fool," he muttered under his breath. "She would enslave me." Why did that not offend him as it ought to?

Cordelya led her mount a tiny bit closer to the outcast.

"Catch up with Sir Loyce," he demanded sourly. "I have no wish to talk."

"If that is your wish," she said in Welsh. "But I want you to know, I believe I love you. And I hope that you will someday love me. But I will have you know—there will be no women for you at Breckbryn. Unless that woman is I."

As always, William kept his features blank. Yet he could have jumped for joy. She loved him.

His jaw tilting Cordelya's way, he drank in the sight of her. She looked lovely in the attire of peasantry. She would look more lovely, he would warrant, without a stitch of clothes.

His lust stirred anew. Nay. Was more than lust he felt for Cordelya. He loved her. He should not. She was much like his mother. She would lead him an unmerry race. He adored her.

"I do have something to say, puss." His eyelids grew heavy with desire. "Allow me to worship at your altar. Enslave me to the grail of your womanly delights."

Her heel dug into the palfrey's flank to ride closer to the pariah. The mount refused. Lew took an even wider berth. Cordelya jumped from the saddle and charged head-long to William. She grasped his hand and looked up with pleading eyes. Such lovely blue eyes, such a tender hand.

"William, my knight, my lord. Say naught of pagan altars. I pray you never look upon me with the eyes of an apostate. You would have me without the Lord God's approval, I know, but I beg you, please! Take heed with your mortal soul.''

His soul already burned in hell.

William leaned down to tip Cordelya's chin upward. ''There is a time to love and a time to hate. A time of war and a time of peace. I am more dead than alive, yea I beg your love. I am the most wretched of men, Cordelya. Have mercy on me.''

Her eyes glistened with tears, her lashes swept down over troubled blue irises. She squeezed his hand. ''When we reach Caerphilly, I will see that food is shoved in your direction.''

She rode swiftly away, joining Sir Loyce, leaving William to wonder at her. When her hand had been purchased from King Edward, he had assumed her pliable as clay. Yet she had a soft inner core that belied her bellicose exterior.

If he could mine Cordelya's inner core, as the Mamluke sappers had carved the underpinnings from the Temple of Acre, mayhap William would someday know peace.

Chapter Eight

"You would rub me with nightshade?" William recoiled from the basket of herbs, gaining the corner of his putrid-smelling tent. "Never!"

Cordelya, three days after the spraying, readjusted the basket of clothes and herbs on her arm. "The soothsayer promises belladonna will rid the last of polecat."

"The soothsayers of Britain know naught. Next you'll be telling me how your mother would treat my malady with stewed newt eyes or a pilgrimage to some godforsaken well. Get away with your poison."

"William, I will not poison you." Cordelya smiled at the cornered knight. "Your mother says a caring châtelaine bathes guests of her castle. The out-of-doors is our castle now. I shall assist you at the stream, and see to your comfort."

One of his black brows winged. "I have dreamed of bathing in your chamber at Breckbryn."

Cordelya smiled, having dreamed the same last eventide, after she'd heard tales of a Norman castle with a count and countess who shared great passion. "Pretend you are in my tub. With my own hands I will rub your flesh with herbs and make you presentable."

"I am not good at pretend." A thumb and forefinger scratched the black bristles that had sprouted on his jaw. "But *you* will do the bathing and rubbing?"

"Who would have you, my dear knave-knight, but I?"

He smiled. "Put thusly, how could I resist?"

She led him to the stream that tumbled over rocks and sang gaily down the hillside. A pine marten, surely from the north of Wales, chirped. Vaulting over a fallen log, a red deer made for safety. Cordelya, still garbed in peasant fashion, put down her basket and turned to William. "Disrobe, my lord."

He showed not a modicum of modesty. Off went Uncle Cyfeiliog's too-short habit. Cordelya gasped, not only at the labyrinth of scars on his flesh. Never before had she gazed upon a naked man.

For certes, she had never seen anyone over the age of weaning unclothed. Yea, William de Granville had to be one of the finer-endowed of the knighthood. She'd heard that knights padded their shoulders and hips; William had no need to.

His shoulders reached as if for the eastern and western edges of the earth itself. His arms were like tree trunks, grown mighty and hard. His torso might have been etched by a wood sculptor of grand talent. Below . . . oh, my—

What a long branch!

She stammered, "See to your bathing."

He plunged feet first into the stream, cupping water within his palms and splashing it upon his face. Black curls flattened about his ears, and a smile akin to the devil's cut across his bristled face. "Join me?"

"I think not."

He sat upon a crested wave that flowed over the bedrock,

denying her eyes the feast of knightly crags and crinkled hairs that sprouted from his chest . . . and lower.

"Delya, my puss. You have caroused too much with me. Your scent is no better than mine. Let us wash. Together."

"I think not." For certes, she was thinking *so*.

To bathe with him would be a surrender on her part, she decided. He would still have her for concubine, would begin the enslavement this day. Be kind to him, *modryb dda* had advised. Perchance if she showed kindness, and a willingness to give, he would change his offer to marriage.

More than all else, though, she simply yearned to know the strength of his arms again.

She loved him. Loved him dearly. And yearned for his love in return. "Do you really think I am objectionable of smell?"

"Aye, puss."

She kicked off one low-cut peasant's shoe, then the other. Her big toe dipped into the water. "Brrr. 'Tis cold."

"You must plunge in. Better to take the plunge—then you won't think long on the shock."

"For certes?"

"Shuck your robes first. They will do naught but weigh you down in the water."

Once, when Cordelya had been but a child, she had fallen into the outer ditch, when Breckbryn had been assailed by an August rainstorm. She had near to drowned, her robes having pulled her under. Why repeat that experience? "Turn your head, William."

He complied, to her astonishment.

She pulled off first one garment, then another, and folded them beside her basket of herbs. Without much rumination, she warned, "Here I come."

She jumped at the same moment William uttered, "If only I might wish."

He caught her ere she hit the rocks.

She knew the water was cold, yet it chilled her not. He held her against his warm strength, and her blood flowed like the molten lava that she had only heard of in bard's tales. Her hair waved in the rushing water, and her heart beat like the thrum of Druid chants, as relayed by the bards.

"We should not do this," she said, twirling the tip of her finger in a swirl of his chest hair and losing her grip when his lips nibbled the column of her throat. Boneless with passion she struggled for a moment's sense. "I have vowed to save myself till after you have taken a ladywife. Would you break my vow?"

"I would praise the Maker, if you would weaken to me." William settled back against the bedrock, resting her upon his harder than bedrock person. "Pray keep your mouth shut when I beg you, and I shall take you to . . . Nay. Wait. Let me rephrase that."

"Go on," she prompted with bated breath and gentled her lips to bruises the courser had made on his scarred chest.

He fitted her into the crook of one arm, pulling her knees over his thighs. His fingers caressed her cheek, as his eyes did her features. "Proud princess, Maid of Breck-bryn, I come to you a knave unworthy of your many gifts. I have sinned. And I have been sinned against. I have known war, and little peace. I pray peace. I pray love with you. May we enjoy bountiful harvests for our people, and see to their health and wealth. More than all, I pray the happiness of my woman. These are what I would have, if the Maker is merciful. But . . . you are a warrior, like my mother. I fear harmony beyond our reach, if I am not the one allowed to wear the hose in our household."

"Does one make a household with his concubine?" Cordelya played her queen and hoped to check the rook.

"If you would *chut* when I beg, if you won't beseech me

to matters I cannot abide, if you would be half as agreeable as you are at this moment, I would consider it an honor above blessings on Judgment Day, if I might be your lord-husband."

Her heart beat rapidly, as if it might jump from her chest. "I—I would be honored to be your ladywife. But what if I cannot keep my tongue behind my lips?"

He grinned most wickedly and kissed the tip of her nose. "Then I shall be forced to sic your Isabelle on you."

Overjoyed, Cordelya gave in to mirth and merriment, and shoved William against the rocks. Tickling his ribs, tugging the swirls of crimped hair that arrowed down from his chest, kissing him all the way to his navel. Her juices flowed like the rushing stream. Her tongue darted into the indentation; she lifted her eyes saucily. "Well then, knave-knight, I shall sic my bulldog champion on you!"

He laughed, a boom that rolled over the water and across the forest. "Raise your head, wench. Else, I'll have your mouth so filled that you cannot say one word. Give me your lips. I mean to kiss them soundly, then kiss every inch of your body!"

"If only you would tell me you love me," she said in her native tongue. "I pray you will love me. As I love you."

He pulled her to him, sliding her up his body, settling her in the bough of his trunk, his manly branch cleaving her womanly place, yea not entering. He wreaked havoc with his kisses, his caresses, his attentions to every sensitive spot on her flesh.

He raised her derrière with his broad hands, as if she were no more of weight than a pebble, and took her breast into his mouth. Her head lolled as if it had no neck. Her thighs closed around his waist. Squeezing, squeezing, aching for something she knew not.

"Rub what you would into me, puss. Be it belladonna

or the tasty nectar of your womanly passage. I am yours to rub.''

Like a cat leaving its scent, she arched against him.

"Be my ladywife, Delya.'' He cupped her face between his hands. *"Rwyn dy g aru."*

He spoke in the idiom of a man well-acquainted with— How could she rejoice in his declaration of love, when . . . ? "You knave. You churl. You speak my language. You have understood every Celtic word I have ever spoken to you, have you not?"

"My tongue is gifted.''

"Shall I plunge my dagger into your soft spot now, ye stinking cur, or shall I wait until ye finish yer spilling?'' a voice thundered from the water's edge.

Cordelya froze at those words spoken in Cymraeg. Her face whipped about. Hair wildly braided and his face showing the gristling of too many years spent fighting the English, Morgan ap Maredudd, deposed Prince of Caerleon, stood with legs parted wide on the bank, a mace in one hand, a dagger in the other.

She screamed, spreading her arms to shield her knight. "No, Morgan, no!''

"Who the hell are you?'' William demanded to know. "And what do you want?"

" 'Tis Prince Morgan," she explained.

"Morgan! My brother! At last we meet. How fortuitous. Join us, man. I am William de Granville. The princess and I enjoy a romp to rid a polecat's spray.''

"I thought 'twas your natural stink." Morgan waved the dagger. "Get out of the water. I would hate to sacrifice Princess Cordelya as I defend her honor.''

William's fingers tightened on her protectively. "She is my ladybride, and I—''

"Boff! Ladybride? I have heard the rumor, but the vows

are not taken and ye defile a Welsh princess. Let loose with her, English swine, or I shall beset ye."

Her knight tensed as if to meet the challenge.

"William, William, be prudent." She tore loose. With one arm covering her breasts and the other hiding her pubis, she surged from the water.

Morgan threw her garments at her feet, and she gathered them. With all haste she dressed, and noticed William had risen from the stream. He didn't bother to dress.

"Brother, what have you to say?" William settled back against a boulder as if to bronze his flesh.

"Let me rub your flesh with these herbs." She scrambled for the basket and began to swab William's arms with herbs, making sure to shield her knight.

He shoved gently at her waist. "Thank you, my dearest, but I can fight my own battles."

She expected Morgan to plunge a dagger or to wield the mace, and steeled herself for the first blow to her knight.

William shook his head, droplets of water spraying. "Have you met Sir Loyce de Granville yet, brother?"

The prince shook his own head of hair—his shaggy braids waving—and lowered his arms of war. "I seek the man. Where can I find him?"

"Inside the village, arranging a meal."

What business did Morgan have with Sir Loyce? "William, can you not cover yourself while speaking with a prince of Wales?"

"Cover me with your sweet kisses, puss."

"Ye'd best marry the knight and quickly, Princess Cordelya. He is hot for ye."

She smiled, then shook a finger at William. "I have brought you spare clothes, my lord. Pull them on. Now."

He pulled the tunic over his head. "Satisfied?"

Morgan chuckled. "I see she had you trained, sire."

William sprang, his fingers closing around the prince's throat. Morgan gasped and fell back into a nest of hedgehogs, scattering them, some of their spines no doubt stabbing his backside. He would have screamed if he'd had the wind.

William straddled the prince, squeezing with even more force.

Cordelya lunged to pull her knight away. "If you please, if you please," she pleaded. "Stop! Morgan, I have not trained him." She would not speak falsely, and vowed that from here forward, her words would be spoken with respect to William's wishes. "If aught, he has trained me."

Squeezing hands eased, and William looked over at her, question in his face.

" 'Tis not a loathsome concept," she said, realizing the truth to it. "I am his, and he is mine. You two must quit your fighting. It disturbs me."

William threw his leg from the prince, rolling to his back in the grasses.

Morgan rubbed his throat, pulled quills from the seat of his breeches, and sighed. "Shall we search for Sir Loyce? My stomach growls for food and my pocket yelps for filling."

"Let us be off." Craning to his feet, William reached down to offer the prince a hand, which was accepted.

"Morgan, what do you mean by filling your pockets?"

"Let me answer that." William strode to her. "The house of de Granville has chosen to arm Prince Morgan in his fight against injustice."

A smile broke across Morgan ap Maredudd's gristled face. "*Creoso i Cymru*. Welcome to Wales!"

William bowed. "Thank you, sir."

Her knight avowed peace, yet he would not quail from a fight? His fight went to Wales. At last, after losing her father at Ifron Bridge, after brother Martyn's ultimate sacrifice, after so many years of Uncle Cyfeiliog's schemes and betrayals, after losing her mother, yet gaining *modryb dda*, the Princess of Breckbryn drew her first calm breath.

All would be right in Cordelya's domain.

Thanks to a mysterious knight of the cross.

Her William.

Chapter Nine

The alehouse, snugly tucked inside Caerphilly village, served both the house specialty and the ever-favored mead, along with a dish called *caws pobi*. The establishment was empty of patrons save for the party of four plus Lew.

William's captain and his ladybride, the latter with Lew underfoot, partook of the toasted bread smothered in a sauce of local cheese, while the alewife yapped and yapped.

William had not gizzard for food. He slugged ale, as did Prince Morgan. His mind was not on the alliance with the prince, or with gaining entrance across the moat's lake to Castle Caerphilly, once gizzards were filled.

He had admitted his love. He should not have. With love went honesty. He could not be honest.

Cordelya must never know his secret.

He reconciled his mind. Why would she need know? She did, however, need to know what his mother planned.

The prince leaned to whisper, "If the alewife would quiet and get to her dishes, we will talk."

The pink-cheeked woman, also the cook and foodbearer, having received a compliment to her skills from Cordelya, hovered and droned on about her prized dish, as if naught else in the cosmos was of import. "I add a bit o' fresh milk, and a tad o' mustard, and some o' Seisyll's ale, I do," whistled through a gap in her top teeth. "The trick be to brown the cheese wit'out burning it."

Cordelya smiled her dazzling smile and sipped daintily from a mug of mead. " 'Tis quite nice, mistress."

"If I eat much more cheese, I'll be stove up for a month," groused Sir Loyce.

The gullies in Prince Morgan's face deepened. "Where is your man, goodwoman?"

"Seisyll?" The alewife wiped chafed hands on her skirt. "This be his naptime."

"Join him," roared the prince. Once the alewife scurried off, Prince Morgan pounded a fist on the table. "How many men can I count on?"

"What exactly do you plan to do?" Cordelya asked.

"Take back my Caerleon lands. Red Gilbert stole them. At last I have the means to reclaim what is mine."

Cordelya's face showed a number of emotions. "William, will you fight the Lord of Glamorgan?"

He could deceive, but he wore enough of a hair shirt without adding another. Becoming Welsh, becoming a good husband to Cordelya, William decided, was not going to be as easy as pouring cheese over toast to make Welsh ra'bit.

"Nay, puss. I'll not fight. This is Sir Loyce's battle."

"I seek vengeance against Lord Gilbert," stated the captain.

Cordelya paled; William took her hand beneath the table. She asked, "Why?"

"Brother, this is a family discussion. Could you . . . ?"

"Right." The prince shoved up from table. "Sir Loyce, I'll see you at Breckbryn. Fare thee well, all."

Sir Loyce spoke up, once the door had closed on Morgan. "I am an aunt offended. I have been forced by circumstance to wait many years for my revenge, but I will have it against Red Gilbert. That *fil de putain* tossed aside my dear niece Alice, and made bastards of their daughters."

Cordelya's eyes rounded. "That means you are—"

"Lusignans," William supplied.

Sir Loyce smiled brilliantly. "My family name."

"Lusignan. Now I understand." Studying him as if she had never ere seen him, his puss murmured, "Do you . . . ? Does your mother plan to do Lord Gilbert or his family bodily harm?"

"Nay."

"We will have a wedding, is what we will have," Sir Loyce explained. "A glorious wedding of a Lusignan in the castle where my niece should bear the keys."

Cordelya glanced down. "Was I but a pawn in this game?"

"More of a convenience," Sir Loyce stated before William could stop her. "You were our pick. By luck, you live nearby to Lord Gilbert."

Cordelya slipped her trembling fingers from William's grip, but he pulled them back and gazed into her eyes. He had to make her understand that their love would not be affected by his captain's quest. "We will be married, for no other reason than the right of it."

"Children, we must present ourselves at the gatehouse ere dusk. The Lusignans come calling."

They were welcomed with pomp and circumstance. The long drawbridge lowered, banners and guards lined their way to the castle of many turrets that dominated the bowl of the vale and had been built by Red Gilbert after he had banished Alice de Lusignan. It was a grand and magnificent fortress fit for a Lusignan.

Torches were lit. Musicians were summoned. So were castle dwellers, led by Lord Gilbert and his beauteous countess. A feast of many courses was laid out in a great hall of grand proportions. Fine wines were poured. Toasts were offered to the bridal couple. Cordelya excused herself early, and did not have to deceive when claiming an unsettled stomach.

Abed and alone, Cordelya felt the full surge of a dilemma of mixed proportions. She was Welsh. She should be pleased to know that Morgan would have a chance at his vengeance and that those of her own had supported him.

Yea though Lord Gilbert had never done her ill, save for bringing William to her, and was that so terrible?

Was it?

The worst part, she decided, was having been deceived, both by Sir Loyce and William himself. How little she knew of the man and mother she loved.

They should have been honest.

"I sense a hesitation in you," the Countess of Glamorgan observed as she followed Cordelya on a dawn walk along an upper parapet of Castle Caerphilly. "Where do your loyalties lie? Do you resent the marital arrangement? Do you have bridal jitters?"

Cordelya turned to the sloe-eyed daughter of King Edward. The countess, barely a score of years in age, was great with her third child. Would Red Gilbert someday turn her and her children out, as he had done Alice de Lusignan?

Of course not.

Longshanks's furies would reach him, would bleach the roots of The Red's rufous hair and fling him by that hair as if pitched from a siege engine. Then again, the English king had done as much with imprisoning his son by law, yea the lord Gilbert thrived.

Gilbert de Clare did not need the buttress of an impoverished Welsh princess.

And, furthermore, why should Cordelya feel sorry for Alice de Lusignan? Well, she did. Mayhap it was the draw of relation that had softened her stance. The Lusignans were not all bad. And perhaps history had been unkind to Alice.

If Cordelya had worn Sir Loyce's gauntlets, she would wish retribution for her own.

She had a different subject to discuss with Joan, though, one that had nettled her. "Why did you ne'er tell me you are styled Joanna of Acre, that you were born in Jerusalem?"

"I do not remember the Holy Land. All I know is what my grandparents in Castile told me as a child. You did know I spent most of my childhood in Las Huelgas, did you not?"

"Sir Loyce did mention that Queen Eleanor's mother and father adored you." Her parents, especially Longshanks, had taken an odd stance with children, according to Sir Loyce. When his father had died, Longshanks wept, when he had not wept at losing more than one male heir. When asked, he had answered that the Lord God who gave him sons could give him more, but he had been blessed with but one father.

Such devotion from a son was commendable. How would Longshanks have reacted now, were he in the same situation? He and his adored queen, now dead for going on three years, were blessed with many children, mostly girls. The surviving son, a child, Sir Loyce had told her, who was given to giddiness and lacked the presence necessary for a royal heir.

"Neither my parents nor my grandparents said much about the Holy Land," Joan said as they walked the allude. The smile she turned to Cordelya carried the fire of Castile and Norman vitality. "Cordelya, forget Jerusalem. Think not of the Holy Sepulchre." A gust of wind blew her wimple away, exposing a shock of rich black hair, showing the soul in her features. "Jerusalem lies in the heart, not in the campaign."

What a womanly way to look at it. Cordelya was unconvinced.

"You skirted my earlier question," Joan pointed out. "Are you attacked by bridal jitters?"

"I have no fear of marriage. William and I are well suited, and my loyalties lie with him and his family."

Running her palm over her bulging stomach, Joan said, "Then you should take yourself to your chamber and ready for the ceremony."

It was easy to shrug a shoulder at a powerful baron, yea Cordelya looked upon a friend. And she worried. This castle was a fortress beyond compare. Howbeit, if an adequately supplied Morgan were to besiege it, what would happen to Joan and her children? "Did you know my husband is of the family Lusignan?"

Cordelya expected shock, yea did not receive it. Joan's lips turned upward at the edges. "How could I not know? My father . . ." She glanced at the hills cloaking her castle. When her gaze soldered to another princess's, her eyes bore witness to a bloodline of kings who had conquered and conquered and conquered. "Gilbert is being punished. You know this. Part of his penance is to beard the lion of Lusignan. I should say 'lioness.' Cease with the glum look. I know I will have Lusignans to meet and greet hereafter. Royalty forms alliances with foes. The strong accept this, use it to advantage."

"And if the alliances are weakened by intrigue?"

"The strong survive." Joan lifted her arm, waving her hand. "Come, Cordelya. Let us make the most of our alliance. I shall attend you myself as you dress for your wedding."

Cordelya lifted her own royal chin. *I will be meek when I must with William, I will honor his mother as mine, but I will survive on my own terms as a princess.* There would be no Lusignans married at Caerphilly Castle. "I will wed at Breckbryn, my home. My own domain."

All her life Cordelya Howel had worshiped in Breckbryn Abbey and now that the abbot was gone, she took full comfort in the sanctuary. This mid-morn, the choir sang and Glynis played the harp. Shards of sunlight bled through stained glass images of Saint Dewi and lit the tombs of princes of Breckbryn who had gone before, including Princess Eleri.

Cordelya had never seen the abbey in such a glorious light. Arrived was the prince of her heart. Mam smiled in that heart.

". . . In the name of the Father," the priest intoned in Latin, the scent of incense wafting.

Shyly, Cordelya glanced at her Lord William. So handsome, he. So right for her. Mayhap she should pen King Edward a note of thanks for sending Sir William de Granville to her. Nay, she would thank the Lord God, and the saints . . . and her *modryb dda* for her good knight.

"I weary of feasting," William whispered in Cordelya's ear, tickling her senses, as if they needed more tickling! They sat the lord's table, the floor beneath the dais having been cleared for the evening's entertainment. "We have made banquet all day, have danced and sung, then eaten more venison and mutton and salted fish. We have drunk broth till it floats us. We have further titillated our palates with jellies and cakes and pudding." He swept his fingers along her thigh. "When is this going to stop? It seems we are now amid competition."

"*Eisteddfod,* my dear lord husband. Contests of poetry and music. *Eisteddfod* carries on into the dark of night, till the last torches and candles have burned down."

"Enough." William rose to stand. "Friends, family, her ladyship and I bid you good-eventide. Carry on with your celebration, but I shall . . ." He winked down at Cordelya. "I shall carry my ladybride upstairs for a good . . . sleep."

A roar of ribald laughter.

Then William swept her into his arms and started the climb to the lord's chamber. He reached the chapel floor, and stopped to press his burden against the wall. "I should have a kiss. I can go no further without a kiss."

She pursed her lips.

And he kissed them lavishly.

"I could take you here," he said, groaning. "I have longed for you since the first moment I laid eyes on you."

"And I for you. I fancy being ravished in your strong arms."

"My arms have but a part to play in ravishment. You do have a lot to learn."

He set forth to teach her. Up the stairs he continued, kicked open the door to the lord's chamber, and she barely noticed that a fire had been laid in the hearth. She cared not to eye the decorations, but did note that a corgi and bulldog were snoozing peacefully, curled with Lew's head on Isabelle's hock, on the wolf-skin throw of the lord's bed.

"These shall be set outside," William promised, first placing Cordelya at the bed's foot. He grabbed a canine under each arm, then banished them to the staircase and dusted his hands in accomplishment. " 'Tis time to forget dreams and make love."

Cordelya trembled in anticipation . . . and in sudden fear of the unknown. While the ladies of the chamber had bathed her, Sir Loyce had stood by, giving advice and trying to give the bride comfort in "the night to come."

Sometimes even motherly advice had its drawbacks, even though Sir Loyce had promised that the marriage bed would hold joy, once this night were over.

Cordelya trembled.

William strode toward her. She loved the way the candles lit his form, the way he walked, the . . . everything of him.

He stroked her cheek. "Shall I call for a lady of the chamber to assist you from your wedding finery?"

Cordelya wrung her fingers in her lap. Her chin ducked. "I . . . I—nay. Sir Loyce says there is much to be enjoyed if you disrobe me. And I believe that to be true, given our previous moments of disarray."

William twisted round to sit beside her. "What else does my mother tell you?"

"She said concubines trained you in the art of lovemaking, or at least that is what she suspects, since several of your conquests at King Edward's court bragged on your prowess."

"Did she tell you anything else about the . . . concubines?"

"Nay." Cordelya lifted her gaze to his. "Is there more I should know?"

"Not this night. I have told you I sinned, and have been sinned against. I pray you accept me as I am. Most unworthy of your affections."

"I love you most dearly. You are fetching enough. I will take you as you are."

He lifted her hand, kissing her fingertips. "Thank you, princess bride. I am grateful for your favors."

"Do you think I would be wanton if I would kiss your flesh as I did in the stream?"

He grinned. "May I kiss you first? I shall start here." He lifted her wedding mantle, set it away, then tangled his fingers in her hair and kissed a lock of it. "And here." He stretched to kiss her forehead. "And here." Next he pressed his lips to her eyelashes. "Such lovely eyes, yours. May all our sons and daughters have your eyes."

"I should like a few to inherit your dark gaze."

"No more than five or six."

"No more than five or six," she echoed with a chuckle. "Husband, I am ready for more sweet ravishment."

"Sweet? I fear 'twill be more bold than sweet."

Her pulse raced, for she fancied the idea of William's boldness. She yearned for more of their heat that had been stoked many times, and knew her own passions were stirring to flames. Cordelya tugged at the hem of his surcoat. "Let us find our pace, husband. Sweet or bold, or somewhere betwixt."

Chapter Ten

"A pace bold or sweet. Whatever it takes," William promised, "I will please." He gazed yearningly at his ladybride. "You've always had a tart prickle to you. Keep it, my love!"

"I thought you cared not for prickles."

"An occasional prickle I wouldn't mind."

"Like thus?" She slipped fingers beneath his codpiece.

Desire threatened to break loose within him. It whirled much as a great sandstorm, blinding him, sweeping him into the eddying clouds, promising to carry him to the heaven of blind ecstasy. Yet he grabbed reason. He must be tender with his virgin bride, for she was western, most western, and even though debauching seemed not to frighten her, he was eastern.

It took deep thought, deeper prayer, and vast concentration to call upon skills learned in first one oasis, then others. The art of love centered on the lady's fulfillment, for in hers, a man gained his greatest satisfaction.

Tenderly, he stripped her attire and caressed each exposed limb with his eyes, his lips, his fingers. And when she lay nude amid the wolf-skin throw, a feast without comparison, he begged her assistance to remove his own clothes.

She plucked at his tunic, pulled at his hose; he felt the rush of her breath, smelled the pleasant scent of a hot cat, and saw fire in her gaze. He heard her sighs and whispers, felt her brazen touches. But he would not be touched; he had to touch her.

"Lie quiet," he crooned. "I shall banquet at your table."

He started with her toes, then the arch of her foot, and moved upward, never gaining an inch before knowing she enjoyed the journey. "Your ankle," he whispered, "is most perfect."

"I need more, William. Show me more." She grabbed his ears. "Much more!"

He gave as bade, yet his powers of concentration vanished. He enjoyed the suckling. Damn, but did he enjoy it! His fingers stroked her tender flesh, while his lips took and took.

And she squirmed beneath him. "Make me your wife."

What an offer. He would have given his head on a silver platter to please her. "Not yet." He lowered that head, and when he knew she would feel no pain, he made her his wife.

And to the glory of The Maker, it was beyond belief.

This was where William would spend his life, fulfilling Cordelya, and gaining his own gratification, both spiritual and mortal. He prayed she would never be taken from him.

May faded to June, then July settled in. Summer's dog days flew by. Arrived were a litter of four pups, each of strange face and markings, yet strong with the blood of bulldog and corgi, each adored by all at the keep.

The grange grew high, the livestock wide; September began most pleasantly, Michaelmas ending on an even fairer note. The whole of autumn went by most pleasantly. Isabelle's pups were taken in by Taffy, by Cadawon, by Adam, and by the captain of archers and his new wife, the meadmaster's daughter.

The stores were plenty for winter; Breckbryn bore the season well. Then came spring. The principality's axmen and archers were fatter than the sheep, given the lack of attention to their trade. Even though Sir Loyce had financed new arrows, bows, and cudgels for Morgan ap Maredudd, there had been no attacks against Caerphilly. And Cordelya had not widened with child, for which she pined.

Did that account for the odd feeling that gripped her?

"Why are you glum?" William asked her one eventide in the lord's chamber as they enjoyed beakers of mead and the company of pets with Sir Loyce.

A fat pup from Isabelle's second litter bounced in Cordelya's lap. "Joan is big with her fourth child. I wonder when we might enjoy our first."

One odd little bitch perching his shoulder, William stretched a leg toward the hearth. "Not for lack of trying."

"Children!" Sir Loyce hid a blush behind a lifted goblet.

Cordelya turned her own pup to his belly to tickle pink flesh. "I feel as if a storm brews. Morgan hasn't moved against The Red, and I . . ."

"The prince is in the North," William said. "Madog ap Llywelyn summoned him. They plan attacks. Morgan to the south, Madog in the north. Unfortunately, the princes fought amongst themselves, as Welshmen are apt to do, so both have retreated to the hills to lick wounds and replace dead warriors."

Sir Loyce said, "It's enough to make me sick, waiting

for war. Lord Gilbert nests with his countess. I want my revenge."

"Captain, what you need is patience."

Cordelya set the pup on the rushes. During her year of marriage, she had never once mentioned her favorite subject, and was proud of that. Yea the fire still burned. "Husband dear, I wonder if we should take our leave, ere the clouds burst. I have yet to make a pilgrimage. I wish to."

Mother and son exchanged a look that spoke volumes, not a syllable having to do with penitential sojourn.

"Think I'll take *my* leave." Sir Loyce stretched to stand and saunter off. "Yours is a matter for husband and lady-wife."

Cordelya caught the arm that was no longer chained in mail. "Why do I feel I am unaware of something I should know?"

"Ask your husband." Sir Loyce made a fast retreat.

William set the perched bitch pup to her paws. "Puss, I have been waiting for the ripe moment to tell you. We have received edicts from the king. He seeks taxes for a war in Gascony. Taxes and soldiers."

"Gascony?"

"He traded his duchy for the hand of a French princess. Alas, the young princess balks at marrying an old man. King Philip the Fair has kept Gascony. And his sister Blanche."

It was as if winter had swept from the North Sea. "You will be forced to fight in France."

"Could be asked."

"I cannot stand the thought of losing you!"

William left his own chair to draw her into his arms and to sit the both of them on a coffer, she in his lap. Stroking her cheek, he said, "I cannot fight, Cordelya. My fight is gone. I spent it in the land of the Mohammedans. On jihad."

"What is jihad? I have heard this word, yea no one will explain it to me. Husband, I make few demands of you, but I do demand to know why you are beaten by such as jihad."

Jihad. William could speak in the parables of Omar Khayyam. But he was not a knight for parables, for they did not suit him. This was a night for straight truth. Too long William had deflected it, in hopes that he would never reveal his past.

He knew he should hold his wife as he explained himself, yet he needed distance. He withdrew from her warmth and trudged up and down the rushes, pausing at the garderobe. This was where he would end up. Down the sewer drain.

What a weakling. Aye, he was weak. He had been beaten in the Sinai, humbled in Egypt, and had known the lushness and wisdom of the tribes on the Euphrates. Then his odyssey had begun again, save for the lushness and wisdom, after his capture by the Mamlukes. It was a long time ere he rode at the head of another Christian force.

For Delya, he must be strong enough to accept himself as he was. "Jihad is to strive in the way of the Creator, to further the realm. Holy war."

Cordelya braced her hands on coffer edges, puppies nipping at her knuckles. Dancing flames from the hearth made an aura of her golden head, as if she were an angel, and, forsooth, William thought her so. Her eyes never left him.

"Then jihad is from the Saracen point of view," she said.

"Aye."

Cordelya rose, taking a boar-bristle brush into hand. The litter of mutts reared their necks to hang on her every word. Yet William dreaded her words, dreaded his own, both with good reason.

"I have a solution," she said. "It spares you war. We shall undertake a journey. A great journey. To visit your Lusignan relatives in Cyprus. Sir Loyce says the island is a restful place. You can walk the hills, while she and I go on to Jerusalem."

William had no trouble forming a vision of his ladywife and captain waving broadswords. He could not, however, imagine his mother going along with this particular fight. "You've discussed your plan with her?"

"Not yet."

"I thought not."

Cordelya gave her hair several brushes. "My uncle has reached Armenia, while we languish in the outer wards of Christendom. Uncle Cyfeiliog has no doubt prayed over Christ the Lord's tomb, while I hunger for it. 'Tis an injustice."

"And when was the world just, puss?"

"I am going to speak with Sir Loyce. If she is agreeable to the journey, we are going."

"Nay. Not now. Not ever."

Those regal shoulders drew up, bold as any Lusignan. "I will fight you on this, William. You gained your own path to glory. I will pave mine."

"Then go to one of those wells you Welsh call holy." There were several, William had been told by Breckbryners. "Go to St. Non's Well. Go to Rome! Go anywhere but the Holy Land."

"No."

"Then forget pilgrimage and give thanks for being a princess blessed with a husband who adores you."

Brush swinging at her side, puppies trailing at her hems, she approached him. " 'Tis not enough. I need more."

"Cordelya, it has to be enough." Why, oh why, must he

have to tell his ignorant wife *everything*? "No Christians pray over the sepulchre. All is lost. Jerusalem fell to the Mamlukes."

"You lie."

He glared into her flashing eyes. "You have sat upon your high Welsh mountain, witness to naught but the small world around you. The western world is one of ignorance and disease and poultices of fat puppy skins. You know nothing."

"Dare you mock me!" She swung the hairbrush.

The back of it slammed against his jaw. He was beyond feeling pain.

"Do not dare play dead, sir. If you do, I will carve your heart into small pieces for Isabelle's pups."

"I am already dead."

"Do not make jest."

"I have been dead for most of my life." William turned away. He went to the windowsill to stare out, yet he looked upon naught. His head bowed. "God forsook the Christians, Delya. As He did in the arenas of Rome, He showed no mercy. The lions of the Saracen did slay Christ's own. In Acre. Then in the rest of Jerusalem. The Holy Land is lost. Forever."

"I do not believe you. You are a knight of hoaxes."

William flexed his fingers. Pressed his palms above the windowsill to support the weight he could no longer carry. His eyes were as if scalded as he admitted, "My mother took me to Cyprus when I was but a lad. She yearned to Crusade, just as you do. She bought favors from our kinsman, and was knighted. She had me knighted. We sailed to Antioch. Went ashore to war, child and mother. I was not the only child. She was not the only mother. Many women and children sought the Holy Land. Dame Lois de Granville, in a man's guise, and I were not the only ones separated by jihad."

He heard his wife's sharp intake of breath.

He said, "A storm blew our ship off course. We made land near Jaffa, and our men were jubilant to have lived through the tempest, to be so near to the Christian stronghold at Acre. We made our way north in the Judean desert toward the capital city. The desert . . . desert sands bore into our eyes, our ears, our mouths. We were watched. And when we were most desperate, Mamlukes surrounded us."

"You lived. And your pilgrimage was just." Cordelya lifted her fingers in the comfort William couldn't abide. She said, "You and Sir Loyce are proof of the Almighty's benevolence."

"That is one way to look at it. I can look only from my own perspective. There, on the Judean sand, I took a Mamluke dagger to my chest. My mother could do naught. Our men were dead, one after another. She was left standing. She had to flee. How could she have ministered to a dying son, or have arranged Christian burial?"

Cordelya knelt at his feet and pressed her cheek to his knees. She squeezed his shins most tightly. "All was not lost. You lived. And were reunited."

"Aye. Twice." William exhaled deeply. "You wish to know of jihad. Sit, ladywife. You will need to sit."

She settled.

"Jihad. The last jihad." He paced. He kicked rushes. "The sultan Qalawun, heir to Baibars, died on the march from Egypt. Qalawun's son, Khalil, stood at the head of forty thousand mounted soldiers. Near to two hundred thousand followed by foot. They were Mamlukes. Have you heard of Mamlukes?"

She shook her head.

"I thought you had not." William ran a hand down his troubled face. "They are slaves. Men of western birth. In service to the Saracen."

"Christian men serve sultans?"

"Aye. And the prophet Mohammed. They are taught to fight in the sultan's barracks and are led to Islam. They fight with no conscience, save for the worship of Allah."

Cordelya said nothing.

"I will never forget—'twas the eighteenth day of May, 1291. A Friday. Mamlukes had besieged the walled city of Acre for weeks. Kahlil ordered sappers to dig beneath the holy temple, to undermine the supports. An awful sound, hearing those many shovelsful of sand being tossed away. The Mamlukes dug on, despite the cries and pleas of the Christians."

"Oh, William, how that must have frightened you."

"Aye, I was much frightened." His eyes closed. " 'Twas as if the world collapsed, when the temple walls broke apart. They sank toward the sea, burying many who had huddled for divine protection. There was nothing left but a gaping hole where Jesú's faithful had sought comfort. The rubble covered Saracens as well. All as one, the children of God."

"But the Christians made the greatest sacrifice. You should take comfort in that."

"I take comfort in nothing. I still hear the great silence. Not even a wave lapped, not a bird sang, not a word was spoken."

"And then? And then?"

"There came the great whoop of the Mamlukes. They poured like roaches into Acre, killing most, capturing the rest, and taking great relish on the sweet-tempered young king of the Christians."

"Your cousin?"

"Aye, my cousin. I was with him when he died. So young, King Henry. A Lusignan lost to the cause. Henry III's skull, like most of the Christians, dangled as trophy. Those not killed were sold on the blocks in Cairo and Damascus."

"How can I help you recover from the pain?" Cordelya's eyes were squeezed closed. Nestling her cheek against him, she said, "Allow me to give you strength. And know that all is not lost. You are here, and I will say no more of pilgrimage. God's will be done."

The lord's chamber grew as quiet as the Acre that William had described. He moved away. Went to the set of armor that stood in a corner. He kicked it with every bit of his might. Steel came loose from bindings, folded into a heap. "That heap is my heart, ladywife."

Then William turned. He jabbed his own chest. Over and again. "Why are you blind? Why must I have to tell you? You are not a village idiot, Cordelya. Open your eyes. Listen with your ears. Must I have to tell you in so many words?"

"I think you do."

"I am the Mamluke."

Chapter Eleven

When Cordelya Howel had been a child, her mother asked two promises. Never marry an Englishman. Never enter a convent. Cordelya had not questioned Princess Eleri's reasoning, and would not now, in this her darkest hour.

Yet she needed the comfort of a nunnery, for she had much to pray on. She had given her heart to a heretic, a slayer of Christians. An infidel. She undertook a pilgrimage.

"What is the purpose of this?" Sir Loyce asked, not the first time, as she followed Cordelya to the rocky coast of southwest Wales.

Each time, as she did now, Cordelya said, "Mam said two visits to St. David's cleanse the soul, as one visit to Rome."

"I have been to Rome. The only cleansing I got was in a nice warm tub of rosewater."

"Well, *modryb dda*, 'tis all I have, this holy place in Wales.

I would not stray too far from William, even for the holiest of crusades."

"Then you should have stayed at Breckbryn."

"Nay. I could not." She eyed the walls of St. Non's Chapel, where legend said Saint Non, sister to King Arthur, had birthed the patron saint of Wales. "I wonder at the sacrifices she made for her son. Saint Dewi must have had a strong mother, such as you, sir."

"I may be strong, daughter, but unwise. If not for my bid to travel to the East, my youngest son would not have known—"

"Please." Cordelya lifted her hand in a gesture to pray quiet. "I will hear no more. E'er."

Nary once since William had confessed his terrible sin had she questioned the captain. To know him, she believed, was to hate him; she wished not to hate her husband. She pitied him. "Will you join me, sir, in prayer for his soul?"

They prayed.

Afterward, they walked to the holy well, where both offered pins and pebbles in the tradition of Welsh pilgrims seeking serenity. Cordelya tossed many pins and pebbles, for her heart and soul were greatly bruised. She almost cared not if the wounds healed. Although no Saracen stood with blade drawn, barring her from holy pilgrimage, she had seen the eyes of Satan.

Seen it in the black of her own lord husband's gaze.

"Shall we carry on to the cathedral?" Sir Loyce asked.

Cordelya brushed tears from her cheeks.

Modryb dda and daughter of the heart could descend the steep hill into the settlement of St. David's, where the great cathedral and Bishop's Palace rose majestically. Cordelya chose not to. It was not the journey that saved the pilgrim. It was the purpose.

She eyed the silver-haired captain, who wore hauberk

and carried a sword, and knew she must change her mind and soul. "Let us sit on the cliff and look out at the sea. I would wish to know William so that I might understand him."

Great waves broke on the cliffs below as they talked. Sir Loyce, in a voice wrought with sorrow, admitted, "I left him for dead in the Judea. I managed to escape, made my way north to Acre. Was taken in by my cousin the King of Jerusalem. Three years later I heard of a Christian boy who had turned up in Baghdad, had been sheltered by a caravan. I knew he was Will. Deep in my mother's heart, I knew. I was fired to save him, and went to lengths to find him. I walked amid the Saracen. But Will's mind was bent by the desert and the influence of the sultans. He broke my heart."

Moved to more tears, Cordelya slipped her arm around the quivering shoulders. " 'Twas too late to help him."

"He had the mind of an infidel. He had learned the symbols of figures and a concept beyond my understanding, called algebra. He knew mysticism and the cosmos. He was of the mind of jihad. So . . . I left him once more in Saracen hands. But I made certain that if he were ever to change, I would make his return easy."

"And you did, *modryb dda.*"

"I did. I'm glad I did. As he held a dagger to the throat of his cousin, Henry of Jerusalem, my son withdrew. He dropped his blade. As did Christ on the cross, William cried, 'Lord God, why have You forsaken me?' "

William, poor William. Cordelya lifted her eyes to the blue sky and felt the power of purpose enter her soul. It was then she felt the miracle of Saint Dewi. "My lord husband has been much forsaken. If he will allow me, I shall bring him peace."

Sir Loyce tightened her steel-gloved hand on Cordelya's wrist. "Give him peace. Love him and bear his children, and be a comfort as you both meet the challenges of Breck-bryn."

Cordelya stood and brushed loam from her robes. "Let me help you to stand, great mother. Let us go home to Breckbryn. To William."

"To arms, man!"

Hair wild, his beard grown wilder, his eyes aching from lack of sleep and hope, William lifted his cheek from the trestle table, where he had drunk the night away.

Morgan ap Maredudd stood in the doorway with another who looked feral enough to be a Welsh prince. The Breck-bryn whelps surrounded them, tails wagging.

"Take what you want, brothers. But leave me be."

"Ye did not make much of a Welshman is all I can say. Come, Madog. Let's be glad we at least got arms out of the de Granvilles."

Prince Morgan and his follower marched from the great hall.

William shoved to stand, wobbled. He yearned for Corde-lya but warned himself to stop. She was gone. A pilgrim gone away from a heretic. He must not wish her home, for what kind of home could he provide a saint? "Just don't let her be dead!"

He struggled up the stairs, and reached the fourth before he nearly toppled. The dogs barked furiously, then with joy. He then heard his name called from the great hall's archway.

"William, I am home."

Cordelya. Delya!

He called on eastern concentration, refusing to allow his heart to sing with joy. "Aye. You are home. I bid you welcome, princess. 'Tis time for me to go."

"I would prefer you stay."

The waft of her sweet scent came to William as she climbed one step and the next. She touched his arm. Spoke his name with such love that he lost his power of concentration. He whirled to her, grabbing her into his arms, squeezing her tightly, with Lew and Isabelle and the lot of their whelps dancing about the steps.

"I thought you were lost to the Holy Land," he whispered. "I feared you would seek to pay for my sins."

"You have paid enough. I have learned many lessons, William. Most particularly that Jerusalem is not a place. It beats within us." Cordelya lifted her hand and laid it where both their hearts met. "Let us honor and praise Him as He wishes us. As husband and wife, blessed with many riches. Content within our home."

"In Jesú's name I pray. Amen."

Author's Note

Breckbryn lives solely in the imagination. Red Gilbert, his countess, and her father—and Joanna of Acre—lived as I have tried to describe them, taking literary license.

Before Madog ap Llywelyn burned Caernarfon Castle, Morgan ap Maredudd rose up against The Red, and got his revenge by sacking the great Marcher border lord's villages and castles, one after the other. Gilbert de Clare and his countess were forced to flee to London, into her father's shelter, and one has to wonder how The Red felt about yet another humiliation.

Morgan's triumphs, however, were short-lived. The following year Longshanks took control of the situation, as he did all situations save for Gascony, and stood down the Welsh prince in person. His demands were met, his son-in-law's estates returned. The great age of the native Welsh prince was truly over, as were the Crusades.

Gilbert de Clare died in December 1295, age fifty-four, leaving his countess with five small children. Much to her father's displeasure, Joan of Acre soon married a squire who had been in service to her lord husband. Ralph de Monthermer was much reviled for having the audacity to marry the king's daughter, when he wasn't even a knight.

Gascony was forever lost to Longshanks, although he did manage to wangle Philip the Fair out of a sister, but not Blanche. Longshanks married Princess Marguerite of France in 1299, and begat more children, although his surviving son by Eleanor, later known as Edward II, was the first English crowned Prince of Wales. He was invested at the restored Caerfarnon Castle, in 1301.

The son and heir of Red Gilbert and Joan of Acre, Gilbert Fitzgilbert de Clare, fell from his horse and was bludgeoned by Scotsmen at the battle of Bannockburn, 1314. Yet Caerphilly Castle stands to this day. The castle was used as one of the settings for the glorious film *Restoration*.

I wish to thank a noble Welsh knight of the Internet for rushing to the aid of this dame in distress. Martin, you are in no way responsible for any errors in fact to this story, and if anything good has come of it, it's thanks to you. Wendy, this Texan curtsies to you for collecting Glamorgan history, as well as for rearing a son any mother would be proud of.

I would also like to recommend the wonderful work collected on the 'Net by Jeff Thomas. Visit his site at http://www.castlewales.com. And to my own *modryb dda*—no, two of them—Lois Atherton and Ernestine Wilson, I owe a lifetime of care, keeping, and motherly devotion. Happy Mother's Day! Happy Mother's Day to you all.

Martha Hix
http://eclectics.com/marthahix

ROMANCE FROM JO BEVERLY

DANGEROUS JOY   (0-8217-5129-8, $5.99)

FORBIDDEN   (0-8217-4488-7, $4.99)

THE SHATTERED ROSE   (0-8217-5310-X, $5.99)

TEMPTING FORTUNE   (0-8217-4858-0, $4.99)

Available wherever paperbacks are sold, or order direct from the Publisher. Send cover price plus 50¢ per copy for mailing and handling to Kensington Publishing Corp., Consumer Orders, or call (toll free) 888-345-BOOK, to place your order using Mastercard or Visa. Residents of New York and Tennessee must include sales tax. DO NOT SEND CASH.

ROMANCE FROM JANELLE TAYLOR

ANYTHING FOR LOVE   (0-8217-4992-7, $5.99)

DESTINY MINE   (0-8217-5185-9, $5.99)

CHASE THE WIND   (0-8217-4740-1, $5.99)

MIDNIGHT SECRETS   (0-8217-5280-4, $5.99)

MOONBEAMS AND MAGIC   (0-8217-0184-4, $5.99)

SWEET SAVAGE HEART   (0-8217-5276-6, $5.99)

Available wherever paperbacks are sold, or order direct from the Publisher. Send cover price plus 50¢ per copy for mailing and handling to Kensington Publishing Corp., Consumer Orders, or call (toll free) 888-345-BOOK, to place your order using Mastercard or Visa. Residents of New York and Tennessee must include sales tax. DO NOT SEND CASH.

ROMANCE FROM FERN MICHAELS

DEAR EMILY   (0-8217-4952-8, $5.99)

WISH LIST   (0-8217-5228-6, $6.99)

AND IN HARDCOVER:

VEGAS RICH   (1-57566-057-1, $25.00)

Available wherever paperbacks are sold, or order direct from the Publisher. Send cover price plus 50¢ per copy for mailing and handling to Kensington Publishing Corp., Consumer Orders, or call (toll free) 888-345-BOOK, to place your order using Mastercard or Visa. Residents of New York and Tennessee must include sales tax. DO NOT SEND CASH.

YOU WON'T WANT TO READ
JUST ONE—KATHERINE STONE

ROOMMATES (0-8217-5206-5, $6.99/$7.99)
No one could have prepared Carrie for the monumental changes she would face when she met her new circle of friends at Stanford University. Once their lives intertwined and became woven into the tapestry of the times, they would never be the same.

TWINS (0-8217-5207-3, $6.99/$7.99)
Brook and Melanie Chandler were so different, it was hard to believe they were sisters. One was a dark, serious, ambitious New York attorney; the other, a golden, glamourous, sophisticated supermodel. But they were more than sisters—they were twins and more alike than even they knew . . .

THE CARLTON CLUB (0-8217-5204-9, $6.99/$7.99)
It was the place to see and be seen, the only place to be. And for those who frequented the playground of the very rich, it was a way of life. Mark, Kathleen, Leslie and Janet—they worked together, played together, and loved together, all behind exclusive gates of the *Carlton Club*.

Available wherever paperbacks are sold, or order direct from the Publisher. Send cover price plus 50¢ per copy for mailing and handling to Kensington Publishing Corp., Consumer Orders, or call (toll free) 888-345-BOOK, to place your order using Mastercard or Visa. Residents of New York and Tennessee must include sales tax. DO NOT SEND CASH.